Red Pandamonium

A Queer Humorous Urban Fantasy

Roan Rosser

Rainbow Dog Books

Your Free eBook is Waiting

No resources? No opposable thumbs? No problem for this band of furry thieves

Sign up for my newsletter to get Diamond in the Rat for free. Available at http://bit.ly/344KD

Contents

1. Haunted House   1

2. Good Bean Water   15

3. Which Witch   25

4. Not a Minor Power   39

5. Shoestorm   53

6. The Broken Seal   65

7. Carriage Trouble   83

8. The Barcade   97

9. The Vampire Sunshine   113

10. Betrayed   125

11. Unicorn Impound   135

12. Like a Super Soaker   149

13. Saturn Devouring His Son   163

14. Cue Training Montage   177

15. Even You Won't Date Me   191

16. Levitation Sounds Fun   199

17. Unicorn Poop   207

18. The Exchange   217

19. The Fight   227

Epilogue   241

ALSO BY ROAN ROSSER   244

ABOUT THE AUTHOR   245

I

Haunted House

A PLATE WHIZZED BY the side of my head, grazing my ear before smashing into the cupboard next to me. I turned, suds dripping from my hands, expecting to see my roommate, Brandon, in the kitchen with me, except, from what I could see in the dim light coming through the kitchen windows, I was alone.

"Brandon?"

"Upstairs, hold on!" he yelled back from a distant part of the house. It couldn't have been him then, unless he'd flown. Or teleported. Weird, but story of my life.

I shrugged and turned back to the sink, but there was a loud ping, and the tile beneath my feet cracked. I stumbled and caught myself on the lip of a drawer. The drawer creaked and slid out of place, dumping its entire contents and me onto the floor. The far end of the drawer caught the edge of the counter as it popped free. With an ominous crack, the linoleum countertop snapped in half, sending my clean dishes and the broken plate sliding back down into the sink.

Then the sink pulled free of the wall and fell, narrowly missing me and smashing down onto the tile with a crash that shook the entire house. The buckets of water I'd been using to clean dishes sloshed out all over me, covering me with suds and dirty water.

Not again.

"Max, what was that?"

"Nothing," I yelled back as I climbed to my feet. This kind of thing was a daily occurrence for me. Besides, the sink had missed me and I was unharmed. Mostly.

Each step groaned as Brandon ran downstairs. The farmhouse we were squatting in had been abandoned and was in poor shape. He entered the kitchen and stopped short, his eyes widening. His eyes roved over the mess as I rolled my sopping wet t-shirt over my head and wrung it out.

"Are you hurt?" he asked, his gaze lingering on my chest for a moment before he met my eyes.

"Like I said, it's nothing serious." I fingered the nick on my ear, which stung as the suds from my hair dripped onto it. I also had a few cuts on my arms where the broken pieces of that first flung plate had landed on me when the sink fell.

"Good," he said with a deep sigh of relief. "That was too close." Then his cheeks reddened. "I mean, we can't afford another urgent care visit this month."

"I know." I picked through the wreckage and found a sizable chunk of the flying porcelain plate and shook water off it, curious where it had come from.

Violets decorated the edges, and I recognized it as a piece from the china cabinet in the dining room, off-limits because of a giant hole in the middle of the floor. There was currently no way to access the cabinet against the far wall, so how had the plate gotten launched at me in the kitchen? Probably another improbable Rube Goldberg sequence of events.

I tossed the pieces back on the floor. When we'd first moved in, before the floor had collapsed during another one of my bouts of bad luck, I'd taken a piece out to be appraised. They were basically worthless, not even worth the effort of removing them.

I wondered how this house hadn't ever been cleared out by looters. It had been abandoned for ages, with everything left as if the owners had just stepped out. Then again, it was a good thing that it hadn't. I'd been slowly going through and selling anything of value. Mold and the damp had ruined a lot of the furniture, but I'd still made a pretty penny cleaning up and selling things like the vases, the antique light fixtures, and crystal doorknobs.

"Do I want to know what happened?" Brandon asked as I stood up and wiped my hands off on my jeans.

"The usual," I said with a shrug.

"It's a miracle you didn't get hurt." Brandon took a step towards me, hands outstretched as if he were going to hug me, but then clenched his fists and backed up. "I... need to make a call." The steps groaned as he went back upstairs.

I got my crime scene tape and used it to make a big X across the kitchen door. Brandon had given me the tape as a gag gift last Christmas. It got a lot of use. Half the doors in the house were now taped off.

We were down to the living room, my bedroom on the first floor, and Brandon's bedroom upstairs. Both bathrooms, the dining room, the basement, the other two bedrooms, and now the kitchen had suffered unfortunate accidents.

Upstairs, I heard Brandon talking to someone on the phone. I returned the crime scene tape to my room and changed into dry clothes. The stairs creaked as Brandon came back down, so I went out to ask him if he wanted to watch a movie with me. But to my surprise, he had his suitcase with him. He set it on the bottom step when he saw me.

The sun was going down, bathing everything in red light, and making Brandon's red hair practically glow like it was on fire.

God, he was handsome. The way the harsh light lit up his cheekbones made my stomach flip and made me want to forget that he had rejected me when we were teens. Our friendship was purely platonic.

"Work emergency. I have to go out of town a few days," he said.

"A *welding* emergency?" I asked, raising my eyebrows. In the four years he'd been working this job, starting with an apprenticeship, this was a first.

"Yeah, it's uh..." he started stammering. "Something broke," he finished with a nervous laugh.

"Okay..." I didn't know much about his work, but I knew he'd only recently graduated from his apprenticeship to a journeyman. Maybe this was part of his additional duties. "So, when will you be getting back?"

"Not sure. Not more than a few days. A week at most." Brandon looked at me, biting his lip. His eyes shone, and he stepped closer to me, leaning towards me. "Max, I..." Color rose in his cheeks, turning them almost as red as his hair. He reached towards my arm and leaned down, as if he were going to kiss me.

My breath caught in my throat, and my heart pounded. I'd been in love with him since high school. I'd have thought this was a dream except for the stinging cut on my ear. My lips parted, and I tilted my head back.

Brandon's hand brushed my arm, and he jerked, stumbling back as if he'd been shocked.

I swallowed my disappointment as Brandon flexed the hand that had touched me before he picked his bag up again. "Max, if I don't come back..."

A car honked outside. Brandon checked the time on his phone and cursed. "That's my Uber. I need to go. Be careful. Please?" he said the last part with a pleading note.

He headed for the back door. The front door worked, but we didn't want to be seen going in and out.

"If you don't come back?" I asked, trailing after him. "What are you expecting to happen on a work trip? Speaking of

4

which, don't you need your tools?" I asked as he put his hand on the doorknob.

"Right. Thanks. Can't forget my work tools." He gave a nervous laugh and headed up the stairs, returning a moment later with his tool bag, welder's mask hanging from the side.

As he passed me again, he paused and bit his lip again. "Max, I love you, and—" The car outside honked again, cutting him off, and he left without finishing the thought.

"Safe trip," I said to the closed door, my heart still pounding. Brandon loved me? He had to have meant like a brother, right? And if he meant romantically, why wait until now?

Six Months Earlier

I hugged my knees to my chest and stared into the darkness. From the other campsites, I could hear the murmur of conversation, almost drowned out by the roar of the cars on the freeway below. We were camping in the forested strip between the road and the neighborhood behind us, along with about a dozen other people.

Footsteps crunched through the underbrush and then Brandon sat down next to me. He juggled two cans of beer and offered one to me with a half smile.

I scowled and scooted away from him. "I don't deserve that after losing us *another* apartment." After three apartment fires, a flood, and an exploding fridge, all in the short six months we'd lived there, the apartment complex had declined to renew our lease when it ran out. With our terrible rental history—inevitable when you lived with me and my terrible luck—we'd been unable to find another apartment that would accept us. So now we were officially homeless. At least because of the fires, we didn't have many possessions left to worry about.

Brandon set my can down in the dirt next to me and popped his own open, taking a sip before answering. "Max, it's not your fault."

I dug my bare toes into the dirt, refusing to look at Brandon. "Doesn't change the result, does it? You should leave me here. Without me weighing you down, you should be able to find and keep an apartment."

"Don't be ridiculous. You're not weighing me down." He picked up my beer can and pressed it into my arm until I took it, then clinked his can with mine.

"So you don't mind camping along the freeway with me?" I shifted to sit cross-legged and twisted the unopened can between my hands.

"It's just for tonight," Brandon said. I shot him a questioning glance. "I have a surprise to show you tomorrow." He refused to elaborate further.

The next morning, he dragged me up to north Portland and led me to the house. It wasn't much to look at: a two-story farmhouse with boarded-up windows, a hole in the roof, peeling siding, and a no-trespassing sign in a yard that had long ago gone to seed.

"What do you think?" he asked, looking strangely proud of himself, chest puffed out and hands on his hips. "It's all ours. Plus, no worries about destroying this house, as you can see."

I popped my rolling suitcase up on its wheels and shook my head. "No way there aren't already people squatting here."

"There aren't. I checked the inside when I found it. Empty. I asked around, and apparently it's rumored to be haunted.

Keeps out the squatters." Brandon winked at me. "Unless you're worried about the ghost."

"I doubt a ghost can do worse to me than my bad luck curse," I said with a snort, giving him a half smile. Brandon knew what I thought about the supernatural. A bunch of BS. My friend Ynes from the Saturday Market was a big believer, and had kept giving me remedies for my bad luck. None of which had worked, of course, because magic didn't exist.

I always found it spooky when I was alone in this house, like someone was constantly watching me. After I went to bed, my bedroom door swung open, and then slammed shut with a bang. Repeatedly. Four or five repetitions later, I resigned myself to no sleep.

I got out the cheap tablet I'd gotten from the pawnshop and played games on it. On the screen, digital zombies attacked my house, and I fought them off with exploding peas and snap dragons powered by sunflowers. The game was silly and mindless, just what I needed right now as the bedroom door continued to slam.

Eventually, the door slamming stopped, but then the staircase groaned as if someone walked up and down it.

I must have dozed off, because the bedroom door slamming again woke me with a start. The tablet next to me fizzed and popped, then smoke started trickling out of the casing. Great... There went twenty bucks that Brandon had encouraged me to splurge on it. Still, it had at least given me a few days of entertainment before my bad luck curse killed it.

I set the broken tablet aside and picked up my sketchbook. Char marks stained the lower edges where it had caught on fire during one of my incidents. But unlike the tablet, my trusty sketchbook had been salvageable once I'd beat out the flames. Part of the reason I ended up sketching and reading a lot. Electronics were just too delicate to survive around me long.

Although, or maybe because of this, they fascinated me. I loved sneaking into the arcade in the mall downtown, listening to the pings and bleeps as I watched over other player's shoulders until I was always inevitably caught and thrown out. They had banned me, for obvious reasons, a long time ago.

I flipped my sketchbook open to the page I'd been working on earlier that day. The Portland Zoo had new red panda cubs, and I'd spent the day at their enclosure, filling half my sketch book with pictures of them. Weekends I drew caricatures of tourists, but weekdays—short of summer holidays and spring break—there weren't enough tourists to make it worthwhile, so I liked to visit spots around the city to practice drawing.

I turned the camping lantern up as bright as it would go and started fleshing out the best of my red panda sketches and adding color. Reds, oranges, and blacks. I was head down, concentrating on getting the highlights of fur right, when a feeling of euphoria washed over me. I'd felt nothing like it before. The feeling swept up me and ended in my hands.

My colored pencils flew over the drawing, each stroke making it more and more lifelike, until the red panda drawing turned its head and stepped off the page, peeling away like a sticker that popped into reality as it tore free. When the red panda was fully there, the feeling of euphoria finally passed and I slumped over on my bed, exhausted. My heart beat fast, like I'd just run to catch the bus.

The red panda and I stared at each other nose to nose for a moment; me gasping for breath, the red panda panting with wide eyes. Then the red panda dashed away, blunt claws scrabbling on the hardwood floor. A bushy striped tail flashed through the halo of lantern light and disappeared behind my suitcase laying open in the corner.

I got up, half thinking it had been a hallucination. Yet two little eyes still glittered at me from the shadows. Maybe a raccoon had gotten in through one of the broken windows, and I'd been so focused on my drawing that I'd mistaken it for a red panda.

I picked up the broom from the corner and prodded towards the glittering eyes with the bristles. "Scat," I said.

The creature bared its teeth at me, fangs flashing white against the dark. "Why don't you scat, Intruder. This is my house."

"Who said that?" I whirled, broom held over my shoulder like a sword.

"I did. I've been trying to scare you away for months," the voice said.

I spun again, seeking the speaker. A shape loomed up behind my suitcase, arms raised above its head, and waddled out into the light.

I blinked and lowered the broom at the sight of the red panda doing its best to look scary with its paws in the air. Orange, fluffy, and as real as the ones I'd seen at the zoo.

"You sure are a hard scare, Kid." The red panda's mouth moved. It was the one talking?

"What are you talking about?".

"The banging doors? The creaky stairs? The flying dishes?" The panda's triangle ears perked forward, and it cocked its head to the side.

I shrugged. "That's my life."

"Plates throw themselves at you all the time?" The red panda rocked back on its haunches and lowered its arms, orange-striped tail swishing behind its head.

"Not exactly like that, no," I admitted. Then my eyes widened. "You were the one that threw that plate at me earlier today?"

"Yeah, I was trying to get your attention. Didn't work, but you're listening to me now, at least. So pay attention." The red panda barred its teeth. "This is my house, and I want you and your ugly bird gone, got it?"

"Bird? We don't have a pet bird."

"The bird, Brandon."

I puzzled over that. I would have described the handsome, red-haired Brandon as a fox trickster or kitsune rather than a bird. I even jokingly referred to him as Reynard sometimes.

The red panda raised its arms again and started waddling towards me once more. "Now go away! I'm scary. Rawr!"

I crouched down and booped its nose with one finger, something I'd wanted to do all day at the zoo.

"Knock it off," the red panda growled.

"You're such a cute red panda," I cooed and rubbed it between the ears. The fur was so soft and deep, like petting a pillow. I'd wanted to pet the ones at the zoo so badly. And now I could! I guess my luck wasn't all bad.

I considered how many tourists would pay to have their picture taken with a talking red panda. Then I discarded the idea. The camera would never last long enough around me for me to actually extract the pictures.

The red panda batted my hands away with its front paws. "What's a red panda?"

"Hold on, I'll show you." I grabbed my sketchbook from my bed and then crouched down to hold the picture I'd been working on up at red panda height. That sketch it had come from was gone, but the others on the page were still there.

The red panda reached a paw out and touched the page. "I look nothing like that," it huffed.

"No, you look exactly like that." It did too, exactly like my drawing, right down to the placing of its markings that I'd copied from my favorite of the red pandas at the Portland Zoo named Moshu.

"No wonder you aren't afraid of me now." The red panda fell back to sit on its butt and crossed its little paws across its chest.

"Yeah, you're way too cute to be scary." I tossed my sketchpad onto my mattress, then held out one hand to the red panda. "I'm Max. What's your name?"

"Pog." The red panda touched a hesitant paw to my fingers. I gently took it and shook.

"What did you used to look like?" I rested my hands on my knees so I could stay crouched.

"Nothing. Everything. Whatever I wanted." The panda waved its little black paws around in the air. "I was the house..."

"Like a ghost. Or a house spirit." I pursed my lips. "Wouldn't a house want people to live in it?"

"Only the family that created me. And that isn't you two." The red panda grimaced and showed me its teeth. "A wizard and a monster. You shouldn't be here."

"And which of us is which?"

The red panda stared at me, its little brown eyes wide. "As if you don't know."

Before I could formulate an answer, the skin of my hands began burning. The tingles shot up my palm, straight to my brain. I cried out in pain and clutched my head. I fell sideways and landed half on and half off my mattress. Spasms wracked me, making me arch my back, fingers digging into the mattress so deeply that I tore a chunk of foam out. I screamed.

The world pulsed.

A wave rolled out from me, changing everything it touched. My camping pad turned into a bed of vines, and the chunk of foam in my hand turned into a mushroom. My cheap flip phone laying on the sheets next to me turned into a leather notebook.

The wooden floor transformed into dirt. Rivulets ran down the walls as if they were candle wax. The plaster of the ceiling twisted into beams, and some of the furniture from the room above mine fell through the now open parts of the floor. A rotting dresser smashed into the floor at my feet and burst into butterflies. The cloud twirled out and away through the hole in the ceiling.

Then it was over. My head was back to normal, the pain gone.

Pog scrambled onto my bare stomach, claws digging into my flesh, irritating my top surgery scars, and grabbed my face with its paws. "What did you do?"

I sat up, and Pog fell into my lap. I clung to that anchor of reality as I stared at my room. The changes extended out into what I could see of the hall, and craning my neck to see up, as far as the lantern illuminated in the room above me.

The only thing unchanged besides the lantern was my sketchpad, looking incongruous laying in the greenery. My bad luck seemed to have taken a very definite turn for the worst, but at least this was as bad as it could get.

"Brains," a man moaned.

The moan came from down the hall, followed by a shuffling sound.

"Wait here," I told Pog and picked up the camping lantern. I held up the light and peered around the corner. A zombie—gray skin, ragged clothing and all—shuffled down the hall towards me, arms extended. "Brains," it said when it saw me, though it didn't react to me in any other fashion. There was a second one about ten feet behind it, identical looking to the first.

"What the hell?" I stammered, staring at it. The dirt floor continued out here as well. Vines with teeth at the end grew on the floor along the hall. They snapped at the zombie's legs as they shuffled, taking out a chunk with each bite.

The smell wafting towards me was absolutely putrid. I gagged and backed up, trying to think about what I could do. Fight or flight?

I wore nothing but pajama shorts and there was nothing in my room that I could use to fight off zombies. So, we needed to run.

"Shit, Pog, we need to go."

I scooped Pog up into my arms, struggling to hold both it and the lantern as Pog struggled. The shuffling sounds were getting closer. Finally, I gave up and dropped the lantern so I could get a good grip on the squirming red panda. Taking a deep breath to build up my courage, I dashed out into the hallway.

The zombie was almost to the doorway and grabbed at me as I ran by. It clawed at my back, but wasn't able to grab hold.

With zombies between me and the back door, I dashed for the front. The vines lashed out and nipped at my bare legs as I ran by, but I was faster than the zombies and the plants moved slowly enough that I could avoid them.

I exited out of the hallway into the entryway. The stairs now ran in a loop, like an M.C. Escher painting or an amusement park ride. The chaos ended right before the front door; dirt turning back to hardwood a few feet from the threshold.

"Not outside!" Pog said as I headed for the front door. "I can't leave the house."

"What?" I stopped and looked down at Pog.

"When I've tried to go past the end of the porch, I fade away and re-materialize back in the basement," Pog screamed, flailing and scratching at me.

A moan came from my left where the kitchen had been. A zombie was right on the other side of the crime-scene tape. I could hear the tape slowly tearing free, though I couldn't see much more in the dark.

"We can't stay here! You'll have to risk it. Worst that happens is you appear back in the basement!"

I hugged Pog closer as the red panda struggled, blunt claws scratching my arms. It took me a moment to find the doorknob in the dark while trying to hold onto the red panda. The crime-scene tape gave way with a last tear and then shuffling moved towards me in the dark.

I finally found the knob. The rusty hinges screamed as I forced them open with strength born of panic. I slammed it behind me and a moment later, something thumped hard into the door. Scratching and moaning cries for brains came from the other side.

"We need help, and I want to get farther away from the house," I told Pog. We couldn't stay here. What if the door didn't hold? Besides that, we needed to find help.

Pog nodded and covered its eyes with its paws. "Just do it quick."

The panda's long striped tail batted at my legs and threatened to trip me, but I made it to the bottom of the steps without incident. I ran down the walk, then carefully stepped over the broken remnants of the gate. Usually, no matter how careful I'd been, I would have gotten a splinter. Or stepped on a sleeping wasp or something. But nothing. Disbelieving, I picked up one foot and then the other, twisting to look as best I could while cradling the panda.

"I'm still here," Pog said with wonder and craned its head around to look at the front yard.

"I'm glad." I was too. Not just because of the warmth the red panda offered against the cool morning. It was nice to not be alone right now, standing on the sidewalk in my underwear, my house infested with attack plants and zombies.

II

Good Bean Water

THERE WAS A PORCH light on in the house next door, so I decided
to try my luck there. The cold from the asphalt seeped up my
soles as I walked. By the time I mounted the wooden steps
to the neighbor's porch, I shivered violently. Pog remained
content to hang from my arms, bushy tail brushing my knees.
Its claws dug into my skin, but I didn't mind with the warmth
it provided.

My hand shook so badly that it took me three tries to press
the doorbell. It buzzed, sounding loud in the pre-dawn quiet.
Since we'd been squatting, I'd avoided meeting any of the
neighbors. I hoped whoever lived here wouldn't be angry at
me for waking them at such an early hour. And, glancing at
my top scars that had turned a bright, angry red in the cold

air where they extended beyond Pog's fluff, I also hoped that they weren't transphobic.

"Put me down." Pog wiggled, so I bent down and set it on the porch. It stood up on its hind legs and looked up at me. "What are we doing here?"

"Looking for help," I said, glancing down at it. "My house was full of zombies. Not to mention everything else."

"Yeah. Why'd you do that anyway?" Pog tilted its head and pulled its ears back.

I stared at it. "Me? What makes you think I had anything to do with that?"

"I might not be entirely myself right now, but I know what I saw and felt. That magic came from you." Pog crossed its paws, black eyes drilling into me.

"Don't be crazy. Magic isn't... real..." I blinked, realizing I argued with a talking red panda and had a house filled with zombies. Pog thought I could do magic? It sent a little thrill through me.

Something inside the house creaked, a minor bit of warning, before the door opened. A man with tousled long blond hair wearing bright red silk pajamas opened the door and blinked out at us.

"What?" he growled, but then he stopped and looked at me. His scowl turned to confusion.

"I need some help," I said, teeth chattering, and then paused, at a loss for what to say. I hadn't really thought about how I was going to explain why I was almost naked on their porch in the middle of the night with a red panda.

"I'll say." He moved to the side. "Come in out of the cold and tell me what happened."

I went inside, still shivering. The man went to shut the door, and I realized Pog was still outside on the porch. "Hey, wait! Pog, come on!" I yelled. The blond man paused long enough to give Pog time to scamper inside, its long tail held straight up in the air.

"What is that?" he asked as he shut the door.

"That's my pet..." I paused. I needed a story. I doubted it was legal to have a pet red panda. "... Raccoon."

"I thought you said I was a red panda," Pog said, ears skewed.

"Cute." The man seemed un-phased by Pog talking. Maybe I *could* explain about the zombies after all. "What's your name?" he asked Pog directly.

"I'm Pog." The red panda thrust out a paw. My neighbor crouched down and gravely shook.

"Pleased to meet you, Pog. I'm Kay." He glanced up at me with a questioning look.

"Oh yeah, this guy is Max." Pog flailed a paw in my direction.

"Does anyone really buy the raccoon story?" Kay asked with a laugh as he stood back up.

"I... don't know..." I bit my lip and looked around, hugging myself. I was still cold, but was slowly warming up now that I was inside.

"I've never met a red panda shifter before." Kay said, looking at Pog with one eyebrow raised.

"What's a shifter?" I asked.

Pog scratched one ear. "I'm not a shifter. I tried. I'm stuck in this form." Pog flicked its tail. "Not that I mind since I got to leave the house."

Kay pursed his lips. "You look frozen. I'll make some tea while you tell me why you're on my porch in your boxers at four in the morning with a red panda."

I bit back a yawn and sat at Kay's kitchen table while he bustled around, filling an electric kettle and turning it on.

Pog was on its hind legs pulling open drawers to examine the contents. Kay patiently shut each one after Pog moved on.

He handed me a mug, then sat down across from me. Pog had tired of inspecting drawers and was now trying, and failing, to open the refrigerator doors. We both ignored it.

"So what's the story?" Kay asked, sipping at his tea.

I turned the warm mug around in my hands, contemplating lying. But if I wanted Kay to accompany me back home to kill the zombies and retrieve my things, it'd be pointless to lie about it. "My friend and I have been squatting in the empty house next door—"

"The haunted one?"

"Not haunted anymore," Pog said. Little paws appeared over the table edge, followed by two large black and white ears, a red face, and brown eyes. "This joker magicked me into this form."

"You're the ghost?" Kay burst into laughter, holding his side.

I stayed silent. Maybe I had, but I had no idea how.

"Did Brandon see this too?" Kay wiped tears of laughter from his eyes.

"Wait, you know Brandon?" I asked with a start.

"Yeah, he came to see me for a reading."

I stared at Kay.

"My mother was a witch. I have a minor gift of prophecy." Kay put a hand to his chest and gave me a sly smile. "I do tarot card readings, mostly."

Why would Brandon have needed a reading? "Brandon's away on a business trip. Can I use your cell phone to call him? Mine kinda... turned into a notebook."

"Sure, but first, let's go next door and see how bad the damage is."

I winced. "Probably should have mentioned the zombies first."

Then Kay wrinkled his nose as what I'd said sunk in. "Zombies? Are you joking?"

"No... I don't know where they came from. Or the bitey plants... Or the swarm of butterflies... or—"

"I get the idea." Kay stood and ruffled the fur of Pog's head. "At least I'll go over with you and check it out. If it's really that bad, I know some people we can call. You wait here and drink your tea. I'm going to go get dressed. I think I have something that'll fit you, too."

Once Kay left, Pog scrambled up into the empty chair. Sitting there, its head barely cleared the table. Pog huffed and then got up onto its hind legs and rested its front paws on the table. "I want tea too."

"No, I don't want to poison you by accident or something."

Pog slumped across the table, back legs and tail hanging off the edge. "Meanie."

I rolled my eyes. Kay returned fully dressed in tight jeans and a low cut v-neck shirt with a peacock feather pattern on it. He'd pulled his blond hair back into a tail at the nape of his neck. He held out a set of pink sweats to me, along with a small brown pouch on a leather cord. Ugh, pink. Still, better than what I wore right now, which was basically nothing.

"What's this?" I asked, picking up the pouch. It smelled of leather and something musty and unfamiliar.

"A protection pouch. To ward off evil. I want you to wear it." He gave me puppy dog eyes. "Please?"

"Alright." I didn't believe in that sort of thing, but maybe I should start. Either way, it couldn't hurt to humor him.

"There's a bathroom down the hall, first door on the right. And wear the pouch inside, against your skin!" he called as I headed down the hall. I waved over my head without looking.

The bath was the pinkest thing I'd ever seen. Pink curtains, pink rug, pink marble counter, pink towels. I had a feeling I could guess his favorite color.

The sweats were too large. Kay was taller than me, but not by much. They'd work until I could get back some of my clothing.

When I returned, Pog stood on a chair, happily lapping from a bowl of dark liquid set in front of it. Kay had one leg thrown up over the table and lounged back, sipping at a cup.

"Coffee?" I asked, recognizing the familiar smell. I normally hated the stuff, but I was exhausted from my sleepless night and worried about the house. The pick-me-up from the caffeine would be worth the bitter taste.

"Pour yourself a cup. We aren't in a hurry." Kay waved at the coffee machine. "I also texted Brandon while you were changing."

He had Brandon's phone number too? How come Brandon never mentioned Kay to me? I thought we told each other everything. I turned this over in my head as I got myself a cup of coffee.

"So, Pog. I don't want to mis-gender you. I've never met a house spirit before. Is it he or she?" Kay asked as I rejoined them at the table.

"House spirits don't have human gender," Pog said before going back to lapping at the drink. "This bean water is fantastic."

"You gave him coffee?" I picked up the bowl. "I don't think red pandas can drink coffee. They eat bamboo." At least that was what the informational plaque in front of their exhibit at the zoo had said.

"Not him, and not really a red panda, remember? Magic," Kay said, taking the bowl from me and putting it back where it had been. "No gender..." Kay picked up his cup and tapped the edge. "Pog, how about using eiy, eim, eir for your pronouns?"

Pog lapped up more of the coffee, eir head tilted. "Sure, that works."

I shook my head and downed my coffee in two long gulps. I needed about four more of these, but the pot was empty. Despite Kay's languidness, I was worried about the time. What if the zombies broke out?

"You ready to go?" Kay asked as I slammed my mug onto the table harder than I intended.

"Yes. But I'm still not sure giving the red panda stimulants is a great idea." I picked up Pog. Eiy gripped the half-full bowl of coffee, dragging it halfway across the table before I pried it from eim.

We emerged onto the porch. The sun had risen and in the morning light the house looked its usual decrepit, spooky self with siding half-falling off and boarded over windows. Kay took off across the grass and I followed him, carrying Pog. When we got there, he peered in a window through a gap in the boards.

"Is that the sink on the floor?" he asked.

"Yeah, it... fell."

"I see something moving... holy shit." He stumbled backwards with a yelp. "That guy's brain is hanging out."

"Zombie. I told you," I said in a deadpan. I don't know what he'd expected.

Kay gave me an incredulous look. "I'm not going in there. We need to call someone."

Something thumped against the window, and we all jumped back.

Kay said, "That or just burn the whole place down."

"Not my house, you're not!" Pog squealed and flailed against my arms. I hugged eim tight and eiy settled down.

"Then we need to call someone," Kay said, marching away from the house. I followed, but then I heard the telltale scream of the front door hinges. I grabbed Kay's arm and hauled him back against the side of the house. He gave me a startled look, but I put a finger to my mouth, mimed opening a door, and pointed to the front of the house. If a zombie had gotten out, I didn't want it to see us. Kay nodded, eyes wide, and pressed back against the siding.

I heard yelling, and then a shout that sounded like a battle cry. Didn't sound like a zombie. All they'd done so far was moan for brains. I side stepped to the edge of the house and peered around. Kay pressed against my back.

"What is it?" he whispered.

That was not a zombie on the porch. Three gray-robed figures ringed the front door, and a fourth robed figure, a massive giant, wrestled with something in the doorway. The giant grunted and kicked the thing back into the house. Another darted forward and pulled the door shut. During all this, they were arguing in a lyrical language I didn't recognize.

I pulled my head back and whispered to Kay, "I don't know. Not zombies though."

He went around me and I backed up so he could look. He only glanced before whipping back around. "Run," he hissed, grabbing my arm and hauling me away. I stumbled after him, dry grass pricking my feet, wondering what was going on.

We were halfway back to Kay's house, climbing over the remains of the picket fence that separated the yards, when a cry came from behind us. "You there, stop!"

"Run!" Kay yelled and sped up. Of course, he had shoes on. I tried to run faster, but Pog's weight and the rocks digging into my bare feet slowed me down.

A three-foot icicle as big around as my fist slammed into the ground to my left. I glanced behind to see the robed figures chasing us. One lobbed something glowing at us.

"What are they doing?" I wailed as another icicle hit, closer this time.

"Trying to kill us, obviously!" Kay yelled. "Now run faster!"

My palms began itching. A ball of fire flew over my head, singeing my hair. It hit the grass ahead of me and smoldered and hissed in the morning dew. I yelped and wished either I could run faster or for something to slow down my pursuers.

The light morning breeze increased in intensity, roaring past me strong enough to almost pull Pog from my grip. I put my head down and squinted against the wind, intent on Kay's back. He'd already reached his driveway and tapped at the keypad on his garage door. The door rolled open.

I risked a glance behind me. The biggest dust devil I'd ever seen whirled on the dry grass, whipping up a cloud of dust so thick I could barely see the robed figures in the center. I didn't know where it had come from, but it had bought me the time I'd needed.

Kay ducked underneath the rising door as soon as the gap was large enough. An engine revved inside. The garage door was halfway up when I got there. I hobbled inside to see Kay in a red convertible sports car.

What kind of person owned a convertible in Oregon when you could only use it for a few months in the summer? Still, it was one more car than Brandon or I owned. I got into the passenger seat.

Kay reversed before I even got my door shut. The car squealed to a stop in the street as he yanked the steering wheel. He popped it into gear and roared off.

"Shit, how did they find him so soon?" Kay muttered, twisting his hands on the steering wheel. "They must have felt the burst of magic earlier. Dummy. I should have thought of that. We should have left immediately." I wasn't sure he realized he was talking out loud.

The dust devil was dying and behind it, smoke billowed up from Pog's farmhouse and flames licked at the siding.

"My house!" Pog wailed, flailing over my shoulder at the receding sight of the burning house.

"I'm sorry, Pog. It's gone." The house looked like it had gone up like a tinderbox. "Everything we owned was in there," I said, feeling close to crying myself.

I held Pog close and rubbed eir fur as we roared away from both of our whole lives.

III

Which Witch

As Pog's wails wound down, I asked Kay for his phone and sent Brandon another text to let him know about the house. It surprised me he hadn't responded yet. He was always up and out to get to work before dawn. Maybe this special job kept different hours.

"Where are we going?" I asked as Kay passed the movie theater, then turned onto the street that led to St. John's bridge.

I had walked over here a few times to see a movie on the big screen, but my bad luck had meant that each time something had gone wrong—a broken projector once, a snapped film the second time, the third my seat had cracked off at the base, throwing me backwards and giving me a concussion. I'd finally given up.

That Kay's car was still running after I'd been in it for this long surprised me. Buses usually lasted longer, in my experience. Maybe something about the luck being spread out over more people, or that I sat in the middle away from the engine, or that the city maintained them, meant they only broke down on me every other ride.

"I'm taking you to a witch family I know that makes magical amulets." Kay kept his eyes glued to the road. "The Prices."

I knew a Price. She claimed she was a witch. Probably not the same family, though. "So I'm a witch," I said, still trying to get my head around the fact that I could do magic now.

"No, you're a mage," Kay corrected.

"What's the difference?"

"I know this one," Pog said, pulling eir face out of the crook of my arm. "Witches do magic with rituals and tools. They make magically imbued jewelry and potions, that sort of thing. Mages pull magic from the environment to cast spells, like those villains did to my house." Pog barred eir teeth.

"The red panda is correct. Though I'm curious how you know that," Kay said.

The engine roared as we picked up speed on the highway and Pog perked up, staring out the window with wide eyes at the scenery flashing by. "It was a witch that created me," eiy said, climbing to eir feet. "I watch. I listen. I know lots of witch stuff."

"Interesting. We'll have to have a chat about that later," Kay said.

"Then shouldn't we be going to a mage for help?" I asked.

"Look how fast we're going!" Pog whispered and pressed eir nose and front paws to the window glass.

"Nope, bad idea."

"Why? I mean, what if I do—" I waved my empty hand around my head "whatever I did at the house again? If I really can do magic, I need to learn how to control it." The thought sent a thrill through me, followed by a wave of dread. Given my bad luck, maybe having the gift of magic was a bad idea.

But, if I could get a handle on it, I could probably use it to make money. The little I made from selling art to tourists didn't go far.

"Max, as Pog pointed out, those people who burned down your house." Kay glanced at me from the corner of his eye. "Mages are after you."

"What? Why? I'm a nobody."

"You're not nobody," he snapped.

"Can you teach me how to control my magic?" I twisted my hands. If people *were* after me, I needed a way to defend myself.

Kay barked out a laugh, and I jumped at how feral it sounded. "No. Mages are born. You either have the gift or not. Anyone can do witch magic, if you know the spell. But that's the rub, there. Spellbooks are usually passed down within families. Unless you have one of those, true spells are hard to find."

"I'm twenty-two," I snorted. "If I was born with it, why did it wait until now to show up?"

"Maybe you're a late bloomer," Kay said, not sounding like he cared much.

I'd grown up in foster care. That was where I'd met Brandon. I'd always been a little frustrated at not knowing anything about my biological family, but it had been a distant worry. And an ache around holidays when I saw all the happy families wandering past my booth at the Saturday market. Had my parents known what I was when they gave me up?

"Don't cry, Max." Pog turned away from the window and patted my face.

"I'm not crying," I protested, but hugged eim close, wishing the red panda were Brandon. He'd know what to do.

"That red panda is damn cute," Kay said. "Not the most practical form to choose for your familiar, though. Draws a lot of attention. Your raccoon play is a good idea, but everyone knows what they look like. Maybe you could say it's a ringtail instead? They're native to Oregon."

"They're the size of squirrels, so I think Pog would be a bit too big to pull that off." I stroked eir back, considering what

Kay said. "What do you mean 'choose?' I didn't choose Pog, eiy just appeared."

"You must have done it unconsciously then." Kay chuckled.

"Wonderful," I muttered. "So how is a witch family going to help?"

"That charm I gave you won't keep the mage's tracking spells from finding you for long. Herb magic wears out quickly. We need to get you more permanent protection. Then from there we'll figure out the next steps."

Puzzled, I touched the pouch through my sweatshirt. Kay had given me this before we saw the mages. A trilling song came from underneath Pog, distracting me from the thought. Maybe it was Brandon! I fished under eim for the phone and pulled it out.

"That's my text message sound. Can you read it to me?" Kay asked. We were almost to downtown and the rush hour traffic had picked up, slowing us down to a crawl.

"It's not from Brandon." I slumped as I read the screen.

"I know. That's the sound I use for one of my clients. Can you read it?"

"'Kay, where are you?' from a contact listed as the wolf."

"Dang, that's right. She had a reading this morning. Text her back, tell her I'll reschedule with her later."

I did so, then put the phone to sleep. I'd forgotten Kay said he did readings. I'd seen people doing them downtown and at the Saturday market. After this morning, I was ready to believe.

"Okay, so... witches, mages, and familiars are real." I ruffled Pog's fur between eir ears. "How about werewolves? Is that why you call her the wolf and thought Pog was a shifter?"

"Yes. Werewolves are real. They prefer to be called shapeshifters though, since a lot of them aren't wolves."

"Wow. Vampires?" I asked, practically vibrating with excitement. I read a lot of novels, being one thing that my bad luck couldn't interfere with too much, and vampire ones were my favorite.

Kay let out a long-suffering sigh. "Yes, though I don't get the modern world's obsession with the parasites. We actually drove past one of their organizations on the way out of St. John's."

"Under the bridge?" I was at St. John's bridge a lot with my paint and ink. Tourists ate up art of the iconic bridge. There was an enormous structure at the base of the pillars in the middle of the park that I'd always imagined housed secrets, though Brandon had told me it was just where they anchored all the cables for the bridge. Boring.

"No, in Forest Park across the river," Kay said.

Forest Park was a huge natural park that took up a large swath of the hills between Portland and Beaverton, so I could easily picture something like that hidden away somewhere in the trees off the beaten path.

"What does this organization do?" I asked.

"The Paranormal Creature Association, or the PCA. Its goal is to keep supernaturals hidden from the outside world. Mostly it's shifters and vampires that work there, as they're the ones most likely to have negative run-ins with humans that need covering up." While the words were positive, Kay's tone dripped with derision.

"That sounds like a good thing. Why do you sound so disdainful about it?"

"It's the way they go about it. The vampires use it as a cudgel to force the rest of us to follow their orders."

"I see," I said, but couldn't quash my excitement about the idea that I might meet a real life werewolf or vampire. "By the way, what did Brandon need a reading about?" I asked. He'd never really struck me as the type that would be into fortune telling or tarot card readings. He was always so serious and intense.

"Sorry, my readings are confidential. Patient client confidentiality." Kay winked at me. I rolled my eyes.

Kay parked in front of one of the historical Victorians that dotted the upscale Sellwood neighborhood southeast of downtown. Huge old oak trees lined the street, providing a pleasant cover of shade. The house he parked in front of was gorgeous. So much nicer than the rundown farmhouse we'd been squatting in.

A tower anchored the center of the house above a steep gabled roof. A porch with yellow painted decorative pillars and carved railings wrapped around the outside. My fingers itched for my sketchbook and pencils, to get the sharp lines of the old house down in black and white.

Pog clambered up to my shoulder and draped around like a scarf before I got out of the car. My bare feet sunk into the soft dirt under the trees. I followed Kay up the walk, and he rang the doorbell. It bonged, a low deep sound that vibrated the soles of my feet.

A wooden porch swing and matching chairs sat next to the front door, looking out over the street and sidewalk. Everything about this house was adorable. I gripped Pog's tail to my chest and took a deep breath. My palms were getting that itchy feeling again.

"Calm down, Max." Pog rubbed his muzzle against my cheek. I stroked eir head and the itchy feeling faded.

"What's wrong?" Kay asked, but then a young woman with dark, wavy hair opened the front door. She wore lots of flowing, brightly colored fabrics. I also knew her.

"Ynes?" I said in surprise.

"Max?" Ynes blinked past Kay to focus on me. Her glasses accented her widening eyes.

"You're acquainted?" Kay asked in surprise.

"Yeah, from the Saturday Market. Ynes has the corner booth near where I usually set up to sell my art." As well as anything else I could get my hands on, like the things I'd looted from Pog's house. I didn't have a booth; my bad luck made that impossible, but I had a spot that I frequently used to catch the tourists who came to see the market.

The first time I'd done portraits on the waterfront during Saturday Market, she'd come up to me and introduced herself as "Ynes Price. Yes, that Price family. Anyway, I know your father and I recognized you right away, so I thought I'd come say hello." She'd been embarrassed when I told her I wasn't who she thought I was, and then we'd become friends, or at least friendly with each other.

"Wonderful. That will make this much smoother. Ynes, may we come inside?"

"Oh, yes." Ynes stepped back, skirts swirling. "Is that an art doll? It's very realistic," she asked as I passed her.

"Not hardly. I'm Pog." Pog tugged on my ear to stop me and then stuck out eir paw to Ynes.

"Oh my gosh, you're so cute!" Ynes squealed as she shook eir paw. "I can't believe you can talk!"

"Don't familiars usually talk?" I asked as I looked around.

Ynes looked at me over the rims of her glasses and raised her eyebrows like I'd just said something incredibly dumb.

The house smelled of lavender, cherries, and herbs. A thick red runner set with yellow geometric patterns ran down the front hallway. What I judged to be an original oil painting hung over a carved wooden shoe bench that sat just inside the front door. I hadn't known Ynes' family had money. I wondered why she bothered selling at the market.

"Is your father home?" Kay asked as he kicked off his shoes by the front door.

"Nope, just me, I'm afraid." Ynes adjusted her glasses and frowned at me. Her frown deepened as she glanced down and saw my bare feet.

"Sorry, my house burned down this morning and Kay didn't have any shoes that fit me."

Ynes' hands went to her mouth with a gasp. "That's awful!"

Pog's tail tightened around my chest and eiy buried eir face in my neck. Crap, I'd said that without thinking. While I was upset about losing all my things, that house had been Pog's whole life. I rubbed eir head. "I'm sorry. I said that without thinking. Our house burned down this morning. Pog's pretty upset."

"Come into the parlor." Ynes gestured us through a doorway and into a small sitting room with bay windows that looked out over the porch.

Kay sat in the armchair. Ynes took a seat on the far end of the sofa, a huge plush deal, overflowing with throw pillows, that took up most of the far wall. I sat on the other end of the sofa. Pog tried to dash off, but I grabbed eim by the armpits.

"Pog, no. You'll tear up the fabric with your claws," I said, setting eim in my lap.

"He's fine." Ynes patted the seat between us. I let Pog go and eiy scampered off my lap, across the cushion, and into Ynes' lap.

"Not he, eiy," Kay corrected her.

"Is that right?" She grinned and scratched Pog's chin. "So, Max, why did you pretend to not be part of the supernatural community when I asked you?"

"I only found out this morning," I said.

"That's why we're here," Kay said. "I made him a protection pouch, but you know how crap I am at anything to do with spells. There's a reason I stick to fortune telling."

I tugged the little pouch out of my sweatshirt to show it to Ynes.

"No, Max, keep that against your skin until Ynes can get you something else," Kay said.

"What's after him? A demon? Ghost?" Ynes asked.

I waited for Kay to answer, but when he didn't, I said, "Mages."

"I knew it!" Ynes stood up, sending Pog sliding down her skirts to the floor. She pointed at me. "I told you it was a curse!"

I rolled my eyes. "Ynes, I know I *joke* that it's a bad luck curse, but it's not a curse."

"Didn't that amulet I gave you help?" she asked, putting her hands on her hips.

"You tell me. I was wearing it during the goose incident." I settled back into the cushions, trying my best to look nonchalant. I knew she'd been trying to help by giving me the amulet, so I'd humored her and wore it on the days when she was working the market, even if it had been super ugly. But because it was so ugly, I'd kept it hidden under my shirt most of the time, so maybe she hadn't realized I'd had it on when everything went down.

Ynes's dark cheeks turned pink, and she pressed her lips together before sitting slowly back down. "I just assumed you hadn't been."

Kay laughed and asked, "Bad luck curse?"

Ynes looked at me, eyebrows raising. "You've been with him for how long?"

"Since just before dawn. So, about two hours now?" I looked to Kay for confirmation. He nodded.

"I guess it hasn't struck yet." She sounded skeptical. She'd seen enough at the market to know how unusual it was that nothing had happened. Unless you counted the zombies or the dust devil. But usually it was less overt and more things breaking at inopportune moments.

While we talked, Pog wandered around the small room, sniffing and running eir paws over every surface eiy could reach. Ynes didn't seem to mind, so I let eim be.

"Yeah, it's been pretty quiet." It was weird. And ominous. When it was quiet like this, it usually meant it was building up to something nasty.

"At least since the house burned down, you mean," Ynes said.

"No, that was the mages," I said.

Ynes' face blanched. "That's terrible," she whispered. "Why would they do that?"

"Sorry to cut this short," Kay said, checking his phone. "But we're pressed for time. Can you get started on that amulet while we wait for your father to return?"

"Sure." She stood and strode out, her feet soundless on the thick rug. She stopped in the doorway and turned to me. "Max, I'll need you to come with me so I can tune the spell to your aura."

I got up and followed her out, Pog scampering at my heels. Kay stood, but Ynes waved him back. "Please wait here. It'll just be a moment and I'll send him back to you."

Kay sat back down, but with narrowed eyes. I don't know why he was so suspicious. He was the one that had brought me here after all. It was just a coincidence that we already knew each other.

Three years earlier

Today looked like it was going to be a perfect day for the outdoor market—blue skies with only a few fluffy clouds in sight.

Since I was stuck on foot, I'd had to leave early this morning in order to get downtown on time. I crossed the bridge on the pedestrian walkway and took the overly steep stairs down to the street level. I'd tumbled down these several times when my bad luck had struck, so I took it slow and steady, trying to keep my breathing even until I reached the bottom.

I was late, having been slowed by my bad luck causing a minor car accident. Throngs of tourists already wandered around the booths. I didn't have an official space—I was a squatter. Most of the vendors didn't like me, feeling like I was stealing business from them, especially the artists. But not all of them.

"Hey, Max!" Ynes waved to me from her booth as I stepped out of the crosswalk.

A steady stream of bikers, joggers, roller skaters, and more moved along the river path on the other side of this end of the market. I had been planning to go directly to my favorite spot to catch their eye, but I detoured up the couple of steps to where Ynes was perched on a stool behind all her jewelry displays.

"I was wondering if I'd see you today," she said with a giggle. "I missed you last week."

She really was cute, with her short wavy hair, her glasses, and her colorful clothing. I'd ask her out, but she'd seen my bad luck in action too many times for me to have a chance with her.

I rolled back my right sleeve to show her the long cut running down the back of my arm. Seven black stitches ran down it, painfully dark against my pale skin. "Had a minor accident. Couldn't hold a pencil."

Her pretty brown eyes widened. "Oh, my! What happened?"

I'd had so many things happen in the week since, that it was a struggle to remember what had caused this cut. When it came to me, I looked back at her. "Streetlight directly above me exploded. Big piece of glass impaled my arm."

"Are you sure someone didn't curse you?" Ynes asked. She slid her fanny pack around to her front and started digging through it.

"You know I don't believe in that." I rolled my eyes. "And if they did, they cursed a baby. Things have been like this since I was a toddler."

"You know, an acquaintance of mine does tarot readings by appointment. He's really accurate," Ynes said. "He'd be able to tell you for sure."

"It's fine," I said, rolling my sleeve back down. It was already hot, and the day only threatened to get hotter, but I needed to cover up the cut so it didn't scare off customers. "Besides, that sounds pricey."

"It's not, Max. You really should get it checked out by an expert." She pulled an ugly medallion on a thick cord out of her fanny pack and thrust it at me. "I know you don't believe in magic, but I'd like you to wear this."

I tried not to scrunch up my nose at the thing. I didn't take it. "No offence, but why? I'm not a big jewelry person."

"It's a charm against dark energy. Curses, that kind of thing. I made it myself." She stood and pressed it into my hands. "You might not believe, but I do. Will you wear it for me?" Her eyes shone behind her glasses, so earnest that I sighed and took it. I supposed it wouldn't hurt anything to humor her. If I kept it under my shirt, no one should see it. I put it on, then wandered around the fountain, looking for a space to set up my folding stool and easel. I'd been too slow, and a juggler had already taken my usual spot.

I only bothered to wear the ugly thing when I did the Saturday Market, keeping it outside my shirt when I arrived so that Ynes could see I had it on. It didn't seem to have any effect. The bad luck was as bad on those days as at any other time.

In fact, after the third stool in a month snapped, I started just sitting cross-legged on the pavement, foregoing the easel, drawing with my sketchbook in my lap, and laying out a few paintings around me for sale.

I was head down, inking, when a shadow fell over me. "Interested in any particular painting?" I asked without looking up.

"These are gorgeous!" Ynes' voice finally made me look up. She'd crouched down in front of me and was looking at one of my paintings.

I realized with a start that the one she was looking at was a portrait of her. I'd tried to change it enough to make it unrecognizable, but her clothing was so distinctive that it was futile. Blushing, I said, "Thank you."

"So, how has the charm been treating you?" she asked, picking up the very picture I didn't want her to see.

I fingered the chain around my neck. What should I say? I didn't want her to feel bad that it hadn't done anything. It wasn't her fault I had terrible luck. "Oh, fine."

She grinned at me over the canvas. "Great!" then she turned the canvas around and posed. "I'm flattered."

"Sorry, I didn't ask permission. I like to paint the people I see around town." I flushed brighter and leaned over to unzip my backpack so she couldn't see my face. "This is one of my neighbors in the apartments," I said, tapping another canvas.

"I don't mind. In fact, I'll take it. How much?"

I waved her off. "You can have it. Consider it a trade for the charm." I kept my head down until she'd stood and walked off. When I did, I found she'd left a hundred dollar bill on my sketchpad. That was too much. More than double my usual price. I should go give her change, but I was grateful for the money. It was enough that I might treat me and Brandon to grocery store sushi tonight. Fancy.

IV

Not a Minor Power

I SHOOK OFF THE memory. Ynes and Brandon had been some of the few people who I counted as friends, everyone else having been driven off by my bad luck. So in that regard, I counted myself lucky.

"My workshop is back this way." Ynes led me through the house. The air was silent and oppressive. In the distance, a clock ticked. I didn't think I could live here. Too quiet, and everything was so perfect.

Ynes cast a worried glance my way as we went out the back door and down the steps into the garden. Massive trees, as big as the ones that lined the street, left the entire yard in shadow.

Colorful bursts of flowers punctuated the neat rows of plants that took up most of the yard. I didn't recognize most of them; they weren't typical garden fare. With an exclamation of delight, Pog ran into the garden and began sniffing furiously at everything with eir little snub nose.

"Where's your boyfriend? Is he okay?" Ynes asked as we headed down the paving-stone path for a shed on the other side of the yard. The shed looked more like a miniature house, with pale yellow siding, white trim, and a white door complete with a little planter box on the window filled to overflowing with yellow posies.

"Brandon?" He'd sometimes come with me on Saturdays around the holidays to help me out selling prints while I did my caricatures. My face heated in a furious blush remembering last night, when I'd sworn he was about to kiss me. I wished. "He's not my boyfriend. We're just friends and roommates."

She paused at the door to the shed, turning to arch an eyebrow at me and give me a half-smile. "Is that right? I guess I just assumed..."

"We get that a lot," I mumbled.

Ynes didn't know what she was talking about. Brandon was straight. Maybe I would have had a chance before I transitioned. In fact, we'd been each other's first kiss one day after school.

The overhead bulb inside Ynes' shed blinked on as we went inside.

Benches lined three of the four walls of the space, covered in half-finished pieces of jewelry, twists of silver and gold wire, glittering stones and charms, a variety of small tools, and a bunch of junk like a burned out match, a mini-slingshot, and a half-disassembled pocket knife.

There was a little plush red velvet bed tucked into one corner. A small fuzzy brown head poked up to peer at us with beady black eyes, nose quivering. A fluffy brown tail uncurled from around it and flicked over its head. Cooing, Ynes went over to the corner and held out her hand. The squirrel hopped from the bed onto her palm and flicking its tail. Ynes smiled down at it, eyes crinkling, then turned to hold it out to me.

"Barnabas, this is my friend, Max, from the Saturday Market. Max, Barnabas. Barnabas is my familiar."

The squirrel chittered. "He says he remembers you. You feed him a lot," Ynes translated.

More like my bad luck frequently caused me to trip and drop my food. But I didn't want to hurt the squirrel's feelings, so instead I said, "It just sounds like he's chittering."

"That's why I was surprised I could understand Pog," Ynes said, nuzzling Barnabas to her face.

"Kay can too. I thought it was normal, but then I just met Pog this morning."

Barnabas gave one last flick of his tail and then leapt from Ynes' hand to the counter, and from there scampered down and out of the shack.

"Why didn't your parents help you summon one when you were little?" Ynes said, watching Barnabas go with a half smile.

I averted my eyes and crossed my arms. "I don't know who my parents are. That's why I didn't even know I was a mage until this morning." I blew out a deep breath.

"Your first spell was summoning a familiar?" She stared at me, then she glanced at her watch. I hadn't noticed it before now, as it had been half hidden under her chunky bracelets. Who still wore watches in this day and age? "If that's true, I need to call the PCA. The zoo has probably noticed a missing red panda by now."

My thoughts spun around at what Ynes had just said. Pog hadn't originally been a red panda. Eiy'd been a house spirit. Maybe eiy had merged with one of the zoo pandas? But then how had it gotten to my house from the zoo? To get to St. John's neighborhood from the zoo, it would have had to go down the highway, through downtown, across the river, and then through several more neighborhoods.

"But Pog just appeared out of thin air," I said.

"That's impossible! You can't make something from nothing. No one can. We call familiars from nature around us. Regular animals that become infused with magic." Ynes threw up her arms. "Even Kay knows that. He should have taken you straight to the PCA. The longer we wait, the harder it's going to be for them to get a cover story into place."

"We drove by it on the way here. He pointed it out, but said it's all vampires and werewolves and that I should avoid it," I said.

"You should take anything a kitsune says with a grain of salt. They're all tricksters," she said with a scowl.

I had no idea what that meant, so I stayed silent. Was that like a witch idiom or something—a way to say someone is not to be trusted? Ynes didn't notice my confusion. She was busy taking pinches of dried plants out of various drawers and dropping them into a little stone mortar. "Do you know why the mages burned down your house?"

"Probably because of the zombies inside it."

"The what?" She gave me an incredulous look and then went back to her grinding. "Not funny. This isn't the time for joking around, Max." Without looking, she thrust out a hand toward me. "Hair."

I sputtered. "What?"

"I need one of your hairs." She snapped her fingers. Shrugging, I plucked out a strand that was coming close to hanging in my eyes and handed it over. She dropped it into the mortar and ground it in with smooth, practiced motions. The scrape of stone against stone set my teeth on edge. My palms started itching.

"I need quiet for this next part. Go back inside and wait with Kay in the parlor. And take Pog with you. I don't want any of the neighbors to see him. Eim." she corrected herself.

"Speaking of untrained, shouldn't I be looking for a teacher? What if it happens again?" I flexed my hands, which still itched. The burning had spread to my fingertips and down to my wrists. Rising panic made my hands shake.

"It won't." Ynes didn't look up from grinding. "I'm surprised you even managed the familiar spell without training."

"But you said most people get their familiars as children. So why would I not know I had magic until now? Shouldn't I have manifested powers earlier?"

"You probably have a pretty minor power. Maybe only a sixteenth Fae. Or less. Another reason I'm not worried."

"I'm part Fae?" I stared at her back. "Like a fairy?"

"Yes and no, but I can't talk now. Ask Kay." She kicked a foot backward at me. "Now shoo. This is delicate work."

What had happened at the house didn't seem minor, but Ynes' clearly couldn't talk right now. I backed away and hugged myself as I left the shed, shutting the door firmly behind me.

While I'd been inside, the sun had risen further, heating the backyard enough that my sweats were now almost too warm. Speaking of sweats, the over-sized pants slid down as I walked. I grabbed for them, but tripped on an uneven paving stone. The rough stones scraped up my hands and knees as I landed. Damn borrowed clothes. I wished I was wearing my familiar hoodie and jeans.

"Max!" Pog called, but it was too late. The itching burn on my hands roared through me. I could feel it expanding out from me like a wave. My sweats transformed like an anime magical girl sequence, changing from pink sweatshirt material into my favorite gray hoodie and blue jeans. The hard rock under my knees turned soft and squishy. The grass in the yard turned purple and the plants in the garden twisted, like the ferns back at the house, turning into cartoonish multi-colored sunflowers with faces.

Then, as suddenly as it came, the magic was gone. Pog threw eimselves against my face. Barnabas dashed around me, chattering.

The sunflowers all started singing in unison, a wordless song that sounded very cheerful.

I was still on my hands and knees, trembling from exhaustion now. Sweat dripped from my face and I was panting as if I'd just gone for a run.

I pushed Pog away and sat up. I tugged at the hem of the hoodie, pulling it out to look down at it. Staring back at me was the faded red logo of the art college that I'd attended for two weeks until they had thrown me out after a disastrous incident with the paints. It was even stained in all the same places as the one left in the house that I'd thought was destroyed by fire.

Though the paving stones still looked like rough stone circles, they were now plush pillows with stone-patterned fabric. Would have been nice if that had appeared a few moments earlier, to be honest. Blood still oozed from the grit dug into my palms, and the knees of my favorite jeans were turning red where I was bleeding through the fabric.

The shed door opened, then Ynes wailed, "My garden!"

Kay came tearing out the back door, then stopped so abruptly he nearly fell face first off the steps onto the paving pillows. "Gods damn it, Max. Might as well have rung the dinner bell and sent up a flare," he yelled, tearing at his hair.

"That is not a minor power!" Ynes yelled, either at me or Kay, I wasn't sure.

"We can't wait for her father to get back. We need to go before your fan club gets here." Kay latched onto my arm and towed me towards the back door. Then he looked at my neck and swore. "Max, where's my pouch?"

I patted at my chest and then my neck. "It must have transformed with the sweats."

"That should be impossible. I charmed it against magic."

I was hearing that word a lot today. I just shrugged, not sure what to say.

He tore at his hair again and looked back at Ynes, who was still staring at her ruined garden. "Ynes, do you have anything pre-made? Any kind of protection charm or magic-dampening amulet you can lend us so he's not completely exposed? Or do you have anything that your father might have left for me?"

"He didn't leave anything. I didn't even know you were coming!" Ynes yelled back.

"Do you have any protection items that could help him?"

"Yes..."

"Go get it!"

When Ynes hesitated, Kay yelled, "Now!" His eyes flashed yellow for a moment. Weird. Either the scary eyes or the terrified look on his face got Ynes moving.

"Fine, but don't get in the habit of ordering me around," she growled as she stomped back towards the shed. She returned a few moments later wearing a fanny pack, sling style, across her chest. She reached around her neck and removed a thick chain that held a copper amulet at the end, holding it out by the chain.

Kay reached for the amulet, but Ynes pulled it back. "Payment will be taking me with you. I like Max and I don't trust you," she said.

"Fine, but we go now." Kay ripped it from her hands and tossed it over my head, tucking it down my shirt. I felt nothing special about this thing, but Kay seemed satisfied. Then he rushed us both through the house and out the front, impatiently tapping his foot as he waited for Ynes to lock up.

"This is a two-seater," Ynes protested when we reached Kay's car.

"Two door," Kay corrected. "I have a truck—" Ynes began, but Kay cut her off. "No time. Max, you're the smallest. You get in the back."

That was debatable, but I wasn't about to make Ynes climb back there in skirts. I popped the seat forward and wiggled through the gap. The top of my head brushed the soft top of the car once I was seated. I felt cramped back in here.

Pog climbed in and plopped into the seat next to me, back legs out in front of eim with eir tail sticking out in between. It looked comical, but I tried not to laugh as I buckled eir seatbelt.

Ynes got in the front seat and set Barnabas in her lap. "Where were you planning to go?"

"I was just going to drive around for a bit while we wait for your father," Kay said as he started up the car and pulled away from the curb. "Moving will make it even more difficult for them to track him."

"Go fast again, Kay!" Pog yelled, vibrating with excitement. Eiy had wiggled out of the seatbelt and stood, nose pressed to the tiny rear side window. Kay ignored eim.

"That was your plan?" Ynes scoffed. "What if he goes nuclear again?"

"I can feel them coming," I said. I rubbed my palms as if they itched, though I wasn't feeling the sensation right now.

"Enough time for me to pull over?" Kay glanced at me in the rearview mirror. His nose had wrinkled up like he smelled something bad.

I shrugged. "Maybe?"

"This is the part where I should probably tell you that my father isn't getting back for two days," Ynes said.

"Two days?" Kay pounded on the steering wheel. "When were you planning to tell me that?"

"After you told me why you needed to see him." Ynes hiked a thumb back at me, voice raising an octave. "But I clearly can't wait. We need to find Max a teacher, before someone gets hurt. He's warping reality, Kay. I've never seen anything like it."

"So call your father and tell him to get back here!" Kay yelled.

"Stop yelling!" I yelled back. "If you're going to be like that, drop me and Pog off here and I'll figure things out on my own." I knew roughly where we were. What I'd do or where I'd go, though, I had no idea.

"I'm sorry," Kay said with a sigh, lowering his voice. "I'm a little stressed."

Him? He didn't just lose everything he owned and learn he had magic all in the same day, but I swallowed back the admonishment. To his credit, he seemed like he meant it. "Alright."

Ynes pulled out a cell phone from her fanny pack and waved it at Kay. "I already texted him, but he drove up to our vacation house to work on something delicate for a client. They don't have cell service out there, so he might not get it until he heads home."

"Wait," I said, furrowing my brow, "how could he have left you something that might help? I just met you this morning."

Kay growled, turning his head so I couldn't see his face from the back seat. "Doesn't matter."

"Odd time to ask about it then," Ynes quipped, head bent over her phone.

Kay twisted his hands on the steering wheel. "I might have had a vision about Max getting his powers. Your father is making something to help him. I would have asked for it first thing, but I thought it could wait. Clearly, I was wrong."

"Then you should have scheduled this better," Ynes said with icicles in her voice.

"I *did*." He paused and took a deep breath, visibly trying to calm himself. His next words were softer. "My vision said it would happen a week from now, not today."

"Gift of prophecy?" I said in a sing-song, trying to defuse the fight I felt brewing. My palms itched. I clenched my hands, willing it to go away.

"Minor. I said minor. Which means I'm not always right, though I usually am," Kay said, waggling a finger at me over his shoulder without looking at me. "Something must have changed after I did the reading..."

"Well, what does your gift say about a place to pull over?" I said as the burning in my hands intensified.

"Are you kidding me? It's been thirty minutes!" Kay's voice went gravely and muffled, like he was clenching his teeth together. "How are we going to survive two days if this keeps happening?"

"So you'll admit you're wrong about him not needing a teacher?" Ynes crossed her arms, looking smug as Kay turned off onto a side street.

"Look, a teacher is out of the question," Kay said, slowing down and scanning the street.

This didn't look like a suitable spot to me. The houses were barely set back from the sidewalk and there were people in half the yards. He pressed a button on the dash and the top started receding. Good idea; the less time it would take me to get out of the car, the better.

After a moment, Kay continued, "I don't know how much you know about mage magic, Ynes, but you need a teacher from your own family or one that has a similar gift. And he doesn't know who his parents are."

"How did you know that?" I flinched.

"Gift of prophecy, remember?" Kay flashed me a tooth-filled grin over his shoulder.

I rolled my eyes, not buying it. Brandon had probably told him we'd met in foster care, so he'd jumped to that assumption. Not that he was wrong, but a flash of jealousy stabbed me. Kay and Brandon must be close friends if Brandon had told him that. Yet, I'd had no idea.

"Are you sure?" Ynes had twisted totally around to kneel in the front seat and was staring at me over the headrest. "When I first met him, I thought he was a Woolven."

"You think I might be related to that family?" My stomach growled, loudly. Maybe after I took care of the magical thing, we could go get breakfast.

"Yeah, I do." Ynes slid back around.

I might not know who my parents were, but I knew they had voluntarily placed me in the foster care system. There was something about knowing you hadn't been wanted that made you bitter about the whole bio family thing. So why this sudden flurry of excitement in me?

I wasn't sure it was a good idea to go to my family. How would we even explain any of this? Besides the fact that they must have abandoned me for a reason, there was also the problem that, as far as they knew, they'd given up a daughter.

I clutched my stomach and wished Brandon was here. I didn't want to meet my family without him there, yet I *needed* a teacher.

My palms seemed to catch fire. I gasped and fell forward.

Pog climbed into my lap. As eir fur touched my hands, the burning sensation faded but didn't go away completely.

"Why is this helping?" I asked, burying my hands in the thick fur of Pog's ruff.

"Familiars help you channel magic," Kay said. "Hopefully that bought you enough time." He pulled over to the curb. "There's a park there, now go!"

I climbed out the back over the trunk and ran, clutching Pog to my chest, aiming for a large swath of grass in a currently unused soccer field. I fell to my knees near the goal, so hungry that all I could think about was food. Even the grass looked like the green candy sticks I coveted from the downtown candy store. If I had a good day at the market, I'd buy some to eat on my walk home.

The smell of freshly cut grass turned sugary as it turned into green licorice sticks, the effect swirling out from me in a circle.

I gathered up a handful and munched on them on the way back to the car. Watermelon. My favorite.

"Is my amulet okay?" Ynes asked as I neared the car. She gripped the car door tightly and her eyes were wide.

"Yeah." I hooked the chain under one finger and lifted it to show her.

"Good." She slumped back, relief written on her face. "That's my personal everyday carry."

"Your what?"

"Besides warding the wearer against magical scrying, it also can function as a flashlight, a screwdriver, a fidget toy, and a bottle opener. I made it myself. It's a prototype." She went back to texting on her phone.

I stared at her for a second, trying to think of a reason you'd want a protection amulet that did such a random assortment of tasks.

"Might as well make it a vibrator too," I joked. I knew her well enough to know she wouldn't be offended.

Ynes just shook her head, a smile tugging at the corner of her mouth. "Not a bad idea," she said back. I only half thought she was joking.

Pog had a licorice stick in eir mouth, I noticed as I lifted eim back into the car. I was tempted to take it away, but the coffee hadn't seemed to have any ill effects on eim, so I let eim be.

As I lifted Pog into the back seat, Kay said, "You're one to talk, eating the grass."

"It's not grass anymore, it's licorice." I held one out between the seats. "Want one?"

Ynes wrinkled her nose and swatted it away. "I saw where you got those from. No thanks."

Kay also shook his head.

"I kinda missed breakfast." I bit off another bite and then stuffed the rest in the pocket of my hoodie, then climbed over the trunk into the back seat.

"I can go through a drive-through," Kay said.

"Please. I'm starving. I don't even care what," I said, glancing at Pog. The red panda was chewing on a stick that was clenched between eir paws like a piece of bamboo. "Speaking of that, what should we feed Pog?"

"I texted the PCA. They're going to contact the zoo and get back to me. I can ask them about getting us some bamboo in the meantime," Ynes said.

"Brandon hasn't texted you back yet either, Kay?"

"No. So I guess the Woolven's it is then," Kay growled. "I don't want to risk this happening while he's in my car."

If we really were heading for the Woolven's, this potential family, I needed to tell Ynes and Kay that I was trans before we arrived, but the words died in my throat. Maybe I should wait until we were there. Then I'd only have to explain it once.

I wished again that Brandon was here. I needed some emotional support. Thinking about Brandon again made me realize that I might have another way to contact him after all. I borrowed Kay's phone again and called Brandon's employer.

The front desk admin answered the phone. It was a small locally owned place, and I'd gone with Brandon to the last few work parties as his plus one, so I knew pretty much all his coworkers.

"Hey, Charlie, this is Max, Brandon's roommate. He's not answering his phone. I know he's on a business trip, but can you pass along a message for me?"

"What?" I could hear Charlie's confusion. "He's not on a business trip. He called last night. Some family emergency. He took this entire week as PTO."

I sat in stunned silence for a moment. Brandon had lied to me? First Kay, and now this. Maybe I didn't know Brandon as well as I thought. And family emergency? I was basically his only family, just like he was mine.

"You still there, Max?" he asked.

I shook myself. "Yeah, yeah. I must have misheard him." Except he'd taken his tool bag. But then, I'd had to remind him of that, hadn't I?

"Alright, I'll talk to you later." Charlie hung up, and I lowered the phone, chewing on my lip.

Why had Brandon lied to me?

V

Shoestorm

WHEN WE STOPPED FOR food, Ynes bought me a pair of cheap flip-flops at a corner convenience store. They were bright orange, but better than being barefoot. The clouds that had been threatening all day darkened, and I hoped we got this done before the rain started, since I didn't have a jacket.

The Woolven family lived in Ladd's Addition, a densely packed neighborhood of turn-of-the-century houses just east of downtown. We couldn't find any parking close by, so we had to walk almost a half mile. Pog draped around my shoulders, eyes closed, pretending to be a toy. Barnabas followed, running alongside the sidewalk looking for all the world like a regular squirrel.

Ynes insisted on walking next to me, I suspected so that she could pet Pog while we walked.

Pog got some odd looks. I repeated the 'art doll' story that Ynes had come up with. People bought it, or at least they walked away, which was good enough for me. A few offered me enough cash for Pog that I almost considered selling him. Almost.

Hmmm that might be a good hustle, selling Pog to people—with eir permission of course—then eim escaping and returning home. But after a moment's consideration, I dismissed the idea. Too much chance of people catching on. While eiy might pass as a really realistic doll even close up, once you held eim and felt eim warm and breathing, it'd be pretty obvious.

The Prices lived in an old Victorian, big, but showing its age. The Woolven's place was a massive neoclassical style mansion set far back from the street. A perfect expanse of bright green lawn bordered the walkway up to the front door. Corinthian columns flanked the front steps, and additional wings expanded the house on either side. It had to be worth several million dollars, at least.

"This can't be the right place." I said, my mouth falling open.

Ynes patted my arm, lingering longer than she needed to. "No, it is. The Woolven family has been in Portland even longer than the Prices. The family is a pillar of the local magical community."

"You really think we're related?" I stared up at the house, skeptical. I could not see this family needing to give up their kid. Unless... No. No parent would be so callous as to give up a child just because of a little bad luck, would they? If that was the case, they would not be happy to see me.

"You could be Mr. Woolven's younger twin. You'll see," Ynes said, starting up the walk.

Kay stuffed his hands in his pockets and glanced at me, jerking his head after Ynes.

I didn't move. "Maybe we should have called first," I said, clutching Pog's tail and swallowing hard. My palms started itching again.

Pog's tail curled around my neck like a scarf. "Deep breaths," Pog whispered in my ear.

I closed my eyes and concentrated on the act of breathing. In and out. The itching reduced a bit but didn't go away. "It's not working," I whispered back.

"Again?" Kay muttered next to me.

I nodded. "Maybe this is the form my bad luck is taking now?" Nothing extremely unlucky had happened since the sink collapse and my tablet shorted out and I was getting more and more on edge waiting for the other shoe to drop.

Kay was silent for so long I thought he'd left. My eyes were still closed as I stroked Pog, trying to calm down. Eventually, Kay whispered, "It was that bad?"

I opened my eyes to look at him. He tilted his head, which sent a long lock of blonde hair that had escaped his ponytail falling across his face. His square jaw had a smattering of stubble on it I hadn't noticed this morning, and his bright blue eyes were focused on me. Damn, he was handsome. My libido was in overdrive today. Concentrate.

"Yeah, it was that bad. When I got a job, I couldn't ever keep it. Buses would break down, bike tires would pop, or chains would snap. Even walking could get perilous. I've had more broken bones than I can count." I rubbed my lower arm where the worst of the breaks had been when I'd been eight. "Then if I managed to actually make it to the workplace, they always fired me within days. Usually because of too much lost inventory."

"Would you say the bad luck happened at the same rate as these magical bursts?" Kay asked.

"I guess?" I hadn't exactly been timing them.

"Interesting..." Kay pursed his lips and looked around. "Until this next one passes, stand in the center of the grass there. Based on the size of the licorice circle, it looks like enough space that you shouldn't hit the sidewalk or the house."

"But that's in full view of the road..."

Kay shrugged. "So? Humans see magic all the time. Especially in this modern age, they're likely to think that they imagined it."

I was starting to understand why Kay was so dismissive of the PCA. "What if they don't? Think they imagined it, I mean."

"Who's going to believe them?" Kay pushed me onto the grass. "Now go. I don't want to see what would happen to me if I got caught in range."

"It doesn't bother Pog," I protested, but walked across the pristine emerald grass to roughly the center of the lawn. I'd never seen such bright green grass. It was lush and almost springy under my flip-flops, and there wasn't a bit of moss in sight.

So far, the magical effects had seemed to relate to what I was thinking, like the grass had turned to the candy I was craving, so maybe I could direct it.

"Pog, what if I tried to expel the magic with purpose rather than letting it just happen? It's like a buildup of magical energy, right? So if I used it, no explosion."

"It is," Pog said, sounding skeptical. "But do you really think you can control it?"

"No," I said truthfully. "But will it really hurt anything to try?"

"I suppose not," Pog agreed.

I turned in a slow circle. Kay and Ynes stood on the mansion's front porch, ringing the doorbell. No one else was nearby. My palms were on fire now. I needed to do this soon.

"Do I need a wand to focus things?"

Pog leapt from my shoulder, then stood up on two legs and faced me. Eir striped tail waved back and forth behind eim. "No. Magic for a mage is all about intent and focus, not the tools."

"Thanks, Professor." I quirked a smile at the diminutive red panda. Eiy looked so serious.

I did some of my hand and finger stretches, like I'd do to limber up before a drawing session. Focus, but on what? I kicked off my flip-flops and let my feet sink into the soft grass.

I wondered if I could turn the cheap plastic flip-flops into tennis shoes like I'd morphed Kay's sweats into my normal clothes. Flip-flops to sneakers. Easy.

I thrust my hands at the shoes. Change! Nothing happened.

In the distance I heard a door open and then people talking, but I kept my attention on the orange flip-flops, vibrant against the brilliant green of the grass.

I could feel that Pog wanted to say something, but eiy kept quiet. I didn't know how I knew that, but I did. And now that I'd noticed, it was very distracting.

Sneakers! I thrust again. Nothing still. The burning moved to my fingers.

"I said I have no idea what you're talking about! I don't have a brother!" a man yelled.

The raised voices caught my attention, and I looked up, chewing on my lip. Ynes was pointing at me. I should have told them I was trans, so they could have explained, but I thought I'd be there with them. Too late now.

The magic in my fingers reached the tipping point, and I fell to my knees with a scream. The fire engulfed me and expanded out. Sneakers! I thought at the magic.

The grass stayed grass, and as I watched, the ugly orange flip-flops morphed into a pair of sneakers. They stayed bright orange, damn it. But it had worked! My first proper spell!

I sat down to put my new shoes on when something rubbery thumped into my head. I winced and turned to look at what had hit me. A right sneaker, white with gray trim.

Pog's eyes widened and eiy dashed under my bent legs as more shoes began raining from the sky. I covered my head with my hands and bent over my legs, trying to shield Pog from the onslaught. They bounced off my back, shins, hands, and elbows hard enough that I was going to be bruised all over.

A nearby window shattered with a crash and I risked a glance out under my elbow to see shoes bouncing off the mansion's roof with solid thumps. Car alarms started going off in the street and there was the sound of more breaking glass. Honking horns and yelling started coming from the surrounding neighborhood.

Maybe my 'create shoes' spell had been a little too successful.

The arguing from the porch stopped as everyone stared in stunned silence at the falling shoes.

After a few minutes, the rain of sneakers petered off.

A Shoestorm.

I snickered to myself at the silent joke.

I found a right and a left of the white and gray rain sneakers. Just my size—at least one thing had gone right—and put them on, leaving the bright orange ones where they lay. Then made my way to the porch, kicking sneakers out of the way as I went. Pog ran along after me, bounding over the shoes like it was an obstacle course. Glad someone was having fun.

On the porch, Kay mimed bashing his head into one of the Corinthian columns. Ynes stared around, open-mouthed at the mess. And the man... he was staring at me. I stared back. He could have been my twin brother, except his shoulders were broader and his face a little rounder. But his hair was the same dark brown as mine and we had the same nose and the same dimple on the left cheek. I swallowed hard, not sure what to say to my maybe-brother.

A sneaker from the roof rolled off and landed on the pavement between us with a loud thump, breaking the staring contest. Pog stood on eir hind legs and tottered up to the shoe with eir front paws in the air.

"Quite the weather we're having," I said to him as Pog pounced on the shoe.

The man jerked his gaze back up to me in shock. "Maybe you should come inside after all."

Inside was even more opulent than the exterior. White marble floors. A grand staircase. Minimalist dark wood furniture decorated the entryway, the dark grain contrasting pleasantly with the white of the floor and walls. I scooped up Pog, terrified eiy might break something.

"Put me down, Max! I want to explore!" Pog flailed in my arms.

The man glared at me. "You made a red panda talk?"

"Not on purpose..." I tightened my arms on Pog and eiy settled down, but eir skewed back ears told me eiy were unhappy about it.

"That's why we're here, Rod," Ynes said, putting a hand on my arm.

"Roderick," he snapped at her. It would have been nice if Ynes had warned me I had a potential brother.

"You look a lot alike," Kay said with dry understatement. More like twins. "Maybe he's a cousin?"

"My father was an only child, as was my mother." Roderick shook his head. "I don't have any other immediate family that I'm aware of."

"That you're aware of." Ynes pounced on that statement. She should have a cat familiar and not a squirrel. "Is your father here? He might know—"

"He's away on business and is out of cell phone range."

Ynes' eyes widened, her mouth turning into a little Oh. Same as Mr. Price. My eyebrows raised. That was an odd coincidence. Yet Kay didn't mirror Ynes' and my shock, instead shrugging like he'd expected that. I felt like I was missing something, or that Kay knew something we didn't.

"Is your mother home?" I asked. Ynes glanced at me and made a 'no' gesture, slashing her neck.

A pained look passed over Roderick's face.

"She died last year," Ynes hissed at me.

"I'm sorry." I felt a pang of loss for the potential maybe-mother that I'd never meet.

"It's fine." Roderick pointed at me with a scowl. "But you're a menace. Ynes, what were you thinking bringing him here?"

"I told you, he needs a teacher." Ynes' phone buzzed with an incoming text message. And then another. And another. Her eyebrows climbed higher as she read each one. Then it rang. "Excuse me." She stepped away, putting the phone to her ear.

"She said you were an orphan?" Roderick turned his attention back to me. Ynes must have told him that on the porch while I was out of hearing range. "You don't have any idea about your family?"

"Not orphan, abandoned. My records are sealed, and I wasn't old enough to remember." Not that I'd ever tried to unseal them, like I'd heard some of the other kids attempting when they turned eighteen. If my family didn't care enough about me to raise me, why should I bother to look for them?

Besides, Brandon had gone through all the effort to get his records only to find he'd been dropped off anonymously at a hospital.

"You were? There is a very strong resemblance, so I suppose you could be a distant relative," Roderick said, crossing his arms with a frown and looking at the ceiling in thought. "I have third and fourth cousins from my grandparents' siblings. When were you born?"

"I'm twenty-two now."

Roderick's eyes scanned the ceiling as he thought, then shook his head. "I don't know of any relatives that could have a boy that age. My father might know more, though."

I took a deep breath and Pog yelped as I tightened my grip on eim. I attempted to loosen up. "They would have given up a daughter, not a son. I'm trans."

Roderick stared at me blankly.

I squeezed Pog again for support. "They declared me a girl when I was born. When I turned eighteen, I started my transition."

"You... you're saying you were a girl?" His eyes went wide and his face pale. "How old when you were given up?"

"About a year old."

"It can't be." All the color went out of his face and he staggered back to fall against the front door with a thump. He slid down it until he sat on the rug, then leaned forward, clutching his head. "She's dead..."

I knelt down next to Roderick, setting Pog down next to me. I expected eim to run off but eiy sat down next to me and wrapped eir long striped tail around my leg.

"Who's dead?" I asked.

"My older sister." He looked up at me now, his eyes haunted.

My ninety percent certainty that this was my brother turned to a hundred percent. I stared at him for a long beat. My heart stuttered and my breathing became ragged as I hyperventilated. My vision started going dark at the edges and I lay on my back to still my swimming vision.

I felt a whisper of the magic itch crawl across my palms, but it was muted and vanished as quickly as it had come. Probably I was spent from the last explosion just a few minutes ago.

"Breathe, Max." Pog scrambled up to my chest and stood there, claws digging into one of my nipples and my scar, muzzle only millimeters from my nose.

"Can't breathe with... you standing on me..." I gasped.

"Ohhhhh..." Pog giggled and slid off.

Kay crouched down with us. "Glad we figured out we're having a family reunion, but we need to do something about him before something else happens."

I rolled my head to the side to squint at Kay. The morning sun streamed in from the picture windows on either side of the doors, and I could have sworn the long shadow extending from him, dark against the bright white marble, had pointed animal ears and a tail. I blinked and Kay's shadow was back to normal. Had I imagined it?

Kay helped me back to my feet.

"Your head alright?" he asked belatedly.

"Yeah, it's fine. I was just dizzy with shock." I scratched at yesterday's scabs, now covered with bruises where the shoes had hit me.

Ynes hung up her phone as she joined us back in the foyer. "Bad news, and potentially worse news."

Kay gave her a dirty look. "And here I thought this day was about to get better. So what's the bad news?"

"The zoo isn't missing a red panda."

We all turned to look down at Pog. Eiy looked back up at us. Definitely a red panda.

"So where did Pog come from?" Roderick growled. "You can't just manifest up something from nothing."

"Yeah, Ynes explained that back at her house," I said. We continued to stare down at Pog. "But then, where did the shoes come from?" I asked.

Everyone turned to look at me. Ynes blinked and Roderick pressed his lips together.

"I thought I was hallucinating from lack of sleep, but I'm pretty sure I made Pog's body from my sketch pad and colored pencils. I turned Ynes' paving stones into pillows, her plants into other plants, kinda, and I transmuted the grass into licorice—"

"You did what?" Roderick yelped. "Not our grass, right?" His voice turned pleading.

I ignored him and continued, "But the shoes fell from the sky like rain. Where did they come from?"

"The clouds," Ynes said. "It had been cloudy when we got to the Woolven Manse. After the shoe rain, it was sunny."

"Boy, is that going to fuck up local weather patterns," Kay said with a laugh.

"That's... not a good thing." I grimaced, not sure why, of all the crazy things my magic had done today, that was the one that Kay found funny.

"What's the worse news?" Roderick asked, ignoring me.

"Oh, right." Ynes looked a bit embarrassed and twisted her hands in her skirt. "The PCA has already gotten dozens of calls about the shoe rain—"

"Shoestorm," I said.

Ynes rolled her eyes. "It's already on the news."

Roderick cursed. "Do they know it was centered on my house?"

"I don't think so. Apparently the 'shoestorm,'" I could hear the quotes in Ynes's voice, "encompassed several square blocks. A news van was on Hawthorne covering something else when it happened. They got the entire thing, LIVE, on the morning news."

I couldn't help it. I giggled. "Really?"

Ynes shot me an exasperated glare. "It's not funny. I had to beg ignorance. I'm already regretting it."

"Thank you," Roderick said. I was surprised.

"What do you care?" I glared at him.

"It wouldn't be good for the family name if this gets out." Roderick sighed. "Declaring you dead and dumping you into the mundane child welfare system. I'd like at least a chance to ask father about what he was thinking before this gets blown wide open."

"Not why?" Ynes asked. She gave me a sympathetic look. I was glad she asked, because I was still reeling from Roderick's bare admission that I was most likely his 'dead' sibling.

"No. I have a feeling I know about the why. Come with me." Roderick headed up the grand staircase.

I glanced back at Kay rather than following. "Do we have time? At Ynes' house, you said we needed to leave immediately..."

"We can't stay long," he said, glancing at his phone. "But the amulet you're wearing should buy us some time—" He jerked, eyes widening. "You still have it, right? You didn't change it into pasta or something?"

"He better not have." Ynes huffed, putting a protective hand on her pouch thing.

I hooked a finger under the chain and lifted it to show Kay and Ynes it was still there under my hoodie. Kay relaxed and headed up the stairs after Roderick. If he wasn't worried, I figured I wouldn't either.

VI

The Broken Seal

THE MINIMALIST DECORATING THEME from downstairs continued through the rest of the house. We passed a sitting room that looked coldly impersonal; like a magazine picture of a room more than an actual lived-in space. I couldn't imagine what it would have been like to grow up here. Nothing about the house looked inviting to children. Although maybe they'd redecorated since then.

The door Roderick stopped in front of looked no different from the rest of the house: carved wood, not painted but made of white wood. The ghosts of where wooden letters had been nailed on were still visible as vague lighter spots, spelling out my original name. Different even than the one they had provided when giving me up. Interesting.

Roderick put his palm against the door with a frown. "This was my older sister's nursery. It's been sealed since before I was born, so I've never been in here."

I'd draped Pog around my shoulders again like a scarf. I know eiy wanted to go explore, so appreciated that eiy stayed with me. The furry weight of eim was like an anchor that kept me grounded when my emotions otherwise might have swept me away.

"If it's been sealed, are you sure it's the same as my magic?" I asked.

"I'm not. That's why I want to open it." Roderick stroked the wood then turned to face us, his expression dark and posture stiff. "But I've picked up bits and pieces over the years about my older sister. People talk. It sounds the same."

"Why seal it off?" Ynes asked, eyes darting back and forth from Roderick to the door to my room.

"From what I understand, there's some wild magic inside that father could never figure out how to clean up," Roderick said.

"This is a waste of time." Kay huffed and tapped his foot. "It doesn't matter if we verify who Max is. You said his type of magic runs in your family. Just teach him some control exercises."

"It matters to me," I said in a near whisper. Pog nuzzled my face, and I reached back and rubbed eim between the ears absentmindedly.

"Exactly." Roderick said. "Mage magic depends a lot on emotions. I'd bet, Max, that a lot of your uncontrolled outbursts of magic happened when you were upset or otherwise having emotional flux."

I thought back. The first one had been close to when I'd found Pog in my room. The red panda startled me when it started talking, and boom. MC Escher zombie house. The giant dust devil had happened when the mages chased me and Kay. At Ynes' house, I tripped and fell. The fourth had happened after Ynes had mentioned finding my family. The last when we'd arrived here.

"Yeah. Except for when Pog materialized," I said. I'd been in my happy place drawing with my colored pencils when I'd made eim. "Pog, what do you remember about how you came to be in my room?"

Pog shifted, fur brushing my neck. "I'd been trying all night to scare you away since the birdbrain was gone. But you refused to leave. So I was lurking on your ceiling, watching you, trying to come up with another plan."

I still had no idea why Pog kept using bird metaphors for Brandon.

"The ceiling?" Roderick crossed his arms and scowled at Pog. "Red pandas can't hang upside down. Besides, he asked what happened before you were in the room."

Pog's fur bristled under my hand. "This was before I found myself in this body."

"Pog was a house guardian spirit put there by the witch that built the house," Kay said. "Though the locals said the place was haunted. That's why it was abandoned."

"I don't know what I was. I just knew I needed to protect the house, so I scared off intruders," Pog said.

"Then what happened?" Roderick asked, eyes wide and staring at Pog.

"I got..." Pog's ears screwed backwards and eir muzzle scrunched up. "Twisted? Compressed? Squished? I don't know how to describe it, but it was like something grabbed my form, even though I was incorporeal, and shaped it into the way you see me now. When it was over, I was on the floor, staring at this one."

"Pog, why didn't you say something?" Ynes said, her voice raising an octave. "I was frantic about the zoo missing a red panda."

"Maybe this form had come from there? How would I know?" I didn't know red pandas could growl but Pog managed it.

Kay lifted his phone and tapped on it. "Tick Tock. Roderick, open that door since you say it's so important."

"What's important is that Max gets a little context. If his emotional state is imbalanced, he'll be more likely to lose control again."

"But you're hesitating," Ynes pointed out.

"I told you my father sealed it." Roderick grabbed the doorknob. "When I break the seal, it will trigger an alarm. I think it will notify my father. Maybe more. I don't feel any other defenses, but it doesn't mean they aren't there."

"Perfect, we want to talk to him anyway," Ynes said.

Roderick made a pained expression that told me he didn't want to do this. "Back up, just in case."

We all took a step back.

Roderick closed his eyes and chanted.

The hair on my arms stood up, like I was getting a static charge. My teeth itched. I knew that was impossible, but it was also true. The charge built and built. Bees stung my arms. I backed up farther. The pressure lessened but didn't go away entirely. I felt like I could practically see the magic radiating from Roderick and the door.

Ynes and Kay seemed to not notice. Kay gave me a curious look as I backed further away.

I felt a crack. The magic became discordant, like someone had strung the wrong note on a guitar, but as something I could feel and not hear.

Then suddenly it was gone. My ears rang in the sudden absence of magic. It had been silent, but that was the only way I could describe the sensation.

"Did it work?" I asked, rubbing down my goosebumps.

Roderick raised an eyebrow at me and pushed the door open, then he stepped back. "Don't cross the threshold," he warned.

Ynes, Kay, and I crowded in a half circle around the door and stared inside. I felt Roderick come up behind me to look over my head. Stupid tall people.

A toddler's bed made of pink painted wood sat askew on one side of the room. A matching pink wooden chest overflowing with children's toys sat along another wall next to a wooden child's size dresser, and a mural of cartoon bears in pastel colors covered most of the opposite wall. But I barely saw all that past the swirling chaos.

More than a dozen twinkling balls of light bobbed around inside. When one hit a wall, it bounced off and changed course. One floated by the doorway. *Twinkle, Twinkle, Little Star* played at a low volume from it. Overtop that was quieter music from one a little farther away, *Blue Boy* I thought, though it was hard to tell. In fact, they were all playing music, different songs with different beats, filling the room with a cacophony of noise.

Interspersed with the balls of sound and light were streaming ribbons that hung from the ceiling and fluttered in an invisible breeze, and a balloon giraffe that changed colors every time it bounced off a wall. A blue spotted cartoon dog cartwheeled across the floor and then jumped on the bed, clapping its paws.

"Come play with me!" the dog yapped at us and waved.

I raised a hand and gave a cautious wave back. The dog wagged its tail and bounced higher, cartwheeling off the bed back to where it had started. "Come play with me," the dog repeated, then the loop began again. The noise of the dog's barking joined the chaos of the overlapping songs.

"What..." Ynes gawked at the chaos. "What are we looking at?" She took a step forward and Roderick lunged and grabbed her arm, hauling her back.

"I wouldn't go in there. Spells keep anything from leaving the room, but," he swallowed hard as he glanced inside, "there are less obvious magical effects, too."

"This is all baby stuff," I said.

"That's why it's so dangerous. Babies don't know what's harmful or not." Roderick frowned. "In fact..." Roderick shooed us all back away and closed the door again. "I actually don't even know if having the door open is safe."

"I'm still not sure what we were supposed to learn from that chaos," I said, waving a hand at the closed door.

Roderick glanced away, his cheeks coloring. "Right, if you were raised by Mundanes, you wouldn't know. Most mage children don't get their magic until seven or eight years old.

The first time is often explosive, depending on the child's power, but at that age they're old enough to learn control. A lot of children are even started on the exercises before they get their power, so they already have a framework."

"That," Kay pointed at the closed room, "was not magic made by a seven-year-old."

"No, that was magic made by a baby. My sister," he cut off again, tension radiating from him. "She got her, his... your magic at six months old, apparently." He gave me a significant look.

Ynes pulled a square of microfiber cloth from her fanny pouch, took her glasses off, and began cleaning them. Kay's mouth opened in a little oh and then closed again.

"And that's bad?" I asked, stroking Pog's tail to calm myself.

"Babies can't learn control," Roderick said. "And they don't have a sense of danger. Like the dog in there. What if you'd seen a crocodile or something else on television and copied it instead?"

"Ah, yeah." I felt dumb.

"So he *is* your brother! Does that mean this is my new house, Max?" Pog said, tugging on my hair.

I bit my lip and glanced at Roderick. From the way his eyebrows drew together and his lip curled, I thought probably not.

"Plus," Ynes said, "the younger a child gets their magic, the more powerful it usually is."

"And you saw that room, that magic is so advanced my father, who is one of the best of the best, couldn't figure out how to dispel it, and twenty some years later it's still active." Roderick blew out a breath, tightening his hands on his arms. "Also, the talking dog?"

We all nodded.

"Transformation mages can't make living things. Only inanimate objects." He pointed at Pog. "You made that. My sister made the dog. It didn't look intelligent, not the way its actions looped, but it's still unprecedented."

"Shit," Ynes said, summing up my feelings perfectly.

"But if your sister," I said, still not able to connect myself mentally to the distant figure, "got her magic at six months old, how is it I just got my magic this morning? Why have I not had it this whole time?"

"I have no idea. On that cheery note," Roderick clapped his hands together, "in order to protect the rest of my house, I'll teach you some control exercises."

"The shoes weren't that destructive," I objected as Roderick headed past me.

Roderick stopped at the top of the stairs and pointed down. "Max isn't going to be able to concentrate if you all are here. There's a kitchen down and to the right," he pointed. "And leftovers in the fridge. Help yourself to anything."

Kay didn't look happy, but complied. Ynes grabbed my hand and squeezed it before following him.

"Him, uh," Roderick stumbled over his words and then pointed to Pog on my shoulder. "The panda, too. Go with them."

"Shouldn't I have eim there to help?" I asked.

"No, a familiar is a crutch," Roderick said with a note of disdain.

"What if—"

"You don't need it," Roderick snapped.

I rolled my eyes and pulled Pog from my shoulder and set eim on the floor. "Pog, are you hungry? Why don't you go with Kay and Ynes and get something to eat besides coffee and candy."

"Fine." Pog stuck out eir tongue at me and then bounded down the stairs after the others.

Once they were out of sight, Roderick went down the opposite hall towards the other wing of the house. I followed him in silence, glancing around at the bland art decorating the walls. Too bad all my finished paintings had been at the house when it burned down. They desperately needed some decent art, and I desperately needed the cash.

Roderick stopped two doors down and hesitated with his hand on the knob. "This is my room, so don't touch anything, okay?" he mumbled, not looking at me. Was he blushing?

"You still live at home?" I asked, trying to keep my curiosity about his room from my face.

"Father insisted." Roderick toyed with the knob. "I just graduated from high school last month. I'm working at his business until I start college this fall. I want to move to the dorms, but..." he trailed off and looked uncomfortable as he opened his door.

Team scarves lined the wall near the ceiling. I didn't recognize most of the team names, but guessed they were soccer teams, since he also had a giant Thorns poster hung over the bed, flanked by a framed Timbers jersey with a sharpied signature scrawled on it. Bookshelves filled with soccer memorabilia covered the rest of the walls. A massive green and yellow shag area rug of the Timbers logo covered the middle of the floor.

Everything was tidy. Even the bed was made, sheets pulled crisp and smooth. Roderick must have gotten all the tidiness that had skipped me.

This bedroom was massive, bigger than the living rooms in many of the houses I'd fostered in. Besides the bed, Roderick had a large desk with a rolling chair and a recliner.

I stepped inside and Roderick shut the door behind me.

"I feel you might like soccer," I joked as I sat down on the recliner, excitement making my hands shake. I was going to learn how to do magic!

Roderick pulled the computer chair around the rug before sitting. "Don't you start," he growled.

I blinked. I'd been joking, but the soccer stuff was apparently a sore spot for him. Given the decorating in the rest of the house, I'd guess his father wasn't a big sports fan. I dropped it, not wanting to rankle him further. Instead, I asked, "What spell am I going to learn first?"

"None. I'm going to teach you how to gain a heightened sense of awareness and regulate your breathing."

"That sounds suspiciously like meditation," I said, narrowing my eyes at him.

"It is."

I flopped sideways over the arm of the recliner with a groan and covered my face with one arm. Brandon got big into meditation over the last year and kept trying to rope me into daily evening meditation with him. I hated it. As a constant fidgeter, sitting cross-legged on a mat with nothing in my hands sent me into a nervous spiral.

"What does that have to do with magic?" My hoodie muffled my words.

"Magic is all about control." Roderick rolled the chair closer and kicked my shin. I lowered my arm and glared at him. Giving me the full brother experience already, it seemed. "Sit up and suck it up," Roderick said.

I sat back up with a sigh and, for the next bit, Roderick led me through some of the same meditation exercises that Brandon had tried to teach me. Though with the extra motivation of not wanting to hurt someone with my magic, I sat through an entire hour of Roderick's lessons until the doorbell rang, saving me from further torture.

"I'll be back momentarily," Roderick said, standing up. "Touch nothing," he warned me again before leaving.

I made it an entire minute of wandering around Rod's room before I was bored. Soccer held no interest for me. The door hadn't quite latched closed when Roderick left, and I heard voices. Out of curiosity, I left and went down the hall to eavesdrop, stopping just short of where the banister started.

"I'm here with a message for Mr. Woolven." The speaker's voice was lyrical and high pitched. Woman? Man? Other? I couldn't guess one way or the other, but it didn't matter. It was a shame the messenger wasn't a radio announcer or a singer. That voice was doing things to me.

I peeked my head around the corner, but from this high angle, Roderick's body blocked my view of the speaker, who still stood on the porch.

"I'm Mr. Woolven," Roderick said.

"I'm sorry, I should specify that I'm looking for your father, Charles Woolven."

"He's away on business. I can handle any matters in his stead." My brother's voice had an authoritative edge to it that hadn't been there before.

I had a brief twinge of guilt for eavesdropping. But then again, wasn't this my family? If not for the quirk of fate that had been my magic, it might have been me at the door.

I wondered what magic my brother had. Transformation magic, like me? He said it ran in the family.

"It would be better that I wait for his return," the messenger said, coldness creeping into the lyrical words.

"He's not due back for days, I'm afraid."

"This is quite desperate. Do you not have any magical means of communication, in case of emergency?"

"I do, but I won't use them if you can't even tell me the purpose of your visit."

The messenger exclaimed. A curse, I would bet, though I didn't recognize the language. It sounded familiar, but my lack of sleep was making it difficult to concentrate, and the last hour of sitting quietly hadn't helped to wake me up at all.

"Fine. Please contact your father and tell him the seal on you sister's magic has been broken. Judging from the shoes that fell from the sky, it seems it already has spiraled out of control. We must act quickly to find her and get her contained before it is too late." The messenger spoke quickly, a note of desperation in their voice.

Then it hit me. That was where I'd heard the same lyrical language. This morning at the house. The robed figures. Now I *really* wanted to know what they looked like. I weighed the risk of trying to take another look. Given that the messenger had used 'her' and 'sister' to describe me, they likely didn't realize I'd transitioned. Plus I wore different clothing than when they'd seen me this morning in Kay's pink sweats.

I moved to the edge of the wall and craned my head around. Roderick had shifted to the side, opening the door up further. Still, the top of the door frame blocked my view of their face and all I could see were their gray robes, embroidered around the edges with golden swirls. Dang.

There was a pregnant pause. I stiffened, sure that Roderick was going to expose me. But to my surprise, he didn't. "I'm afraid you are mistaken. My sister has been dead a long time." He was a decent liar, at least from what I could tell this far away.

"You are the one mistaken."

More silence. Roderick and the messenger stared at each other.

"It is imperative that you contact your father immediately, before the situation escalates. If someone else captures her before we do, we won't be able to restore the seal."

"What seal? And my father knew she was alive?" Roderick asked. "How was the seal broken in the first place?"

"It seems you are not wholly in your father's confidence and I've already inadvertently divulged too much."

Not in his father's confidence was right. Perhaps that was why Roderick had kept my secret. And the way the messenger said it made my head race. So had his father, no, our father, had known I was alive? I moved further out, trying to get a better view, but no luck.

"Do you want me to pass on your message or not?" Roderick said in a cool tone.

The messenger let out a musical sigh. "An intruder entered Faerie and broke the seal. A phoenix named Brandon."

Brandon? My eyes widened. But the name had to be a coincidence. My Brandon was not a phoenix.

They'd mentioned Faerie. Were they a fairy? I wished I could see the messenger.

"Who is Brandon?" Roderick asked.

"Your sister's lover," the messenger said, making me snort. I wish. "We do not know how he found out about the location of the seal, but he is being questioned as we speak. Another communique will be sent should we find out anything pertinent or locate the girl. We have been trying to track her, but something is interfering with our spells."

My head spun, and I sagged against the banister. The name was not a coincidence. That was why Brandon hadn't been answering his phone. He was a prisoner in Faerie. That must have been where he went after he left the house last night. But why had the messenger called him a phoenix?

Didn't matter. The important part was that Brandon had been captured and was being questioned. Did that mean torture? My heart pounded, and it was only by sheer force of will that I wasn't crying. I zoned out as I tried to quell my rising panic.

Seven years ago

The last bell rang right as the teacher wrote our weekend homework on the whiteboard. I jotted it down, then slowly repacked my notepad and book in my ratty bookbag, keeping my head down as I waited for the classroom to empty. The principal topic of conversation was tonight's football game that would kick off the season.

I'd only started as a freshman at this high school four weeks ago, but I already had a reputation. Even the teachers had begun to wince when they saw me coming. So I did my best to stay out of people's way when I eventually left the classroom and trudged down the hall. I moved slowly, dreading what I had to do before beginning the walk back to my foster house.

An overhead light pinged and flickered out as I walked underneath it.

Brandon already waited in front of his locker. With his height and bright red hair, he was easy to spot. He'd shot up this year, and now stood several inches taller than most everyone else. The sight of him made me smile despite the task I had ahead of me.

"Hey, Max!" Brandon said as I joined him by the locker. So far, Brandon was the only one I could get to call me by my chosen name. Hearing it always gave me a little thrill. Brandon gave me a dazzling smile and moved aside. My blouse and jumper dress, decorated with tiny pink flowers, hung inside his open locker.

"Too bad the school day isn't longer," I said, scowling at the garments and making no move to take them. I currently wore a pair of Brandon's old pants, rolled up on the cuffs to fit my shorter legs, one of his school sweatshirts that was hilariously oversized on my tiny frame, and had tied my long hair back and stuck it down the back of the sweatshirt to disguise its length. I didn't pass, but at least I wasn't wearing a dress.

Brandon put his hands in the pockets of his jeans and leaned one shoulder into the lockers while tapping out an uneven rhythm on the floor with one heel. "If you want an excuse to stay, there's always the football game."

I grimaced. Watching a bunch of guys in padded jerseys run back and forth across a field had never been appealing to me, but if I went, I could put off changing back into the dress for several more hours.

"Do you think Thad and Wilma would be okay with that?" I asked, referring to the foster parents we were both currently placed with.

"I can call them and ask." He pulled out the cheap pre-paid flip phone the Pfennings provided us both with, but then hesitated and looked at me. I rolled my eyes and backed a dozen locker-lengths away. "You mock," he said as he dialed, "but how's your phone doing?"

I swung off my backpack and dug it out of the front pocket, then held it up for Brandon to see as he pressed his phone to his ear. My phone was blackened and charred from the fire that started when the battery exploded during world history this morning. I was only lucky I'd caught it in time and it hadn't sent my backpack up in flames with it. Brandon's eyebrows went up, and he shook his head.

After a moment of back and forth on the phone, Brandon hung up and turned to me, grinning. "Good news. Wilma was glad we're getting some school spirit. We just need to be home before ten."

Roughly five hours from now? That was good news. I took the dress out of the locker and stuffed it in my bag, since I wasn't sure if the school would still be unlocked later this evening. Thad and Wilma would flip a lid if I returned home wearing Brandon's clothes. I could find somewhere to change later, even if it was the bathroom in the 7-11.

Then we headed over to the football field. I would have preferred to go somewhere else, like the county library or the park, but I also didn't want to risk getting in trouble, just in case one of the Pfennings's other foster kids tattled on us, or if they came to the game themselves. They liked to be involved in their foster kids' lives. I almost preferred the houses where I'd been ignored.

People milled around, forming little knots of conversation at the edges of the field, since the game didn't start for another half hour.

We found seats at the bottom of the bleachers—no reason to risk injury sitting higher up—but after a few minutes I was recognized and people threw popcorn at my head.

"Get off the bleachers before you make them collapse!" someone yelled at me. Another followed up with, "Yeah, get out of here!"

I pulled the hood of my jacket over my head and hunched my shoulders. I'd found the best way to deal with things like this was to ignore it.

As if to prove my haters right, the metal seat underneath me gave a groan and collapsed at one end, sending all three of us sitting on this end sliding towards the grass. I ended up landing on Brandon and a girl I recognized from calculus hit my side. Brandon gave an ear-piercing scream, then the railing he'd hit snapped in half. He fell the few feet to the grass, catching himself with his hands and turning it into a roll. I grabbed the seat to keep from falling and jumped down, landing on my feet next to him. The girl's boyfriend grabbed her hand and pulled her back up to the unbroken half of the seat. Both of them glared at me.

"You alright?" I asked Brandon. The way he'd screeched, I thought he'd maybe broken an arm or something when he hit the railing.

"Fine. C'mon, let's find somewhere else to watch the game from," he said, offering me an amiable smile as he brushed grass from his jeans. I tried to return the smile, but knew it didn't reach my eyes.

Brandon took off. I picked my backpack up and followed. I thought he'd meant to leave the school grounds after all, but he circled around to underneath the bleachers. A few kids had gathered at the far end, smoking, but otherwise it was deserted. Bars of light from the field's floodlights filtered in through the openings in the seats.

I shivered and hunched over, hugging myself, trying to keep warm. The temperature had dropped rapidly as the sun set. Brandon didn't seem bothered by the cold, even though he wore only a thin rain jacket that he hadn't even zipped up. Bastard.

Brandon seemed nervous, bouncing his leg and constantly running his hand through his short red hair. We stared awkwardly at each other as the bleachers filled above us. I was jealous of his haircut. I'd been begging my foster parents to let me cut my long hair, but no luck yet. Only three more years until I turned eighteen and could do whatever I wanted, and transition for real.

Suddenly Brandon blurted out, "Max, do you like me?"

I stared at him, my mouth gaping open, not sure how to respond. I'd had a crush on him for ages, but had never dared say anything to him because I thought it would be weird. The Pfennings referred to all us foster kids as siblings, so it felt a bit like I was crushing on my brother.

"I mean," he stammered. I imagined I could feel the heat coming from him as his face turned scarlet. "Not like sibling love, like romantic. Because—"

The game started, and the official's whistle cut Brandon off. He bit his lip as talking became impossible with the roaring crowd above us.

I twisted my hands together, wanting to grab his shoulders and yank him down so I could kiss him. But I also worried. We lived together. If this didn't work out, things could get awkward. Yet, I couldn't bear to let this opportunity go. That sealed it.

The band started playing the school's song. I grabbed the openings of Brandon's jacket, drew him down to my level, and pressed my lips to his.

I closed my eyes as our lips met. Brandon tasted of smoke, like a campfire, which was interesting as I'd never seen him smoking. The feeling of heat increased until, if I hadn't known better, I'd swear I stood next to a roaring bonfire. I could even hear the crackling and popping of the flames.

Brandon's arms encircled my back, squeezing me to his chest and pinning my arms between us. My entire body tingled, and I shivered with pleasure, groaning against his mouth.

Distantly above the roar of the flames, I heard screaming and the acrid smell of smoke increased. Had my bad luck done something to the bleachers while we kissed?

Gasping, I pulled back from Brandon and opened my eyes. I hadn't been imagining things. The surrounding grass was on fire, and flames licked at the bleacher's supports. Worse, fire danced on Brandon's head and back. I stumbled back from him, horrified. My luck had never been this bad before.

I hadn't imagined the screams either. The bleachers had cleared of people. Distantly, I heard the blare of sirens.

I tried to call out Brandon's name, but when I opened my mouth, smoke choked me. Someone grabbed my arm and pulled me through the flames and away from Brandon.

After pulling me out, someone else had gone back for Brandon and beat out the flames. Miraculously, neither of us had been burned, although a few people who'd been sitting in the bleachers had suffered minor injuries.

They accused Brandon and me of arson. Though ultimately we escaped punishment, since they never found the source of the fire, they still separated us, and Brandon got moved to a new foster home. Although we stayed in touch, whatever romance might have happened between us seemed to have been burned away in the fire. The next time I saw Brandon, he kept me at arm's length, refusing to even give me a hug.

VII

Carriage Trouble

THE FRONT DOOR SHUTTING snapped me back to reality. Rather than return upstairs, Roderick walked out of my sight. I went downstairs to follow him, but lost him immediately. The hallway he'd entered had multiple doors and he could have gone into any of them.

Portraits of Woolvens, past and present, lined this hallway. As I wandered down the hall listening for signs that Roderick was in one of the rooms, I examined them.

Each one had been painted by a different artist. Unlike upstairs, these were quality paintings, and some were quite old. Each one must have cost a small fortune. Little brass plaques underneath each portrait identified the subject and their years of life.

Roderick's portrait sat at the end of the line. I stopped at the one before that and stared at the picture of my father, Charles Woolven, standing behind his wife, Clarice—my mother—one hand on her shoulder. I ran my fingers along the brass plaque bearing their names.

He looked like Roderick and me combined. Or more accurately, I guess Roderick and I looked like him. Besides the signs of greater age of the man and woman in the portrait—the salt and pepper hair, the severe lines of wrinkles framing his down-turned mouth telling me it had been recently painted. In the painting, his face had a neutral expression, but his eyes didn't show any warmth.

I wondered what it would have been like to grow up here with a normal life. No bad luck. No succession of foster homes, most of whom treated me like a burden. I'd never really dreamed of having a life like everyone else because the thought had seemed so far-fetched as to be laughingly impossible. As realistic as riding unicorns to work or money raining from the sky.

But maybe now a normal life wasn't an unrealistic life. My bad luck seemed to have been banished on Pog's arrival. Had that been because the seal that the messenger had mentioned had broken?

I still stood in front of the portrait when Roderick emerged from a door at the far end of the hall. A sheen of sweat glistened on his forehead and he was perspiring badly enough that he'd soaked through his undershirt, leaving damp patches on the sides of his button-up.

As he joined me, he said, "Sorry I didn't come back. Something urgent came up."

Had he been trying to contact his—our—father? He'd said earlier it was impossible. But apparently not. What about the visit had changed things enough that he felt the need to use this apparently difficult method of communication?

I realized I was staring at him and nodded.

Roderick glanced at our father's picture and grimaced. "I hate that picture. It makes him look so angry."

I didn't respond. I'd never met him, so what could I say? I changed the subject. "I need to go check up on Pog and the others."

Roderick nodded. "Good idea. I'll walk you to the kitchen."

"Do you have a familiar?" I asked on the way.

"No." Roderick placed his hands together behind him and threw back his shoulders in a very formal pose as we walked. Talking to that messenger seemed to have put him in a more formal mood. "Father thinks they are dirty animals and won't allow them in the house. Besides, you don't need them if you learn control early."

I raised my eyebrows at the 'dirty animals' part. I almost felt sorry for Roderick growing up in such a joyless household. At least I'd had my art and Brandon. Despite the bad luck curse, I counted myself lucky to have found such a good friend.

In the kitchen, Ynes leaned on the counter, feeding pieces of an apple to Barnabas, who sat perched on the edge of the sink. Kay sat at the kitchen table dealing out tarot cards in a triangle pattern. He examined the spread as we walked in, sniffed, then swept all the cards together back into the deck before I could see their faces.

Pog sat at the counter on one of the bar stools, a slice of cake in front of eim. Eir long striped tail hung off the edge of the stool, twitching as eiy brought pawfuls of cake to eir mouth. Pink frosting coated the front of eir muzzle.

"More sugar? No." As I reached for the plate, Pog picked up the rest of the piece and stuffed the entire thing in eir mouth. I scowled at Kay and then Ynes. "Pog is going to get sick at this rate!"

"Pog said it smelled good," Kay said, shuffling his tarot deck with deft movements. "And it's not like we had any bamboo handy."

Pog licked frosting off eir paws. "It's yummy, Max."

"You could have at least given eim something nutritious," I griped, taking the dirty plate and putting it in the sink.

"You need to get going," Roderick told us. "Faeries are hunting for you, and it would be very bad if they found you here."

"Is that who was at the door?" Ynes asked, slicing off another piece of apple with her pocketknife.

I propped a hip against the sink and turned to look at Roderick, trying to look curious, like I hadn't eavesdropped on the entire conversation.

"Yes. They suspect you're in the area. You should probably leave before they track you here." Roderick scowled.

"Did you teach Max enough?" Kay asked, the ruffle of shuffling cards punctuating his words. "You only spent an hour with him."

"No," Roderick snapped. "But we're out of time." He pointed to the back door. "Go. Cut through the backyard. They might have someone watching the front."

I took a napkin from the gold trimmed dispenser on the counter, trying not to snort—who the heck spent money on a gilded napkin dispenser—and cleaned up Pog before eiy jumped down. Kay led the way, flipping cards one handed from the top of the deck to the bottom as he walked. Barnabas perched on Ynes' shoulder.

The backyard was far more ostentatious than the grassy front. The back was a flower covered wonderland. A neat little path wound away from the backdoor. Off to the right was a patio covered with wrought iron furniture.

The shoes scattered everywhere ruined the effect a bit. Some flowers had been crushed, and more than one broken branch hung from the trees.

The clouds that had been threatening overhead were gone, and the sky was now bright blue with not a cloud in sight, as Ynes had pointed out.

We walked in silence for a few minutes. Ynes broke it with a curse in Spanish and then said, "What crawled up his ass and died?"

Kay snorted, and even I cracked a smile.

"I think whoever was at the door scared him," I said.

"What did they say?" Kay asked.

I found it funny that Kay assumed I'd eavesdropped. Funnier that he was right. Or had the cards told him? I shook my head. Fortune telling was weird. "They said something about a seal breaking. That I was alive and that his father needed to contact them."

"Who was it?" Ynes asked.

"I couldn't see their face, but they wore the same robes as the ones who chased us this morning," I said. "It scared him badly enough that he went and used some like emergency magical thing to contact his father. That's why he was all sweaty. I think," I amended, realizing I was jumping to conclusions.

"*Your* father," Ynes corrected.

I shrugged. I didn't feel like I had any connection to the stranger in that portrait, even if he looked like me.

"Shit." Kay sped up his walking and hurried us along.

"Yeah. But if he could have done that at any time, why not do it when we first arrived?"

"I think he was upset that your dad lied to him about your death." Kay stuffed the cards in his back pocket. We'd reached a fence, and either needed to go up over it or find the gate. The path ran along the fence, but I couldn't see a gate anywhere.

I frowned. "So he wanted to get to know me?" I asked. He sure had a funny way of showing it. I would have bet money he didn't like me.

"Maybe," Kay said. He crouched and then jumped and landed perched on the top railing. That thing was like a quarter inch wide. I had no idea how he was balancing there.

"He wanted to help. Even if he was a little short with you, I could feel that he wants to make things right." Kay crouched and grabbed the railing with one hand and lowered his other towards me. "Help up?"

"Yes, please." I stood on my tiptoes and took Kay's hand.

The soles of my shoes slipped against the smooth metal until I got high enough that I could wedge my toe against the cross-bar. With a lot of grunting on my end, Kay got me up to the top. I jumped down and landed, stumbling a little yet marveling that nothing went wrong.

Pog wriggled between the bars to join me on the sidewalk. I picked eim up and eiy draped around my shoulders.

"Ynes?" Kay said, extending his hand again. I watched, curious to see how she was going to do this in that skirt.

"I got this," she said, fishing in her pack.

Kay hopped off, landing gracefully next to me.

Ynes pulled out a flashlight. When she flicked it on, a beam of light like a light saber shot out. The blade cut through the metal bars of the fence like butter, making a giant person-shaped hole. The metal in the center tumbled to the ground with a thud. The cut ends of the bars sizzled, red from the heat. Ynes turned off the beam, gathered up her skirts, and stepped carefully through.

I glared at her as she repacked the 'flashlight' in her pouch. "You let me and Kay climb over?" I grumbled.

She just giggled. "Isn't it fun? I made it myself. It also functions as a lighter and a camping stove."

"Show off," Kay muttered, spinning on a heel and prancing off. Like he was one to talk.

We took off down the sidewalk, heading for where we'd parked the car, kicking tennis shoes out of the way as we went. I gathered up a few extra pairs, tying them together with the shoelaces to carry them in one hand. I would have taken more to sell, but with this many sets in this size suddenly available, the market was going to be pretty gutted.

We passed a woman using a push-broom to sweep piles of shoes off of her lawn. At another house a man used a snow-shovel to scoop them into a garbage can. Shoes were piled up waist high in places, looking like dirty white and gray snow.

"Where are we going anyway?" Ynes asked when Kay's car was in view up the block.

"We aren't going anywhere," Kay said. "I'm dropping you back off at home, and then Max and I are going to find a safe place to bunker down in until your dad gets back. I've got some feelers out."

"You aren't ditching me that easily," Ynes snapped, picking up speed to walk even with Kay.

"We aren't hunkering down anywhere," I said. "We're going to Faerie."

Kay stopped so abruptly I ran into his back. My hand brushed something furry on his lower back. Weird. "Sorry, sorry." I stepped back and took a surreptitious look down. Nothing there. Pog's tail was wrapped around my throat. So what had I touched?

He whirled on me. "We aren't going to fucking Faerie. Where did you even hear about it?"

I turned to Ynes with a pleading look. It always worked on Brandon, but she scowled.

"I'm with Kay on this one." Barnabas chittered at me from her shoulder. "And Barnabas agrees. Faerie is wicked dangerous."

"It's important!" I stopped walking and started shaking. My palms itched. Shit. I closed my eyes, pet Pog's tail on my neck, and did one of Roderick's dumb exercises. The itching went away, though my hands still shook.

"Faerie is not like a Disney movie," Kay said. "I know you're excited about finding out supernatural stuff is real, but we're not going on a tour. We need to get out of here if those people really are around here looking for you." Kay's head jerked back and forth, scanning the people working around us. He came between us, and put a hand on each of our backs, pushing us on. Once we got going, he dropped his hand from Ynes but kept it on my back. His hand was warm and solid and definitely not furry.

"Who put Faerie into your head, anyway?" Ynes mused, her skirts swirling a bit in the cool breeze coming in off the river. "I can't see Roderick mentioning it..."

"The messenger."

"Shit," Kay swore and sped us up again, practically running now. I kept nearly tripping on the shoes scattered on the sidewalk.

"What's the big deal?" Ynes asked.

"Brandon. He's a prisoner in Faerie. We need to go rescue him," I said, stopping and clenching a fist around Ynes' protection talisman through my sweatshirt.

"Not going to happen. It's too dangerous. Besides, Faerie is as large as Earth. Do you even know where he is?" Kay asked, pressing harder against my back. I stumbled forward a step, then whirled on him.

"No, but you could tell me." I pointed an accusing finger at him.

"Me?" Kay's eyes widened, and he touched his chest, his expression confused.

"Gift of prophecy. Do a reading, or whatever, and find out." I crossed my arms and glared.

"It doesn't work that way." A vein jumped in Kay's jaw, and I could practically hear his teeth grinding together. "I can't just snap my fingers and know anything." He stalked around me, kicking a shoe on the sidewalk with such intensity it sailed a good half block before landing in the street. He went around, unlocked his car door, and got in.

"Max, you can't even control your magic. How do you expect to rescue him?" Ynes asked as she opened the passenger side door and pulled the seat forward.

I fingered Ynes' protection talisman through my shirt, considering her question. Ynes had her spells and gadgets. Kay... I wasn't sure he'd help, so I discounted him. All I had was my out-of-control magic and a red panda familiar.

Kay leaned into the passenger seat to look up at me through the open door.

"Hurry up. We need to get out of this neighborhood. That talisman may prevent them from finding us with magic, but it won't stop them from stumbling across us by accident," he growled.

A light bulb went off in my head at his words. The people looking for me were the ones keeping Brandon prisoner, and I had something they wanted. Namely, me. Brandon was family, I'd trade my life to save him, no question.

I tossed the shoes I'd gathered into the back seat. Then, I reached behind my neck with both hands to pick Pog up off my shoulder, using the movement to disguise that I popped the clasp of the talisman's chain. Pretending to have trouble getting my hands around Pog's middle, I twirled the chain up around my hand until I had the amulet in hand. Then I lifted Pog up and over, putting eim in the backseat. Pog's long, fluffy fur hid the amulet nicely. I dropped the amulet under Pog before climbing in after eim.

"Max, you—" Pog began.

"You want to sit in my lap?" I asked, scooping eim up and knocking the amulet to the floor. Kay had specified it needed skin contact, but I still scooted to the other side of the back seat before snapping on my seatbelt.

"Max—" Pog started again.

I hugged eim to my chest, cutting eim off. "It's fine, Pog."

Ynes popped the seat back and climbed in. "I'll contact some people I know, see if there's anything they can do," Ynes said as she shut the door.

My resolve deepened. They wanted me to just sit and wait while Brandon was suffering in Faerie. Not going to happen. I twisted around in the seat, looking out the windows, willing the robed figures to hurry and find us before Pog could tell Kay or Ynes I'd taken off the amulet. The itch sprang back to my hands and almost immediately spread down my wrists.

All I could think about was Brandon suffering in Faerie at the hands of whoever had captured him.

"Max, calm down," Pog said, draining off some of the magic. Not enough, but that was fine. A magical blast without my amulet while they were in the area would draw them right to me. Then I could arrange a trade, myself for Brandon.

"Not in my car!" Kay yelled. I heard the front seat ratchet forward, and then Kay grabbed my arms, tugging on me.

Everything felt compressed and muffled, like I was underwater.

Tiny feet ran up my arm, claws digging into my skin. Barnabas was so small I barely felt him perched on the back of my head, but I could feel him trying to pull magic from me. Unlike with Pog, my magic resisted, stretching and then snapping back like taffy.

The passenger side door opened and Ynes hopped out and ran.

Kay climbed into the back seat and clawed at my seatbelt release, but it was too late. The magic was too far gone. It exploded out from me, engulfing Pog, Barnabas, Kay, and the convertible. I clutched my head and held back a scream as it ripped out of me. I wasn't sure if it was becoming less painful, or if I was just getting used to the feeling.

As it passed over Kay, his clothing turned into fur and he morphed from a human into a gold fox with two tails. His new fluffy, white-tipped ears pulled back flat to his head and I swear he scowled at me.

The car lurched and curved around us, changing from a cramped sleek box to a roomy bulb with bright red walls, leather seats, car doors, and stereo system. A pair of reins came in through the dash.

The engine split in half turning white, growing fur and a pearlescent spiraling horn in the center of their horse heads. The new unicorns snorted and pawed at the road, tossing their white manes.

The magic trailed off, spent. I unclipped my seat belt and slid away from a growling fox Kay. Pog moved between me and the fox, standing up on eir hind legs, front paws in the air in a futile attempt to look more intimidating. I popped open the door and climbed down to look for Ynes, accidentally kicking her amulet out of the car. My magic hadn't changed it at all, either because of the magic-resisting properties or some other mysterious reason.

Ynes stood in the yard of the house next door, staring at me, hands clapped over her mouth. I turned around. Kay's car had turned into a cherry-red carriage that looked like a fusion between the red sports car it had been and a high fantasy carriage, with chrome trim, cherry red paint, racing stripes down the sides, and car tires. The carriage was hooked to two gorgeous unicorns whose white coats shimmered in the summer sunlight.

The patch of road surrounding it was now a cobblestone circle, and a nearby tree planted in the verge had become a giant mushroom.

What a day to not have my art supplies. This would make an awesome painting.

The driver of a car passing the other direction stared out the window, so distracted by the sight they jumped the curb and crashed into a tree in a yard across the street.

Growling, Kay moved to the edge of the carriage's rear seat, his twin tails thrashing behind him and his ears pinned flat.

God, now I felt guilty. I didn't care about Kay's car, but I hadn't wanted to hurt Kay.

"I'm so, so sorry Kay. I didn't mean to turn you into a fox. I'll figure out a way to turn you back, I promise," I said to him.

"Kay's a kitsune," Ynes said. She'd walked up to the front of the carriage and was petting the nearer unicorn. "That's his true form. You didn't do anything. The magic must have forced him to change."

"When were you planning to tell me you were a kitsune?" I asked Kay. Ynes' vague warning this morning now made more sense.

"Half kitsune, and ideally never," Kay said, flicking one pointed ear.

A trumpet blast cut off anything else he was going to say. We all turned to look down the block. A green robed figure stood on the corner blowing into a curved horn.

My plan had worked! The robed figures had found us.

"Shit! Everyone back inside the car... carriage," Kay yelled, scrambling over the center console to the driver's seat. I wasn't sure how he planned to drive with paws instead of hands.

The figure dropped the horn back to their belt and ran towards us.

I jogged towards them, waving my arms, and yelled, "Let's talk! I want to propose a trade for Brandon!"

"Max, what are you doing?" Kay barked.

As the robed figure ran towards me, his hood blew back, revealing pointed ears and a face so beautiful that I lost my footing and stumbled to stop. He wore a green doublet with a high collar and polished silver buttons. His long earth-brown hair was pulled back in an elaborate braid threaded with green ribbons and silver charms.

"Fuck, that's Prince Wynne!" Kay yelped.

"Max, come back!" Ynes yelled, chasing after me.

The elf smirked at me and cocked back his arm, looking over my shoulder at Ynes. "As if I need to bargain with you. You're nothing. You and the rest of the girl's protectors. I'll have her soon enough without your help."

Did they think Ynes was who they were after? I felt magic gathering in his hand, an odd sensation since so far I'd been used to feeling it inside myself. Still running at me, the prince jerked his arm. I only had a moment's notice as I felt the magic move to underneath my feet. I leaped backwards just as a spear of rock came up where I'd been standing, shattering the concrete.

Shit. I scrambled to my feet and retreated to the carriage, scooping Pog up as I ran and tossing eim into the open door to the back seat. Ynes quickly turned back and hopped up into the passenger side with Barnabas.

"I thought you said mages were after him!" Ynes screamed at Kay, then pointed behind the carriage. "That is an elf!"

"Elf, mage, who cares? Does anyone know how to drive a carriage?" I asked.

I felt a blast of magic as the prince raised his hand again. A spear-shaped piece of asphalt broke out of the road and flew at us. It hit the back window and shattered it.

I screamed and ducked, covering my head.

"I do," Kay said. His form shimmered and elongated, his gold fur pulling back into his body and smoothing out to pale skin. I blushed at the sight of his bare back and thighs.

"Where are your clothes?" I blurted.

"Someone seems to have magicked them away, along with my phone and my cards," Kay said, tone dripping with derision as he picked up the reins and snapped them. The unicorns pranced to a start, hooves ringing musically on the asphalt.

I risked sitting up and twisted to look out the rear window. Three more robed figures appeared around the corner. The prince was almost on us. I felt magic gathering again.

"Go, go!" I yelled. As if they understood me, the unicorns picked up speed faster than I would have thought possible.

"Max, what were you thinking?" Ynes yelled, twisting around and thrusting her protection amulet at me. "Put this back on, now."

Biting my lip, I took the chain from her and closed the clasp with shaking hands before pulling it over my head. "I thought I could save Brandon," I said, though I wasn't sure anyone could hear me over the chorus of horns and screeching brakes as Kay cut off oncoming traffic.

Kay yanked hard on the reins, sending the unicorns pivoting to the right. The carriage tipped up onto two wheels before bouncing back down.

Ynes screamed and covered her eyes. I would have done the same, except I'd clamped my hands onto the leather seat. I joined her in screaming, though.

"Faster, faster!" Pog whooped. At some point, he'd climbed into the front seat and stood with his front paws on the dash.

The prince appeared behind us, surfing down the sidewalk on a piece of rock. He was actually gaining on us. The prince lifted his hand again and lobbed something at us.

Kay jerked the reins, sending the unicorns into the oncoming lanes. The rock spear whistled past and slammed into the trunk of the car Kay had swerved to avoid.

The unicorns put their heads down, galloping at full speed. We whizzed past traffic, Kay jerking us left and right around cars. The speedometer on the dash inched up over eighty. We started slowly pulling away from the prince on his rock, and then lost him entirely when we crossed the bridge over the freeway.

Pog gave another whoop and this time I joined in.

"As fun as this is, you owe me a new car," Kay yelled.

I laughed. I was homeless, and he knew it. "Maybe you can sell the unicorns for cash instead," I yelled back.

"Don't be gauche, Max!" Kay flicked the reins again.

VIII

The Barcade

"WHERE ARE WE GOING?" Ynes yelled as we took an almost out-of-control turn around a corner and off Cesar Chavez.

"Your house, where I'm dropping you off," Kay said, not taking his eyes off the road. "Then, if you don't mind lending me some clothes and a less conspicuous vehicle, Max and I will be out of your hair."

"Like I said before, not going to happen." Ynes crossed her arms. "If we're taking my truck, then I'm driving."

Kay snarled, but didn't object. When we got back to the Price house, Ynes got out and ran around to open the back gate. Kay drove the unicorns and carriage right into the backyard. It barely fit, and the top of the carriage was still visible over the fence, but it was better than parking on the street.

"Max, you unhook the unicorns while Ynes finds me something to wear," Kay told me as he hopped out.

Ynes unlocked the back door and led Kay into the house.

The unicorn's coats were silky smooth, and they smelled like lavender. Even after that run, they weren't lathered or winded.

I wondered if they could talk like Pog. I kept up a friendly chatter of conversation with the red panda, hoping one or both of them would join in, but to my disappointment, the unicorns only made horse noises.

The unicorns wandered over to the transformed plants of Ynes' garden and started munching away. I didn't think Ynes would mind. The sunflowers screamed as the unicorns ripped off chunks, but maybe it was for the best that they didn't survive.

I located a hose and filled a few buckets with water for the unicorns to drink, then gave them both one last pat on the nose. I wanted to touch their glittering horns, but refrained. I wasn't exactly a virgin. They hadn't minded me so far, but I didn't want to take chances.

"Time to go," Ynes called from the backdoor. I went inside.

Kay wore a pink skirt that went down to his ankles and a flowing white blouse. He'd also let loose his long blond hair from his ponytail and it curled around his shoulders. When he saw me looking at him, he blew me a kiss with a wink. I blushed.

"We need to talk about what happened back there with the elves," Ynes said, crossing her arms and glaring at me and Kay in equal measures.

"Since you two wouldn't help me go to Faerie, I thought maybe I could bargain with them to take me to Brandon," I said, ducking my head to avoid Ynes' gaze. Pog padded over and hugged my leg. I stroked eir head, the simple pleasure making me feel better. "But apparently, they aren't interested in talking."

Kay snorted. "Yeah, elves, especially noble ones, aren't known for their reasonableness. They're used to barking orders and being obeyed. I'm honestly surprised he even said that much to you."

"Did you know it was elves after Max, not mages?" Ynes turned pointedly to Kay.

Kay flipped his hair over one shoulder. "I'm not sure what difference it makes. Besides, we should get going before they track us here."

"He put the amulet back on," Ynes said, pointing at me.

"Yeah, but we have a bunch of magical constructs in the backyard made with Max's magic that aren't shielded." Kay put one hand on his hip and pointed out the back window at the unicorns. "Best if we aren't here when they come sniffing around."

I frowned and looked down at Pog. "Wait, could they be tracking Pog like that too?"

"No," Ynes and Kay said at the same time. Kay winked at Ynes, who rolled her eyes.

"Pog's your familiar," Ynes said. "So the protection from my amulet will cover to eim as well."

Ynes drove an old pickup truck with only three seats in the cab. I'd seen it before at the Saturday market. I got wedged in the center, holding Pog on my lap. Barnabas perched on the dashboard, chittering happily. As she'd promised, Ynes drove.

"Where to?" Ynes had asked Kay as she turned on the truck.

"The Barcade. It's downtown," Kay said.

I cocked my head and stared at him. "You want to go to an arcade... that's also a bar?"

"I was hoping we could lie low until I could..." Kay glanced at me and I could tell he changed what he had been going to say, "If Max really wants to go to Faerie, we'll need protection."

"I'm still not following," I said around a yawn. Kay's coffee had worn off, and the surge of adrenaline from the chase was fading. I was wiped.

"Barcade is where all the supernatural mercenaries hang out," Kay said.

"Mercenaries work for money," I countered. "How am I going to pay for that? I'm not exactly rolling in the dough."

"Don't worry. Money isn't everything. A few people owe me some favors." Kay put a hand on my arm and squeezed gently. "Relax."

"Why are you doing all this for me?" I asked.

"I made a promise to someone that I would."

"Who?" I blinked. "Brandon?"

Kay shrugged and said nothing else.

As soon as Ynes turned onto the main road, traffic came to a stand-still. We inched towards downtown at a snail's pace in the bumper-to-bumper traffic.

"This is boring. I want to go fast again. Like Kay did!" Pog stood up on two legs and balanced eir front paws on the dash next to Barnabas. Eir fluffy tail waved in my face.

"Absolutely not. Now sit back down. What if someone sees you?" I said.

Pog huffed and flopped back down into my lap. "Spoilsport."

"Where did you even learn these words?" I rubbed eir head.

"From you. You and the bird were always watching movies on the wall," Pog said, referring to the projector Brandon had purchased for me. We'd discovered that there was a range to my bad luck, so the projector was perfect, allowing me to watch movies without ruining the electronics. "I was the house, so I saw them too. I really liked the one with the cars sliding around the parking garages and jumping off bridges, especially now that I've ridden in one." Pog held up eir paws like eiy were holding a pretend steering wheel and made vroom noises.

"You let eim watch *The Fast and the Furious?*" Ynes asked, incredulous.

"I didn't know eiy existed!" A massive jaw cracking yawn cut off the rest of my protestations.

"You can get some rest at the safe house I arranged after we pick up our additional protection. If we ever get there. Where did all this traffic come from? It's past when rush hour should have ended," Kay said. He leaned across me to turn on the radio. I blushed and tried not to pay attention to how wonderful he smelled as he flipped through the channels until he found a traffic report.

"—things are *still* snarled from the movie promo stunt with the unicorns on Cesar Chavez earlier today," the radio announcer said, then began listing routes to avoid. A very long list. Long enough that it might have been quicker if he'd said what streets weren't backed up.

"Movie promo?" I asked, staring at the radio like it could give me the answers.

"Probably the cover story the PCA cooked up to explain the unicorns and carriage," Ynes said.

How much magical stuff had gone on right under my nose all these years? I supposed that was the point, but it still irked me. Why hide it? Magic was wonderful, dare I say, magical. Humans could learn to live next door to witches, wizards, and kitsune, right?

"I wonder what they said about the shoes," I giggled. Maybe a promotional thing by the shoe company?

"It's not funny, Max," Ynes growled. "After that stunt on Cesar Chavez, every PCA agent in the city is going to be looking for us. And they're GOING to know it was us. Do you know how many traffic cameras are on that street? Not to mention the goddamn *unicorns* in my backyard!" Ynes was yelling by the end, then she slumped over and banged her forehead against the wheel when we stopped at a light. "My dad's going to kill me. And if there's anything left of me after that, the PCA will have our hides."

"Like they'll be able to catch me." The expression on Kay's face, teasing and playful, really reminded me of a fox. I don't know how I didn't see it before.

I settled back, closed my eyes, and tried to nap until we finally arrived at Barcade near dark. Ynes parked in the lot. Kay threw open his door and hopped out before she'd even put the truck into park.

"C'mon, Max," Kay said, making a come-hither flirty gesture.

"I'm going to stay here," Ynes said, making no move to undo her seatbelt. "The crowd in there can be rough."

I stared at her. "It's a video game arcade." I could even see the glittering and flashing lights of the machines through the glass windows.

"That's a favorite hangout of all of Portland's toughest supernaturals." Ynes gave me a significant look that I couldn't interpret and put a hand on my arm. "I'm staying. You can leave Pog with me if you don't feel comfortable taking eim inside."

Probably a good idea. I wouldn't want to leave Pog alone in the truck; I suspected eiy might try to drive it. Ynes still had her hand on my arm and squeezed it gently as she leaned towards me. Was she trying to tell me something?

"Kay, can I have a word with Ynes for a moment? I'll be in right after," I said.

"Fine, don't be long." Kay threw up his hands. "And don't do anything stupid..." he glanced at me, "stupider," he amended before shutting the door and stalking towards the arcade.

Ynes and I watched until he disappeared through the glass door.

"Do you really believe he changed his mind about taking you to Faerie?" Ynes said as soon as it closed behind him.

"Not really," I admitted, hugging Pog. "But I also don't really have many other options. Those elves were serious, and I believe he wants to protect me, for whatever reason that I don't understand yet."

"That's fairly self-explanatory if you ask me," Ynes said with a giggle, running her hand down my arm.

I gave her a questioning look.

"It's not true for all of them, but there's a reason folklore depicts kitsune and foxes as tricksters. And your magic so far has been chaos incarnate."

"That's true." I couldn't help but join in her laughter as I remembered the shoestorm.

"I propose we ditch him and go to the PCA for help." She squeezed my hand, then pulled back, blushing. "I bet they might even set up a diplomatic talk with the elves so we can try to work things out."

I had to think about it for all of three seconds. "Let's do it."

Ynes grinned at me, cranked the shaft into drive, then floored it out of the parking lot with a squeal of rubber.

"This is what I was talking about," Pog cheered and jumped up and down. I had to grab eim to keep eim from tumbling off my lap.

Even I was cheered until a crack appeared in the road and tore towards us, sending chunks of pavement spiking up. Ynes slammed on the brakes.

"What's tha—" I began. The crack went under the car. The ground rumbled under the stopped truck, then a spike of earth burst up from below us, piercing the truck's engine and hood.

"Run!" Ynes screamed, undoing her seatbelt, throwing open her door and grabbing my hand. Barnabas jumped on my shoulder as she hauled me and Pog out of the car. Luckily, she'd taken off so quickly that I hadn't had time to put my seatbelt back on.

Three people in gray robes, hoods pulled low to cover their faces, ran toward us. We turned and ran back towards the Barcade.

"How'd they find us?" I patted at the charm Ynes had given me. It was still there.

She cursed in Spanish. "They must have had someone staking out the Barcade. If they're using magic to move around the city..." she trailed off, huffing from the effort of the run, but I got her meaning. Once they got word, they could be here in an instant.

The glittering lights of the arcade teased us from the corner half a block down. My arm wrapped around Pog's middle, holding eim to my chest, eir back legs and tail dangling. Barnabas chittered and clung to my hair.

Ynes was already panting and gasping for breath, so I slowed down. I could have run faster, even with Pog's weight slowing me down. One benefit of walking everywhere, I guess. And proper footwear.

"Should have ridden the unicorns after all," I muttered. *They wouldn't have gotten speared.* Ynes gave me a dirty look.

The bells over the door to the arcade tinkled merrily as Ynes and I burst inside. I didn't quite understand the point of the bells, since the chaotic sounds of overlapping video game jingles drowned them out. A man in a dirty baseball cap barely glanced up from his game of Tekken as we ran by.

The front of the place was packed with an eclectic variety of games, from the classic to modern, and even a few pinball machines. I kept running, pausing only to glance up and down each aisle, looking for Kay.

We emerged from the games into a more traditional looking bar area in the back. A velvet rope separated the tables from the games, with large 'No one under 21' signs at the gap. Kay sat at the bar, chatting with the bartender. He hadn't noticed us yet.

"Kay," I yelled. "Trouble."

He spun around on the stool, his eyes widening at Ynes, who'd bent over her knees huffing, trying to get her breath back, too winded to speak.

Pog wiggled from my arms. Eiy landed with a thud, then dashed across the bar, weaving through the table legs until eiy reached Kay and tugged on his skirt.

"The elves found us!" I gasped. "The truck's toast."

The glass at the front door exploded. Ynes shrieked and ducked, pulling me down with her. Even as far back as we were, a few shards flew over our heads. Almost everyone in the bar area jumped to their feet, including Kay.

The bartender ducked under the bar. I expected he'd emerge with a shotgun or something, but he came back up clutching a long gnarled staff taller than him, topped with a twist of silver wire that contained a ruby the size of my fist.

Around the bar, hands went into jackets and under tables into bags. As many guns came out as wands. A few people inexplicably began undressing.

The few patrons who'd been at the arcade machines came running back to the bar, all except the man in the baseball cap. I couldn't see the front past the machines, but I heard a roar and sounds of a scuffle.

The bartender came around the end of the bar and planted the staff with a thump. "This is neutral territory!" he yelled. The ruby on his staff burst into flames.

A bolt of lightning came arcing over the arcade games. The bartender's staff sent out a pulse of light and the lightning splashed against a red shimmering barrier that flowed from his staff to engulf the bar.

"Max, Ynes, get behind me." Kay widened his feet and extended his hands, rotating them in a circle before bringing them to his chest. Tiny balls of blue fire sprang up in a circle around him. He threw his hands out, and the fire blazed away, the little balls spinning around each other as they flew away through the red barrier. At the front, someone screamed in a musical tone.

I shoved Ynes towards Kay. We huddled behind him and the bartender. My palms itched, my heart beating fast. I hoped Kay'd had time to find a mercenary to help us, although from the look of things, maybe it didn't matter.

"What's neutral territory?" I asked, gasping and flexing my hands.

"It means that the attackers are breaking a peace treaty. It was a warning that we'd respond with force," Kay snarled. More blue fire blazed around him, revealing fox ears and twin tails, invisible except for the back-lit blue outlines before the wisps flew away. "Normally, magic is forbidden in the building."

I wanted to ask more, but all the magic being thrown about was making my magic blaze in sympathy. Or maybe I was bleeding some magic off all the spells. Or both. I didn't quite understand how magic worked yet. All the power flowing through me hurt and I fell over, groaning, clutching my hands to my chest.

"Do your exercises, Max." Pog put a paw on my arm, drawing off some of the magic.

I nodded and began trying to count through the exercises that Roderick had taught me. Four in, seven out. Concentrate on my breath, not the magic burning at my palms.

Ynes' hand dove into her bag and she pulled out the pocketknife she'd used earlier and flicked it open. But instead of a blade, a twist of wood popped out. Did she really make a multi-tool pocketknife-wand?

Pointing her wand in the direction of the arcade machines, Ynes stepped up to stand on Kay's other side. She muttered a spell and flicked her wand. A sparkle of light zipped from the tip and arced over the arcade game. I winced at the sound of the explosion that followed shortly after. Those poor machines.

One of the woman customers of the bar finished stripping down and fell to all fours. Fur sprang up from her skin even as she began growing in size. The sight distracted me so much I lost track of my counting, instead breathing hard as I stared, wide-eyed, at her transformation.

Her face pushed out into a snout, and her muscles bunched up and grew. She threw back her head and howled, now an amalgam of wolf and woman with huge teeth and razer-sharp claws. She bounded past Kay and swiped a huge paw at a robed figure coming around the corner of the machines.

The figure jerked back out of the way with superhuman speed, so that the werewolf's claws only caught the edge of the hood. Her claw snagged, dragging the robe off as the figure darted backwards and revealing the elf prince who had chased us earlier.

The werewolf threw the cloak aside and swiped at the elf. He darted to the side, but not quick enough; her swipe caught his arm, tearing three gouges down his green doublet. He cursed and disappeared back from where he'd come.

I hunched over, closing my eyes, trying to go back to counting breaths, but the screams, roars, crashes, and sizzling of Kay's firebolts and Ynes' sparkling explosions made it hard to concentrate. Besides, I wanted to watch the magical battle.

The brown-haired prince emerged from behind the arcade games again. He didn't have a weapon, but punched with arms that were now bulky and brown. The werewolf's claws scratched him again, but left only light marks on the hard rock that now covered his skin.

More robed figures came around the machines behind the prince, throwing spells. One threw fire, another bolts of ice, and a third ragged yellow lightning, all of which bounced off the bartender's red barrier. However, after the last bolt of lightning, the red light in the gem flickered and died at the same time as the shimmering barrier. The bartender lowered the staff and darted back around the bar and out through a swinging door. He didn't come back.

The rest of the bar's patrons ran after him. The werewolf, hulking and massive, stayed, stalking back and forth in front of us on two massive clawed feet. Between her, Ynes' bolts, and Kay's fire, they were able to keep the elves at bay. The elves batted away most of Kay's fire and the bolts like they were mere snowballs, but the effort slowed them down and left them vulnerable to the werewolf's attacks.

"Time to go!" Kay snapped, taking a moment to glance at me. His eyes widened. I glanced at my hands to see that they were glowing gold with magic. "Shit," he swore. "Ynes, run."

Ynes lowered her wand and looked at me over her shoulder. Seeing me crouched there, she snapped her wand closed and darted around the bar to the door that led to the kitchen. I heard her rattle it and then she came back around the bar. "It's locked!"

"Those bastards," the werewolf growled before darting forward to drive the elves back with frantic slashes of her massive claws.

I groaned and closed my eyes. Pinpricks of pain were going up my arms.

"You might want to run, Ynes!" Pog called.

Ynes dropped to her knees, flicked her pocketknife open to a piece of chalk, and started doing something on the floor around her.

"Think of something to take out the elves," Kay yelled at me as he melted into fox form.

Like I knew how to do that. So far, I hadn't exactly been successful at directing my power. I wished I could fight like the characters in Tekken, or do actual useful spells like a video game wizard. I focused on that thought as the magic roared out of me.

The werewolf scrambled away with a yelp as the arcade consoles melted, reforming as characters from their respective games. Suddenly, the four elves were surrounded by a literal army of people. When the magic washed over Ynes, a shimmering barrier reflected it from around her.

The elves formed into a circle with their backs to each other, hands held at spellcasting ready, facing the video game characters. I couldn't name them all, but I saw Donkey Kong holding a barrel over his head, the green lizard from Rampage whose head brushed the ceiling, Pac-man, and the blue wizard from gauntlet. However, the characters all just stood there, swaying slightly as each of them acted out their idle animations.

"Why aren't they doing anything?" Kay whispered, padding towards me on four legs. His tails wagged behind him and his ears were pulled back.

I palmed my forehead. "They're video game sprites. They need someone to control them."

The elves too had figured this out, and started pushing the motionless people out of the way to blaze a path in our direction.

"Run!" Kay darted at me, nipping at my leg when I didn't move.

I got to my feet. My legs were shaky and felt faint.

Ynes ran and threw her arms around me. I hugged her back, glad her spell had protected her from my magic and she hadn't been hurt. After Brandon, she was probably my best friend. Not to be outdone, Pog stood on eir backlegs and hugged my leg.

As tired as I was, I wasn't going to be moving fast, and the idle characters were going to slow us down as much as the elves. My magic had to have included a way to control them, right?

I cast around and spotted a line of consoles and mini televisions at the side of the bar. Perfect. This place had everything. I pointed to them as I staggered in that direction. "Everyone, grab a controller!"

"What?" Ynes asked, but I didn't have time to explain. The elves were almost on us.

"... donkey kong!" I yelled as I picked up a wireless controller and started mashing buttons. The ape was the closest to the elves. Kong brought the barrel down on the head of the nearest elf. The barrel exploded into fragments and the elf fell to the floor, hopefully out of the fight tonight for good.

"Why do you know the gorilla's name?" Pog asked, sounding jealous. I ignored eim and tossed a controller to Ynes.

While I was distracted, Donkey Kong stood motionless again, and the prince whirled around and punched the gorilla in the face with his stone arm. Kong fell backwards unconscious, blinking red before vanishing. Shit, my character!

I scooped Pog up onto my shoulders, and then handed eim a controller. "Push buttons," I told eim. Pog sat behind my head hugging it, eir tail wrapped around my neck. Eiy set the controller on my head and began bashing it with a paw. A big muscled character in a loincloth wielding an axe started swinging, taking out two other video game characters next to them, but also forced the largest of the robed elves, who still had its hood up, to turn and engage. The massive elf pulled a sword out from under their cloak and used it to keep the whirling axe at bay.

The werewolf patron howled and leapt into the fray, forcing the group of elves back.

The blue wizard jerked to life and lifted his staff, blowing fire. That must be Ynes. I focused on the giant rampage lizard and started tapping buttons as our group edged our way around the crowd toward the door.

The elf woman shot lightning from her hands at the wizard. The wizard flashed and then disappeared with a video game death sound. But no matter. My lizard stomped towards them, causing video game carnage as it ate half the characters it passed by. Oops.

We reached the door and got outside.

The lot had emptied out. The neon Barcade sign above the door was half smashed and hanging at an angle.

Screams and the sounds of fighting came from inside the arcade as Pog, Ynes, and I continued to attack with our video game avatars to keep the elves busy. However, the crowd was rapidly thinning out as character after character fell to the elves' magic.

"What about the werewolf?" I asked. She was still going at it with the massive elf, though the axe fighter Pog had used at first was gone.

"She'll be fine," Kay said, padding away from the arcade. "Werewolves are tough and almost impossible to kill in wolf form."

"Where now?" I asked Kay. "This isn't going to work for much longer and they destroyed our vehicle."

"I've procured us a ride." Kay darted across the parking towards a black hearse that was parked on the street with its lights on.

"Funny, it looked like you were just flirting with the bartender to me." Ynes snapped as we hurried after him.

"It's called gathering information." Kay sniffed and put his muzzle in the air. "I was trying to find out who was available for work."

I rolled my eyes at him. Sure.

As we approached, the driver's side window rolled down. A very pale woman lowered her sunglasses to look at us. She had red hair cut short and spiked up, and gold studs lined her ears. "Kay? I thought you were going to follow in your own car?"

"Everyone, this is Sunny. And there was a slight change of plans. Add it to my tab." Kay said, jumping in through the open window and prancing across Sunny's lap to sit in the passenger seat. She glared at him and I swore her eyes flashed red for a moment. But no, her eyes were green. They must have caught the reflection from the nearby stoplight.

"Whatever, but the rest of you ride in the back," she growled at us, hooking a thumb at the rear of the car. Then her eyes widened. "Is that a red panda?"

"Yeah..." The covetous glint in her eyes made me nervous, and I put a possessive hand on Pog's tail. "My familiar."

"The red panda can ride up here with me," Sunny said. I ignored her, keeping a tight grip on Pog.

I didn't really want to ride in the back of a hearse, but I didn't really have many other options. Actually, I had no other options. Ynes popped the back open, and we all piled inside. Sunny peeled away the moment the back door closed.

IX

The Vampire Sunshine

BASED ON THE HEARSE, and Sunny's general scowling demeanor—seriously, I think she spent half the ride glaring at me in the rearview mirror—I'd been sure we were going to pull up in front of some crumbling manor like Pog's former dilapidated house. But she took us to an upscale condo in the heart of downtown with parking in a private, underground lot.

The elevator ride up from the garage was tense. Kay was still in fox form; I suspected I'd zapped away his clothing again. That or he just enjoyed being a fox. Pog seemed fascinated by Kay's two wagging tails and kept trying to bite them.

The elevator door opened up into a swanky apartment that could have been on the cover of a home design magazine, though not as ostentatious as my father's mansion. Sunny's living room actually looked lived in, with throw blankets over the brown suede couch, and lamps that cast a cozy glow over the room. She had covered the polished wooden floors with a decorative red throw rug in a brown geometric design. Dark curtains covered the windows.

Pog bounded past everyone to run inside. Barnabas chittered and leapt from Ynes's shoulder, bounced off the wall, and landed on the hardwood in a scrabble of claws, then chased after eim.

"Take off your shoes," Sunny growled as we stepped off the elevator. She took up position blocking the end of the small entryway and pointed to a shoe rack bench, the threat implied.

I kicked off my tennis shoes, leaving them in a heap on the floor. Ynes sat on the bench and pulled her flats off, then tucked them onto an empty section of the rack. Tisking at me, she picked my shoes up and put them next to hers.

Kay's fox form shimmered and a moment later a fully dressed Kay stood on the rug next to me.

"Why didn't you lose your clothes this time?" I asked.

"Why? Hoping to get another eyeful?" He winked at me and wiggled his hips, making his skirts swish.

"No." I blushed so hard my ears burned. "Just last time..."

"I changed to my fox form before you blew up. My magic means the clothing comes with me. Last time, you caught me by surprise." Kay looped his arm through mine and tugged me into Sunny's apartment.

"That werewolf at the Barcade had to strip before she could change," I told him, raising my eyebrows.

"I'm a kitsune, not a shifter," Kay said with a wave of his hand, like that explained everything.

There was a crash from somewhere in the condo. Sunny's eyes widened. "Not my cars!" I blinked, and she was gone.

"What the hell?" I exclaimed, stumbling backwards.

"Let me introduce our host for the evening." Kay waved around the condo. "Sunshine Love, vampire."

"A vampire named Sunshine?" I said, trying to keep a straight face. I must have failed.

Sunny materialized in front of me with a whoosh of air and thrust Pog into my arms. "Not a joke. And keep a closer eye on your familiar, mage. That broken model is going to cost you."

"My profits from this job are quickly dwindling to nothing," Kay muttered.

What? What profits? What job? But I already knew Kay wouldn't answer if I asked.

"That's... an interesting name for a vampire," I said instead.

"What of it? I like my name, so why should I have to change it just because I turned into a vampire?" Sunny's eyes turned bright red and two large fangs now pressed down into her lower lip, bright white against her red lipstick.

I backed up a step, eyes widening, turning my shoulder to put my body between her and Pog. "Good point," I stammered, heart hammering.

"I really don't want to spend the night with a vampire," Ynes said, also backing away.

"Perfectly safe. Really," Kay said.

"As long as I get paid," Sunshine said, flashing me a toothy grin. Then the fangs withdrew and her eye color faded back to their normal green.

"Besides, Ynes, you were the one that insisted on coming along on this little adventure," Kay said. He went over and flopped back onto the couch and yawned widely. "You got anything to eat here, Sunny? I'm starving."

"I made a grocery order after I got your message, Keiichi." Sunny checked her phone. "My servant should return with it shortly."

"You mean your walking snack," Ynes growled as she sat on the couch next to Kay.

Sunny shrugged. "I only bite the willing." Then she smiled, turning her attention back to me. "It's a very pleasurable experience. Orgasmic even." Her fangs came down again, and she put a cool hand on my arm. "Care to try it?"

"Sunny, no biting my mage," Kay growled.

"It's his choice," Sunny said, smile widening.

"Tempting, but no." I used Pog to push her hand away and joined the other two in the living room. I paced for a moment, hugging Pog to my chest, trying to think. I still thought the best bet was Ynes' suggestion to go to the PCA, but I already knew what Kay thought of that idea.

Kay watched me pace for a moment. "Don't worry, we can lie low here until Ynes's father gets back into town."

"I'm not sure how that will help," I snapped at him.

"Because the cards told me it would." Kay crossed his arms. I glared, about done with this fox not telling me everything.

"How!" I dropped Pog on the couch and then grabbed Kay's blouse, yanking him until we were almost nose-to-nose. "How will that save me and Brandon from the elves?"

"Just trust me." Kay smirked.

"Hey, Max! That's my shirt. Be careful!" Ynes yelled.

I threw Kay back on the couch in disgust.

"Calm down." Kay grabbed the front of my hoodie and pulled. I lost my balance and fell, landing face first on his chest, sprawled between his legs. The ties on his shirt front had come undone when I'd dropped him, exposing skin. Kay put his hand down right on the back of my head and held me down as I tried to get up. "Stop struggling," he said in response to my muffled cries. "You don't want to explode again."

Growling at him under my breath, I lay my arms on either side of him. His legs pressed into my armpits and his groin against my upper chest. He smelled of soap and musty fur. The light fuzz of hair on his chest tickled my nose.

"Yeah, Max, calm down." Pog's furry paw came to rest on my hand, followed by the press of a warm wet... tongue?

"Pog, did you just lick my hand!" I mumbled into Kay's chest. Kay giggled, making his body vibrate under me.

Kay's hand moved off my head, so I sat up. "Hey there," Kay said, fingers trailing along my arm as I pulled back. He winked at me. "You don't need to move."

I blushed and scrambled backwards until my back hit the chair opposite. Kay was cute, but I didn't trust him.

Pog snickered. "Max, your face is almost as red as my fur."

"Shut up," I mumbled, bringing my face to my knees and wrapping my arms around my legs to hide my blush.

"Kay, why are elves after Max?" Ynes asked.

Kay made a show of shrugging. "I think we're all tired after a long day. Let's table this discussion until we've had some food and sleep, hmm?"

"Fine," Ynes huffed.

Sunny sauntered into the room. "There's a queen bed in the first room down the hall, and the couch folds out into a bed. Kay didn't tell me there were three of you, so two of you will have to double up," Sunny said.

"Five!" Pog said, pointing a paw at Ynes. "Don't forget her and the squirrel."

"Right, how can I have forgotten the witch." Sunny's mouth twitched like she was hiding a smile.

"Can I see your coffin?" The words popped out before I could stop them.

Sunny glared at me. "I don't sleep in a coffin. Don't be absurd."

"Oh..." I couldn't hide the disappointment from my voice. What kind of vampire didn't sleep in a coffin? A boring one, that's what.

Kay had graciously taken the pullout bed, while I shared the queen in the spare bedroom with Ynes, Pog, and Barnabas.

Pog sprawled in the center of the bed, snoring softly. I didn't know how eiy managed it, but eiy took up as much room as me.

Despite how tired I was, I tossed and turned. Pog's paws pressing into my back didn't help things either.

I couldn't stop thinking about Brandon, about how alone and scared he had to be as a prisoner in Faerie.

How had he known about the seal on my magic? Why hadn't he told me? I missed him so much it ached. I *needed* to save him. If it weren't for him, my life would have been so much worse.

He'd aged out of the system a few months before me and had invited me to live with him when I turned eighteen and never asked me for rent money.

Despite my bad luck costing us so many apartments, he never abandoned me or kicked me out. Even when it got to where no one would rent to us, Brandon found that abandoned house for us to squat in.

"Max, your tossing and turning keeps waking me up." Ynes yawned and rolled over to face me.

"I'm just worried about Brandon." I sighed and petted Pog. Eiy let out a big sigh and rolled on eir back, sticking all four legs straight up into the air. "Think Kay's asleep? We could sneak out and go to the PCA like we planned."

"Yeah, it's probably the best option to help your friend," Ynes agreed. I heard the rustle of sheets and then the curtains opened. The twinkling lights of downtown far below lit up the room. She wore some of Sunny's pajamas, slightly too small on her. "Let me just change."

I slid off the bed and put my back to her to give her privacy. I'd slept in my jeans and hoodie so I didn't have to do anything.

"How do you suppose Kay planned to find Brandon if our mercenary plan had worked out?" I mused. "Maybe he planned to do a reading to find out." Hadn't he said Brandon had come to see him? Maybe that's how he'd known about the seal and how to find it.

"Honestly?" The rustle of clothing came from the other side of the room. "I'm not sure he was actually going to help you. I think he was just trying to placate you until my father gets back. He seems awful bent on getting you to my father."

I sighed. That seemed like a valid possibility.

Ynes came around the bed, back in her skirt and blouse.

"Quiet," Pog grumbled. "Some of us are trying to sleep."

"Pog, want to go do a little scouting for us?" Ynes bent down over the red panda and cooed, rubbing eir head. Good idea. That couch was almost directly in front of the elevator that served as the front door. We wouldn't be able to sneak out without him seeing if Kay was awake.

"Then will you let me sleep?" he grumbled.

"Of course," Ynes gave eir head one last pat and stepped back.

Pog slithered out of bed with a humph. I got up and cracked the door and eiy padded on all fours out into the hall. Outside, the entire apartment was dark and still. Sunny had retired to her room with the woman who'd brought us groceries when the rest of us had gone to bed.

I waited impatiently, watching the clock. Ynes was more relaxed than me, sprawled on her stomach, scrolling through her phone.

After ten minutes, Pog still hadn't returned.

"Should we go look for eim?" I whispered to Ynes.

She looked up at me and shrugged.

Worried about my familiar, I cracked the door enough to slip out, then tip-toed down the hall to the living room. The pull-down bed was out and the coffee table shoved to the side to make room.

"Pog?" I whispered.

The living room lights flicked on and Sunny came sauntering in from the hall that led to the elevator with Pog cuddled in her arms. Eiy had eir head back, a look of bliss on eir face as Sunny scratched eir throat.

"Traitor," I muttered.

"Your familiar is very cute," Sunny said, stopping in front of me. "A red panda is an unusual choice. Difficult to explain to the mundanes."

"It was an accident," I admitted. "What are you still doing up?"

"Vampire, remember?" She grinned at me, showing fangs and red eyes for a moment.

I swallowed hard and involuntarily took a step back. She scared the shit out of me. I wondered why the lights hadn't woken up Kay and looked over to the pull-down. Because of the angle of the couch, all I could see of the bed was the very end of it, covered in a tangle of blankets.

She twisted to follow my gaze. "I sent him to sleep in my room when Amelie left." She turned back to me with a lopsided smile, Pog still melting in her arms. "Kay asked me to keep you inside."

"Sunny, I have to go." I wondered if vampires could tell if you were lying. The truth would be the best. "I need to go to Faerie to rescue my best friend, but Kay said no."

"Smart. Faerie is dangerous, even if you didn't already have the prince after your head."

"I'm not going to Faerie now. We're going to try the PCA first, to see if they can negotiate with the elves for me."

Sunny shrugged. "Don't care. My job is to keep you here and keep you safe until Kay says so."

I held out my arms. "I guess I'll just get back to bed then. Pog, you coming?"

"I want to stay with her," Pog purred.

Back in our room, Ynes sat up in bed, stroking Barnabas' tail. "I guess I should have figured a vampire would still be up," she admitted.

I just climbed back into bed, then pulled the covers over my head and tried not to cry. Eventually, I drifted off to sleep.

The smell of bacon brought me out of the room the next morning. The curtains in the living room were all pulled tightly closed and secured with black clasps.

Pog sat on the couch next to Sunny, lapping at a cup of coffee on the coffee table in front of eim. Sunny also had a cup in her hands, and relaxed back with her feet propped up on the coffee table, wearing sunglasses and pajamas covered with cartoon red pandas.

"I thought vampires slept during the day," I said to Sunny.

Sunny snorted. "And how many vampires have you met, kid?"

"Counting you? One."

"Yeah, that's what I thought." She sipped from her mug. I didn't want to know what was in it.

I went over and sat on the couch and stroked Pog's tail. "Enjoying yourself?" I asked the panda.

"Can we live here now?" Pog said without glancing up from eir coffee cup.

I shook my head and went into the kitchen. Kay wore a black apron patterned with skulls draped over Ynes's clothing from yesterday while cooking eggs at the stove. Ynes sat at the bar sipping on a cup of coffee and watching Kay cook.

As I came in, Kay thrust a plate into my hands. Bacon, scrambled eggs, toast, and strawberries. "Eat up. Plus there's coffee, too."

"I don't normally drink coffee." I took a seat at the bar next to Ynes.

"You grew up in practically the coffee capital of the world, and you don't drink coffee," Kay said, his voice dripping with disbelief and putting his hands on his hips.

"What can I say, I'm a rebel."

Ynes cracked a smile.

I practically inhaled my food. I didn't think I'd ever been so hungry. Kay cooked me another helping of eggs. Usually, I didn't even eat breakfast. Mostly because I was too poor, but still.

"What's the plan today?" I asked when I finished up. "I was thinking maybe we could go over to the City Target, or that thrift store up in Chinatown to get us all some clean clothes."

"You," Kay flourished the soapy dish wand at me from the sink where he was scrubbing our breakfast dishes, "are not leaving this condo until Mr. Price gets back."

"I'll pick something up when I go out," Ynes said.

"You really shouldn't go anywhere, either, missy." Kay turned the wand to point at Ynes.

"In case you've forgotten, *Keiichi*," Ynes emphasized his name, "We left two unicorns in my backyard. I need to do something with them."

Sunny appeared in the kitchen next to me. I jumped.

"What? Unicorns?" she said, eyes wide. "Cool."

"Oh, he left that part out?" Ynes said, banging a fist on the counter. "What a surprise."

"Ynes, if you give me your address, I can send Amelie over to take care of your unicorns." Sunny frowned. "What do they eat, anyway?"

"Same thing as horses, I guess?" Ynes shrugged. "But sure, if you really don't think we should leave the condo." Then Ynes pointed at me. "I bet he also didn't tell you he has out of control magic."

"If I can't leave, what am I supposed to do if I have an episode?" I asked.

"He told me about that," Sunny said. "I have a private rooftop pool. I'll show you where the stairs are. There's nothing up there you can hurt."

"So you say..." The first blast had covered most of Pog's house. The subsequent ones had been smaller... mostly. Except for the shoe thing. I did not want to add a high-rise condo to the list of things I'd destroyed.

"That's not going to be an issue, *is it Max*?" Kay said with gritted teeth. "You should have it under control now."

I just stared at him. Yeah, I'd trained with Roderick, but I'd still had two more—episodes? Explosions? Outbursts?—after. I didn't know what to call them. I turned back to Sunny. "Maybe you should show me how to get to the roof... just in case."

"Sure," Sunny said.

Ynes's phone buzzed, and she held up a finger, then answered the phone. "Hello Dad. I thought you weren't coming home until tomorrow."

Kay froze at the sink, his eyes widening.

"Is that?" Sunny mouthed at me. I nodded. She looked relieved. I don't think she was as at ease with my chaos magic as she'd pretended.

"The unicorns?" Ynes grimaced and made a face at me. "Those. Yeah... I'm holding them for a friend. I'm sorry they tore up the garden." She mouthed, 'he's already at home,' at us.

"Tell him I'm here, with Max," Kay yelled.

"No!" Sunny growled back. "Don't tell him my address. Amelie can drive you over. I'll go wake her." Sunny disappeared in a snap of air.

"I guess you heard all that," Ynes said into the phone. "Yeah. We'll be there soon. Bye." She hung up and glanced at us. "That's weird. He's never cut a trip short like that. Oh, Kay, he also said he left you a message yesterday on your phone?"

"Oh, you mean the one that Max vaporized along with my clothing?" Kay yanked off Sunny's skull apron and tossed it on the counter in disgust. I winced. I guess I owed him a new phone and a new car.

X

Betrayed

AMELIE DROPPED US OFF in front of the Price's Victorian. I was tiring of this house. Mr. Price better be able to help me get Brandon back. I could deal with my crazy magic. It was far better than my bad luck used to be.

Pog scampered up the porch and hopped on the rocker, sending it swinging with a loud creak. The rest of us were slower. While eiy waited, Pog swung back and forth, giggling.

A severe man with salt and pepper hair opened the front door. He had lighter skin than Ynes, but the same eyes. I stopped, as did Kay, but Ynes ran up the steps and flung her arms around him. "Hi Daddy! How was your trip?"

"Kay, who is this?" Mr. Price said, brushing Ynes off him. Seriously? His eyes immediately cut to Pog, still merrily swinging. His frown deepened. "What the hell is that?"

"It's a red panda," I said. "Pog, c'mere."

"But I'm having fun!" Pog whined. Eiy stood on all fours, tail swinging to keep eir balance as the bench moved.

"Good god, it talks!" Mr. Price started.

Kay grabbed my arm and towed me up the walk, his fingernails digging into my arms like claws. I wondered how much of his form was real and how much was an illusion.

"Hey, Kay, let go. That hurts!" I said.

"You gotta expect some weird stuff with this one around," Kay said. "But I expect you knew that with as much as you offered me."

"What?" Ynes and I exclaimed at the same time.

A sinking feeling grew in my stomach. A lot of what Kay had said over the last day made more sense now. My palms itched, but rather than fighting it, I embraced it. The feeling was already crawling up my fingers.

"Daddy, what's going on?" Ynes followed Mr. Price out onto the porch and clutched at his arm.

"I wish you hadn't dragged my daughter into this." He finally acknowledged her, taking her arm. "Ynes, go to the back and take care of those unicorns. I want them gone by tonight."

Ynes and I exchanged a glance, and I flicked my eyes in her father's direction, then jerked my head at the house. She gave me a quick nod, yanked her arm from his and stomped into the house. Barnabas scurried after her, squeaking.

I hoped she'd gotten my meaning to get the unicorns ready.

"And make them take that damn ugly carriage, too!" he called after her. She shot him a middle finger without looking back.

The itching accelerated.

Pog said, "Hey, Max—"

"And you, shut it!" Mr. Price whirled on Pog, who shrank back, eyes wide, and ears going flat.

I didn't think Pog's tail could go any fluffier, but it did. Pog leapt from the bench and ran down the stairs past Mr. Price. Eiy hit my leg so hard it knocked me off balance and only Kay's grip on my arm kept me upright.

"Don't yell at Pog!" I growled. Pog's touch on my leg was pulling some of the energy back out of me, which wasn't what I wanted right now. I didn't know what was going on, but I knew it couldn't be good. At least Ynes wasn't in on it.

"I wouldn't have had to 'drag her into this' if you'd just been home," Kay snarled.

"Your prophecy said we had at least a week," Mr. Price shot back. "Let's talk about this in the house."

"Dude, his prophecies suck, don't they?" I couldn't help but chuckle.

Kay kicked my shin. "I said, 'a week or so' if I recall," Kay responded, going stiff. "And my prophecies are just fine. How do you think I knew how to break your curse?"

I was so flabbergasted by Kay's admission that I didn't fight for a few more steps towards the house. He had been the one to send Brandon into Faerie.

"I headed back yesterday," Mr. Price said in a gruff voice. "If someone checked their messages, we could have taken care of this last night."

"Sorry. My phone had a bit of an accident named Max."

I twisted against Kay's grip with no success. Kay dragged me up the walk and into the house. It was a struggle to walk with Pog clinging to one leg and Kay pulling me.

"How'd you get word to come home early?" Kay asked as Mr. Price shut and locked the door behind us.

Mr. Price sighed. "I suppose you'd have found out, eventually." He took us into the sitting room we'd been in the day before with Ynes. Roderick and the man from the portrait sat together on the couch. Roderick's eyes widened when he saw me and he shook his head and mouthed 'quiet.'

He'd helped me yesterday, so I could keep my mouth shut. I wasn't sure Pog would, or even could, but eiy currently had eir face pressed into my pant leg and hadn't noticed Roderick.

One corner of Kay's mouth quirked up. "Teaming up with the enemy I see?"

Mr. Price sniffed. "Just because mages and witches traditionally don't get along doesn't mean that it's impossible. This is the modern age, after all."

I couldn't take my eyes off the man sitting next to Roderick. My father, supposedly. Despite Roderick's assertion that he was nicer than his portrait made him look, the deep frown on his face only got deeper as he looked me over.

"The kitsune is trying to get something over on us. This is NOT my daughter," Mr. Woolven said.

I snorted. He was more right than he realized. My hands shook, and the tingles had moved all the way to my elbow. Not long now. What should I try to have the magic do? So far, the unfocused ones had been the most chaotic, so I needed to direct it to something.

My shaking must have gotten the attention of Kay, because he looked at me and then did a double take. "Shit. Do you have the containment artifact? Otherwise, I can't be responsible for what happens."

"This is preposterous! We are looking for a *girl*, Rafa. If this crazy kitsune thinks he can lie to us about this, he's sadly mistaken." Mr. Woolven stood up and stormed past me. Rafa sounded like a nickname. Awful familiar for a business partnership between a witch and a mage. Kay had told me they usually disliked each other.

"Still, just to be safe, maybe we should..." Mr. Price said, and took something from his pocket. A silver bracelet etched with gold runes. He reached toward me with it and I backed away, or tried to. Kay's hand on my arm held me in place.

"What is that?" I asked.

"But if you do that, how will the kitsune prove his little boy here is the real deal?" Mr. Woolven said from behind me and laughed. He came back in with a shot glass filled with dark brown liquid.

"A little early for drinking, isn't it, Charles?" Mr. Price said.

"Put that thing away, Rafa." Mr. Woolven swung his glass at the bracelet, making the liquid slosh. "This is a farce. He's probably conspiring with the kitsune to defraud us and then split the payment. Let the boy pretend to have an episode, then send them away. If you put that on him, they'll be able to string us along longer."

"Wouldn't it have been easier for the kitsune to get a woman for this scam?" Ynes' father asked, but pursed his lips and slipped the bracelet back into his pocket. He made a good point if you asked me.

"Who knows with these people?" Mr. Woolven shrugged and sat back down on the couch next to Roderick.

"You dummies, he's trans!" Kay yelled. They both ignored him.

During this entire exchange, Roderick had sat stock still, mouth pressed together in a line. I exchanged a glance with him. I wanted to warn him about the coming magic, but didn't know how without giving things away.

I didn't really like the other two men. Nevertheless, one was my father and the other Ynes', so I needed to do something that wouldn't hurt them, but would let me escape. I hoped Ynes understood my vague signal or I wasn't going to get far.

My eyes caught on the pillows. The shaft of a feather stuck partway out of one of them. Perfect. Feathers. They were soft and harmless.

I focused on feathers and pushed the magic out. I caught Kay's startled eyes as the magic forced him into fox form, and I stuck my tongue out at him as his now thumbless paw slipped from my arm.

Everything the magic touched turned into feathers. The couch that Roderick and Mr. Woolven sat on exploded into a pile of brown feathers, throwing the two of them backwards onto the floor. The magic kept going, hitting the window and turning it into a flurry of crystal clear feathers. The ceiling, even part of the floor exploded into poofy clouds of down.

By the time it was over, I had to brush feathers from my eyes to see. The entire front of the room was gone, and you could see out onto the front grass, the sidewalk... and Ynes, just pulling up in the red carriage, the unicorns prancing happily, tossing their horned heads.

Kay's gold fox head peered out at me from the feathers, blue eyes narrowed at me. Roderick was almost totally buried; all I could see of him was his hands flailing as he tried to get up from where he'd been dumped on the floor.

Mr. Woolven's eyes were wide as he clutched his drink that he'd kept from spilling. Several feathers floated in it. Mr. Price yelped, head swiveling around as he took in what was left of his front room. Thankfully, everyone was fully dressed. Maybe I was getting a tad more control.

"Pog, run!" I yelled. Pog's ears went back, but eiy darted out the hole and across the grass towards Ynes.

Meanwhile, I waded through the feathers and grabbed Roderick's hand, helping him stand. "Roderick, come with us. Please?" I clasped his hands. "I need you."

He looked around, clearly unsure, biting his lip as his eyes focused on Mr. Woolven. While I was distracted, Mr. Price lunged at me, trying to snap the bracelet on my wrist. Roderick shoved me bodily to the side, sending us both falling into a pile of soft feathers.

While we struggled to our feet, feathers tickled my nose, making me sneeze. Mr. Woolven had come to his senses, dropping his glass and lunging for me. I thought we were done for when a small bag flew in through the window and hit Mr. Woolven in the leg. It exploded, sending pink powder puffing up around him. Mr. Woolven stumbled, eyes sagging closed.

Another bag hit the wall near Mr. Price and I followed its trajectory back to see Ynes standing in the yard outside the hole. I crawled through the feathers and tumbled out, Roderick right on my heels. I guess he'd made his choice. Ynes helped steady me and then pushed me towards the carriage.

"Go!" she yelled, then turned to help Roderick.

Feathers trailed from me like confetti, and a bunch stuck to my clothes. I reached the carriage. Pog struggled to reach the step up, so I picked eim up and tossed them into the front seat, then got in and slid over to the driver's seat. Barnabas stood on the dash, waving at me.

"Sorry about your sitting room," I said to Ynes as she climbed into the front seat.

"Not my house," she said, plopping down.

As soon as Roderick was on the step, hand holding the door, the unicorns pranced away, responding even before I flicked the reins. Almost like they could read my mind. Maybe they could since I'd made them.

"I have a car, you know!" Roderick yelled at me as he clung to the back seat, struggling to get inside as the unicorns picked up speed. I ignored him. We didn't have time to change vehicles now.

We were only half a block away from the Victorian when two figures wearing familiar robes strolled out to stand in the middle of the street. One was massive, standing a head taller than the other, slighter figure.

"Oh, shit," Ynes whispered.

"Don't worry, they'll move," I said, urging the unicorns faster.

Ynes fell halfway into my lap and hauled back on the reins. The unicorns reared and snorted as they slowed.

"Why are you slowing us down?" I yelled. "They'll either get out of our way, or I'm going to run them over!"

"A bit bloodthirsty, Max," Roderick said, slamming the back door. Now that we'd stopped, he'd finally managed to climb all the way in.

"You know what a diplomatic mess it will be if you hit them?" Ynes said back with a scowl.

"They're trying to kill me!" I yelled back. "How's it not a diplomatic mess already? Besides," I said, pointing to the rearview mirror where I could see that the other two elves had blocked off the street behind us. "How else are we getting out of here? Even if I could turn around," which I doubted on this narrow street with cars parked on both sides, "we're surrounded."

The elf coming up behind the carriage lifted her arms. A blast of fire came tearing out, heading for the back of the carriage. The fire hit the back under the window, rattling the entire carriage. If that had hit where the back windshield had been broken out yesterday by the prince, Roderick would have been toast.

"I have another bag of sleeping powder," Ynes said, patting one handed at her skirt pocket. She pulled out a little brown pouch swinging by a leather cord. "But you have to get really close to use it."

"Shit. Father is already awake," Roderick said. He'd rolled down the window and had his head hanging out, looking back at the house.

I glanced up at the rearview mirror. Mr. Woolven and Mr. Price stumbled out into the street between us and the rear elves. Feathers stuck out all over them.

"It was hard to see with all the feathers," Ynes said with a scowl. "If I'd gotten them in the face, they would have been out at least a day."

"Rod, can you do anything?" I asked. I still wasn't sure what his magical powers were.

He grimaced and lifted his hands. "I'll try. Get the unicorns going faster. Head straight for the elves."

"Are you sure?" I asked, but flicked the reins. "I don't want to start a *diplomatic incident*."

The unicorns snorted but started off at a trot, hooves ringing on the asphalt.

Roderick didn't answer. He lifted his hands and started chanting.

My hands were shaking almost as much as the carriage. Behind us, Mr. Woolven knelt down, placing his hands on the ground as the two robed elves advanced on them. Fire burned in the hands of one elf, and a miniature whirlwind came tearing from the hands of the other.

The feathers around the mage and witch swirled away into the maelstrom as the magic tore towards them.

Mr. Woolven stood and raised his arms above his head. A wall of asphalt shot up from the street between them and the wind. Meanwhile, Mr. Price pulled jewelry from his pockets, putting on a necklace and rings with shaky hands.

There was a thud at the door on my side. I jumped and whirled back around. Pog climbed in my lap and stood on two legs to look out the window. It made it hard to steer with him standing between the reins like that.

"Hi Kay!" Pog waved at the window.

A massive two tailed white and blond fox the size of a horse ran alongside the carriage, snapping at the door. I hadn't realized he could grow to be a giant-sized fox. Kay rammed the side of the carriage again.

"Kay, stop! You're going to make us crash!" Pog yelled out the window at the massive fox.

"I think that's the point, Pog," I said, risking a glance down at the red panda.

"Well, that's just mean," Pog humphed, and finally sat down in my lap.

Kay threw himself at us again, smashing into the side of the carriage with a thud and sending us jerking to the side. The unicorns whinnied, but kept running.

Ynes crawled over into the back seat and rolled down the window. She lobbed the sleeping pouch at Kay. The bag hit the side of Kay's head and exploded, covering his golden fur in pink powder, and a pink mist formed around his face.

I snapped the reins over Pog's head. The unicorns picked up speed.

The fox snarled and threw himself at the carriage one last time before we left him behind. The back of the carriage rocked, but he only caught the bumper and the hit had little force behind it. In the rearview mirror, I saw him stagger and fall onto his side, taken in by Ynes' sleeping powder.

"I think he's pissed we ruined his payday," Ynes said.

"That, and technically we're stealing his car," I said, glancing at the leather seats of the Audi carriage. The dash still even had the Audi logo on it above the stereo.

"Bye Kay!" Pog said, climbing up my shoulder to wave at Kay out the rear window. Eir waving tail partially obscured my vision.

In front of us, the large robed figure threw back its hood, revealing blue skin that shimmered in the sunlight, large pointed ears, and two tusks thrusting up from their lower lip.

"Rod, that's a troll!" Ynes yelled as the troll drew a massive two-headed battle ax from her back.

Frost formed on the edges of the blade as she hefted it up and took a wide-legged stance. Next to her, the second figure threw back his hood. Prince Wynne grinned and moved out of the way, looking smug.

"Keep going!" Roderick yelled, interrupting his chanting. Then he pressed his hands together and resumed chanting. A shimmering field formed in front of the unicorns.

I threw a wide-eyed look at him over my shoulder, but flicked the reins again, trusting he knew what he was doing. The magical barrier looked pretty insubstantial compared to the very large battle axe and the massive troll that wielded it.

We were almost on top of the troll now. She hauled back her axe and swung at us. The axe hit Rod's shimmering barrier and bounced off it like it was made of solid steel. The troll spun back, and then the full barrier plowed into her just ahead of the charging unicorns, sending the already off-balance troll flying away into a neighbor's grass.

I caught the prince's open mouthed expression as we buzzed by him, then I hauled on the reins. The sharp turn sent the carriage up onto two wheels and threw Ynes sideways into Roderick. They slammed into the door in a tangled heap. Then the carriage rocked back onto all four wheels and they fell back into the seat, Roderick falling on top of a very unhappy looking Ynes.

XI

Unicorn Impound

"WE'RE SO CONSPICUOUS IN this thing," Ynes said as we made our way out of the Sellwood neighborhood.

"Hold on, I can take care of that." Roderick licked his lips and started chanting again. Another shimmering field enveloped the carriage, though this one felt different to me in a way I couldn't describe.

"How's that going to help?" I asked. I fumbled around for seatbelts and pulled mine on before making Pog sit down in the middle seat and having Ynes do up a seatbelt around eir lap.

"I can't see like this, Max." Pog crossed eir paws across eir chest and pouted.

"You need to be safe. After we stop at the PCA we'll get you a car seat so you can see out but still be safe." I glanced at Ynes. "Directions?"

"Turn north onto McLoughlin Boulevard," Ynes said.

I did as she directed, turning out of the neighborhood and onto the main road, then waited for the screams, honking, and smashing metal like yesterday, but nothing. I stopped at a light. A car pulled up behind us. I looked out the window at the car stopped next to us in the left lane. The driver, an older woman, was checking her makeup in the mirror. I waved at the teenager in the passenger seat. He rolled his eyes and flipped me off.

"Roderick's probably doing an illusion around us. They'll just see a car. Maybe longer and taller than normal, but just a car," Ynes said by way of explanation.

I wrinkled my nose. "Boring. Does that mean he's going to chant like this the entire time?"

"Probably. That's why I like witch magic better, personally," Ynes said. "I can do almost everything with potions and artifacts."

The light changed, and I flicked the unicorns forward. I really didn't know what I was doing, but they continued to read my mind.

"How come I don't have to chant like that?" I glanced back at Roderick. He had his eyes shut, a look of deep concentration on his face.

"I don't know," Ynes said. "Mages and witches tend to keep to themselves. I only know Mr. Woolven and Roderick from going to council meetings with my father."

"This is boring. I liked it better earlier when you were going fast," Pog cried as we slogged our way through downtown traffic. "Or yesterday when Kay drove."

I hated agreeing with him. I was driving a magical, unicorn-pulled carriage through the city, yet had to obey traffic laws. Boring.

"So you're going to help me rescue Brandon?" I asked.

"First, let's focus on rescuing you," Ynes said. "Turn here onto the highway."

I wondered if the unicorns could go fast enough to keep up with highway speed traffic, but, recalling Kay's driving yesterday, I was pretty sure they could. They had started life as the engine of a sports car. I wondered idly if they could break a hundred miles per hour. After all, it wasn't like I could get a speeding ticket in this, could I? It's not like we had a license plate... or maybe we did. I hadn't checked to see if it had survived the transformation or not.

I flicked the reins, and the unicorns sped up to a gallop. At least that calmed down Pog, who cheered and craned his neck to watch the tops of the buildings blurring past out the window.

Right before we got to the St. John's bridge, Ynes directed me to turn into the parking lot of the tow truck company that backed up to Forest Park.

"Tell Roderick he can stop the chant now," Ynes said as I pulled the unicorns to a stop behind a line of parked cars in the lot, concealing us from the road.

"You don't have to tell me anything. I'm not deaf," Roderick snapped. The moment he stopped chanting, the shimmer around the carriage vanished, taking the buzz of magic on my skin along with it. "All your chatter did was make it really difficult to concentrate on my spell."

It disappointed me I didn't get to see the illusion for myself.

"Why are we here?" Roderick growled, looking around at the used car lot.

"To see if they'll help us with our elf problem," Ynes said. "Why were our dads trying to buy your brother, anyway?"

"I'd like to know that too." I undid Pog's seatbelt and eiy scrambled out of the car.

Roderick slumped back in the seat and thumped his head against the side window. "The money was a finder's fee, not a purchase. Not that it really makes it any better..."

"A finder's fee?" I pursed my lips. "Why?"

"It's because of me." Roderick scowled.

"What?" Ynes turned and slung her arm over the seat.

"The Woolven family is one of the premier mage families on the east coast. I'm the only child, ergo the 'heir.'" He made air quotes with his hands.

"I can see why they're so revered. The way you deflected that giant elf—"

"Troll," Ynes corrected.

"Troll's axe, and the illusion that got us all the way here were pretty bad-ass."

"Illusion magic like mine is low-tier." Roderick let out a deep sigh. "Besides which, by any standard, I'm not that powerful. I can't even keep a spell going without chanting, as you so tactlessly pointed out on our way here."

"Okay..." I drew the word out and exchanged a look with Ynes, who shrugged and held up her hands.

"Father can do spells like you, with just a thought. Not a lot of mages can." He reached for the door, then paused. "That, and the family magic, is transformation magic, not illusions. I'm a throw-back. Some ancestor of ours was apparently not quite truthful about their Fae heritage."

"Wait, that explained nothing," I said.

"Yes, it did," Ynes said. "Mr. Woolven isn't happy having such a weak mage as his heir, but with only one child he doesn't have a choice."

"But Roderick isn't an only child," I said, looking back and forth between them.

Roderick made a finger gun and pointed it at me. "Exactly."

I made an oh of understanding. "That's why you didn't know his plans. But then, why were you with him today?"

"He knew I'd talked to the elf messenger and gone into your old room. Though he mixed up the order those things happened in, he knew I'd put two and two together. He thought to placate me by bringing me along."

"That's cold," Ynes said. I agreed. I liked Mr. Woolven less and less the more I found out about him.

"What was that bracelet Mr. Price tried to put on me?" I asked. "It had runes engraved on it."

"I'd have to see it to know. We use runes in lots of spells," Ynes said with an apologetic shrug.

"So how is Kay involved?" I asked. Other than sending Brandon in to break the seal. But I didn't understand the bigger picture.

"I can answer that one." Ynes sighed. "If the seal on magic did what I think it did, you would be invisible to magical tracking or locating spells. And Kay has a reputation in the magical community for being the man to see if you've lost something... or someone."

This was too much. I popped the door and got out. Pog and Barnabas were sniffing around the gravel lot.

After closing the door, I leaned against it with a groan. I needed something else to focus on. "I thought we were going to the PCA," I said to Ynes as she got out of the carriage. "This," I waved at the rows of parked cars, "is a tow lot."

A man walked across the gravel towards us from further in the lot, wiping off his greasy hands on a towel. His eyebrows raised as he looked over the unicorns and the carriage. "This is the PCA, but I don't have a place to keep unicorns," he said.

"This is just temporary," Ynes told him. I didn't know what she thought we were going to do with two unicorns, though.

"Better be." He frowned deeper when he spotted Pog at my feet.

"We're going up to the office. We'll take them when we leave, don't worry." Ynes picked up Barnabas and put him on her shoulder, then looped her arm through mine. "Roderick, you coming?" she called.

She towed me away, our feet kicking up dust as we walked through the gravel. Pog darted around my feet, nose to the ground, investigating the mysterious smells of the tow lot. Roderick trudged behind us. He didn't seem happy to be here.

Ynes and Roderick were seriously sweating by the time we hiked up the hill to the office. Even Pog tired of walking and demanded I carry eim about halfway there.

Then, when we got up there, I saw there was a road and a parking lot.

"What?" Roderick growled and pointed at the parked cars. Not that I cared, but he and Ynes were clearly exhausted. Interesting that he hadn't known about the parking lot either. Had he never been here?

"The road up here is pretty wind-y and narrow. The carriage and unicorns wouldn't have fit," Ynes said as we went up to the door and knocked.

A voice came out of a speaker on the wall. "How can I help you?"

"I'm Ynes Price, a witch." She pulled me closer. "This is Max Woolven—"

"Greenwood," I corrected her.

She frowned at me. "And Roderick Woolven, mages. We need some help."

The door buzzed and popped open.

I expected to be greeted with a wondrous sight, but the mundane slapped me in the face again. Inside, it looked like any generic non-profit office I'd ever been in. Peeling paint on the walls, a chipped Formica countertop, and a few plastic chairs that had seen better days lining the far wall of the waiting room.

A young black woman stood in front of the counter facing us, her arms crossed and foot tapping impatiently. Her heels clacked with each tap. Her already narrowed eyes narrowed further when she saw Pog.

"Hello, Ms. Williams," Ynes said to the woman, eyes downcast, clearly cowed by the thunderous expression on Ms. Williams' face.

"So you're the boy who summoned the red panda familiar that Ynes called me about yesterday," Ms. Williams said. "And since I just got informed about a red Audi carriage pulled by unicorns parked in our lot, I'm also guessing you three must also be the trio who took it on a joyride down Cesar Chavez yesterday."

Roderick held up his hands. "I just want to clear the record that I was not involved in that."

"That's good to hear, Mr. Woolven," Ms. Williams said, then turned her laser gaze on me. "I've been dying to know where you stole the red panda from."

"I... don't have an answer for that," I admitted, hugging Pog to me. "I think I made eim."

"Aside from the fact that it's impossible—" Ms. Williams said.

"It's not impossible," Pog said, flailing in my arms. "Max, put me down. I smell coffee. I want some."

Ms. Williams gasped and took a step back. "He talked."

"Eiy's name is Pog." I looked down at the panda. "And I don't want you wandering."

"Max, you're no fun," Pog said, but stopped struggling.

"The red panda isn't important right now," Ynes said. "The reason there has been so much chaos the last two days is because there are four Fae after Max. They attacked us in Rod's neighborhood yesterday, last night at the Barcade, and again this morning at my house."

"They burned down Pog's house, and took my friend hostage," I said. "But I thought you called that one a troll. Is that a Fae too?"

Ms. Williams turned gray, the color leaching out of her dark skin. "There's a troll in Portland?" she whispered.

"The troll is with Prince Wynne. It's not like it's running around wild," Roderick said, sounding nonchalant.

"Fine. Come with me. We need to talk about that and the Barcade." Ms. Williams stalked to a door at the far side of the lobby and gestured us through. We followed.

"Kay said not to trust these people," I whispered to Ynes as we walked.

"And I told you not to trust Kay," she hissed back. "Which one of us do you trust now?"

I chewed my lip.

Kay wanted money.

I trusted Rod to work in Rod's best interests. I was pretty sure he wanted to be the heir, which meant getting rid of me. But I also got the sense he felt guilty about his father dumping me as a baby.

But Ynes... I didn't know what she wanted. I'd been friends with her for almost four years now, yet we'd never hung out outside the Saturday Market. For a casual friend like me, she was really sticking her neck out.

Ms. Williams led us into a dingy office decorated with forest scenes. It smelled like wet dog. "Ignore the smell," she said, lighting a scented candle. "I share the office with a werewolf in the evenings. Take a seat."

There were only two chairs. Ynes sat in one and pulled me down with her. Roderick shut the door behind him and moved to stand behind me.

"So, Roderick Woolven," Ms. Williams said as she took a seat behind the desk. "Heir to the Woolven mage clan. I never thought I'd see someone so distinguished in this office."

Roderick just scowled at her.

Her gaze moved from him down to me and Pog in my lap. "Now, you. Ynes here introduced you as Max Woolven?"

"No," Roderick and I both said at the same time. Finally, something we agreed on.

"Jinx," I said with a laugh.

Roderick leaned over and punched me in the arm. Ms. Williams looked confused.

"I'm Max Greenwood," I told her. When I'd been left with the foster system, they said my last name was Greenwood, and I wanted to stick with that. I wasn't sure I wanted to be part of the Woolven family.

"Alright. Where did the unicorns come from?" Ms. Williams leaned back in her chair.

"That's not what's important," I said. "We need help rescuing my friend from the elves."

Ms. Williams sighed. "Fine, what's your friend's name?"

"Brandon Dempsey," I said, wishing I had my phone so I could show her his picture.

She spun and tapped at her keyboard for a moment and then frowned, shaking her head before turning back. "Sorry, nothing I can do there. The elves filed a formal arrest order for him yesterday."

"What!" I shot to my feet. Ynes grabbed my hand and pulled me back down, then kept it there when I sat back down.

"The claim is that he broke into Faerie and destroyed an important cultural artifact. If you want more information, you'll have to go talk to the Fae." She fixed me with a glare. "Now, about the unicorns?"

Cultural artifact? That could have only been whatever they were using to seal my magic. Ynes squeezed my hand, and I counted back from ten, trying to keep calm before I answered. "I magicked the unicorns from the engine of an Audi convertible sports car."

Ms. Williams wrinkled her nose like she'd just smelled something bad. I had a feeling she wasn't buying my story, true as it was. "You made living creatures? With magic? That's impossible," she said.

"That's probably why the elves are after him," Ynes said. "And us."

Ms. Williams shook her head and stood. "You kids are too old to be playing pranks like this."

"It's not a prank!" Ynes removed her hand from mine and pointed at me. "He has chaos magic!"

"Alright, show me," Ms. Williams said, drumming a hand on her desk.

Three pairs of eyes turned my way.

"I can't do it on command," I said. I could barely do it not on command.

"Yeah, that's what I thought." Ms. Williams pointed at the door. "Out."

"Don't you want to know what happened at the Barcade?" Ynes said.

"I know what happened. I've already talked to the bartender and the patrons. They told me about the elves. I know you two," she pointed to Ynes and me, "were there, along with Keiichi Miura. I just wanted to hear your take on things, but clearly, you can't be trusted to tell the truth, what with that wild yarn you're trying to sell me about the unicorns."

"So where *did* the unicorns come from then!" Ynes yelled, jumping to her feet and slamming her hands down on Ms. Williams' desk.

Ms. Williams gave Ynes a death glare until Ynes sat back down. "I'm guessing you stole them from the elves, which is why they are chasing you. Probably during the same incident that got your friend Brandon arrested. We're going to have to impound the unicorns. What was your name again? Max Greenwood?"

I nodded.

Ms. Williams bent over and tapped at her computer. The printer whirred to life and spit out two pages. Ms. Williams thrust one at me and one at Ynes. "These are the fines for your little stunts. When you see Keiichi again, tell him I've got one for him too."

I crumpled the paper up and stuck in my pocket without looking at it. I couldn't have paid a fine of even a dollar right now, so the actual figure on the paper mattered little.

"I appreciate you coming in and admitting your involvement, though it wasn't necessary as we had all three of you on video," Ms. Williams said, then stalked over and opened the door to her office. "Thank you all for coming. We'll make sure the unicorns get back to their rightful owners."

"That was kind of our ride..." Ynes half-heartedly protested. I don't know why she bothered. As far as I was concerned, this solved one problem.

"I'll need the red panda too," Ms. Williams said, stepping in front of me as I went to lead the group out of the office.

"No way." I hugged Pog to my chest.

"You can't carry a red panda around town," Ms. Williams put her hands on Pog and tried to take eim.

"No, I want to stay with Max!" Pog howled, digging eir claws into my hoodie.

"Especially a talking one." Ms. Williams tugged harder.

"Besides being Max's familiar, Pog is a sentient being," Roderick said. "You can't just decide for eim."

"And how are you going to explain him?" Ms. Williams said, but she let go. I think Roderick had known what magic words to say to her to get her to back off.

"I've been pretending!" Pog exclaimed proudly. "See? I'm just a plush toy." Eiy crawled up onto my shoulders and draped themselves around me like a scarf, then closed eir eyes and went limp, like eiy'd done when we were walking around Portland yesterday.

"And that works?" Ms. Williams asked. She sounded skeptical, and I didn't blame her, but I also didn't want to lose Pog. Eiy was growing on me. And they were my familiar.

"I mean... mostly. Besides, Rod... Roderick is right. It should be Pog's choice." I stroked eir head. Pog's eyes opened and eiy pushed eir head into my hand.

She scowled, but stepped back out of the way. "Is he really your familiar?"

"Yes, not that it's helped me much with control." I sighed.

"How old are you, Max?"

"Twenty-two, why?"

"You should have gotten lessons ever since you manifested your first magical ability."

"You mean since yesterday?" I snorted. "Roderick gave me some tips, but..."

"Yesterday?" She regarded the three of us again.

"Yeah."

"Must be a pretty weak power, then."

Ynes looked like she wanted to scream, even though she'd told me the very same thing yesterday morning. This clearly was not going the way she'd thought it would.

Ms. Williams held out a business card to me. "Here's my number if you need me. In the meantime, I'm going to be calling around to figure out where your red panda came from. It didn't just manifest out of nowhere, despite your claims. Is there a number I can reach you at?"

"Either of theirs for now. My phone was... destroyed." An understatement, but Ms. Williams didn't believe us already, so I felt no need to say anything more. I stuffed the card in my pocket with the ticket.

Back outside the PCA, Roderick smiled, too nice to say I told you so, though it was clear from his smug expression. Pog sat at my feet, happily lapping at a cup of coffee I stole from the break room on the way out.

"We don't even have a ride now," Ynes huffed.

"Probably better this way. I honestly had no idea what we were going to do with those things," I said. "Unless there's a unicorn rescue farm out in the country?" I joked.

Roderick shot me a baffled look. "No. I'd never even seen a unicorn until this morning. They're only found in Faerie."

"How did they get into public lexicon, then?" I asked. "All the myths about them?"

"Sometimes they slip in through spontaneous, temporary portals that open between the realms. Same as dragons and a lot of the other mythicals," Ynes said. "Normally they're only found in Faerie."

"Lame." I'd really wanted to see a dragon.

"What are we going to do now?" Roderick asked.

"I don't know," Ynes said, looking stricken. "I thought the PCA would just, I don't know, swoop in and fix everything. I don't even know what to do now..."

"Ms. Williams said we should contact the Fae. They can get us in touch with the elves, I should think," I said.

Ynes nodded, looking unsure.

"They have an office downtown," Roderick said. "But I'm not sure what you could say to them to get them to let your friend go."

I flexed my hands and looked down at the top of Pog's head. "I had the idea before to try to trade myself for Brandon. Of the two of us, I'd bet they want me more."

Ynes touched my arm. "I'm not sure that's a good idea, Max."

"I don't have any better ideas, do you?"

Roderick frowned and shook his head. Ynes stepped in front of me and held out her arms, glancing at me in a wordless question. I nodded, and she wrapped me in a hug. We were almost the same height, and her poofy hair tickled my nose. She felt nice, and I felt myself relaxing into her embrace.

"I don't like it, Max. I can't bear the thought of losing you," she mumbled into my hoodie.

"I just feel helpless knowing my best friend is in trouble and I'm out here doing nothing," I said, hesitantly putting my arms around her waist.

"Roderick, you were with Mr. Woolven. Did you hear anything?" Ynes asked, pulling away slightly to look over at Roderick.

Roderick's cheeks heated up, and he glanced away from us. "No more than you already know."

To my disappointment, Ynes dropped her arms and stepped away. "We can't stay here. If Ms. Williams really is going to contact the Fae Embassy, the prince will be on his way here. They know the unicorns were with us."

"How? They took our carriage and unicorns," Roderick said.

"I saw a bus stop right out front. We can catch that back to downtown," I said.

"I don't think you should go into the Fae office," Ynes said as I crouched down to pick up Pog's coffee. Pog could walk. Carrying eim was getting tiring.

"I wasn't planning on it. We can call and leave a message," I said, standing up.

"Then what's downtown?" Roderick asked as we began the long walk back down to the highway.

"A friendly red panda lover, who hopefully might let us crash there for tonight while we figure out a plan," I said. "Unless you'd all rather sleep under the overpass tonight, because it seems all three of us are now homeless."

"Wait, what? Oh my god." Roderick paled and abruptly stopped walking. He caught up with us a moment later. "What was I thinking?" he muttered.

"You were helping your brother," Ynes said cheerfully over her shoulder. "I think it's sweet."

Roderick turned bright red and ducked his head, mumbling something I couldn't hear.

XII

Like a Super Soaker

THE BUS RATTLED ITS way toward downtown. Pog sat in my lap, doing a bad job pretending to be a stuffed toy since eiy had eir muzzle pressed into a coffee cup and was lapping away. I let eim be, since the bus was nearly empty. The only other passenger, an old man with a walker, sat up front near the driver, and we were in the rearmost seats.

I was still thinking about that bracelet that Mr. Price had tried to put on me, and the elves sealing my magic.

Ynes and Roderick had also both been lost in their own thoughts. I don't think either of them had thought about the fact that they couldn't exactly go back home after what had happened with their parents this morning, and now that fact was hitting them hard.

"So, Mr. Woolven... my father..." I said to really no one in particular. "It looks like he paid the elves to seal my magic. Why not just use a bracelet to help control the magic like the one Mr. Price tried to put on me this morning?"

Ynes giggled and scooted closer to me on the bench seat to hug my arm. "You haven't been around little kids much, have you?"

"I have! The foster houses were always full of them, but I mean, faking my death and dealing with elves sounds like a lot more work than just making a magic-controlling bracelet a kid can't take off until he's old enough."

"Or killing you," Ynes added. Roderick turned around in the seat ahead of us to stare back at her.

"Or that," I conceded.

Roderick turned his gaze to me. "You both have really low opinions of my dad."

Ynes said with a shrug, "It's true."

"To change the subject," I said, trying to save Roderick, "I've been thinking. If the thing with contacting the Fae office doesn't work, maybe we can use Kay to find Brandon in Faerie."

"No. Bad idea," Ynes snapped. "He already betrayed you once, Max."

"It wasn't personal." I shrugged. I understood needing money.

"And he said 'no' to going to Faerie," Ynes added, poking my side.

"I'm sure he'd do it if we pay him, though I'm not sure where we'll get the money. I wasn't exactly rolling in cash even before all this. And I never even looked at how much I owe for this ticket."

I pulled the crumpled paper out and smoothed it out on my leg. "Let's see. It's a charge of magical joyriding... and as for the fine..." My eyes widened at all the zeros. "Holy shit." I was *really* glad that they didn't know I'd caused the shoestorm yesterday, too. Or the zombies.

"If you can't pay, they'll let you do community service," Ynes said, taking the paper from me. "How bad is it anyway—Holy shit!"

"What, was yours not that much?" Roderick asked, taking my ticket from Ynes and glancing at it. He shrugged and passed it back to me.

"I didn't look at mine either," Ynes admitted. She took out hers and groaned. "Are you kidding me? It's for even more! In the notes, she said I should have known better."

"Too bad I can't magic up a pile of cash," I said, taking my ticket back from Roderick. Actually, maybe I could... Hmmm... no. I shook my head. The PCA would probably charge me with money laundering or something. And if they didn't, the FBI definitely would.

"I can pay this off for you," Roderick said.

"Using Daddy's money," Ynes scoffed.

"You're one to talk," Roderick shot back. They glared across the aisle at each other.

Their partnership was as shaky as the one between their parents. Speaking of parents... "Why are your dads working together, anyway?"

"Father probably knew he'd need help with Max's magic," Roderick said.

"My dad makes the control collars for the mages in prison," Ynes said slowly, understanding blossoming on her face. Then she turned green. "He wouldn't have, would he?" she whispered.

"Wait, was that what he wanted to put on me in the living room?" I asked, eyes widening. I'd thought it would just suppress my magic or something.

"I didn't see it, but it's possible," Ynes admitted.

Roderick looked away, out the window at the passing traffic.

I shuddered. Tingles started in my palm. I closed my eyes and counted out under my breath, in and out, stroking Pog's back until the tingles faded.

"How are we going to get a hold of Kay?" Ynes asked. "I don't have his number. And how do you know he won't be with our dads? I bet they're using him to find you."

"I'm sure Sunny knows how to contact him." I watched the sunshine coming in through the bus window and realized we might get there too early for her to be awake. "When do you think vampires wake up?"

"You want to go see a vampire?" Roderick scoffed. "That's a good way to get dead or end up vampire food."

"We spent last night at her place. She was nice... ish. She knows Kay," I said. "And she's the red panda lover I mentioned."

Roderick looked stricken, but swallowed and stopped arguing.

We got off the last stop of the bus. To kill some time, we stopped to get a late lunch at one of the cart pods. Roderick paid with my father's credit card. Then we headed to the high rise where Sunny lived. Pog was doing a good job playing a plush on my shoulders. Or as good as a real red panda could. But even with my art doll story, I got more than one offer to buy him and lots of gasps and fingers pointed our way.

Roderick's eyebrows went up as we entered the lobby of Sunny's condo building. Even he looked impressed. Going through the parking garage, we hadn't seen the lobby before. Every surface was marble, with bronze accents that gleamed in the bright afternoon light. A security guard at the front desk frowned at the three of us as we ambled up.

"Hi, we're here to see Sunny," Ynes said.

Pog's tail wagged on my chest. I grabbed it and held it still.

The bored guard sniffed. "Don't know who that is."

"Ms. Love," I said impatiently. "Sunshine."

Roderick choked when I said her name. I don't think he'd put it together until then.

"And who shall I say is here?" the guard drawled.

"This is the red panda team," I told him, improvising since I didn't want to say our names out loud. Just in case.

"Wait a moment." The guard picked up his phone and dialed. "Yeah, I've got a, um, red panda team for you here." A pause while he listened. "Yeah, three of them. Two guys, a girl, and a fake red panda." Another pause. "Sure." He hung up and looked up at us. "First elevator. It'll take you straight there." He jerked his thumb at the elevator bank behind him.

Pog sat up on my shoulder after the elevator doors closed. "Yay, I'm so excited. Max, did you know that Sunny has a driving game? She let me play it this morning while you were sleeping." Eiy held up eir paws like eiy was holding a steering wheel and made vroom noises.

Roderick squinted his eyes at the panda then shook his head.

"Maybe this can be our new home," Pog continued.

Poor Pog. My heart broke; he wanted a new home so badly. I didn't know what to say to him.

The elevator dinged as we reached the penthouse, then opened to reveal Sunny. The vampire was scowling, hands on her hips. "Kay, you little..." She blinked at us as we got off the elevator. "Wait, where's Kay? And who is this?"

"Funny story..." I began.

Sunny's scowl deepened, so I pressed Pog into her arms. The red panda threw eir paws around her neck and rubbed eir muzzle against her chin. Her expression softened as she hugged the panda. "I don't like being woken up," she growled, but led us over to the couch and sat down.

We ran her through what had happened this morning.

"So can you get a hold of Kay for us?"

"No. You won't make it ten steps into Faerie." Sunny rubbed Pog's head. "I don't care what happens to you, but I won't let you drag this little guy to eir doom."

Guess it all rested on the elves being willing to bargain with me. "So we're back to me trading myself for Brandon's life."

Ynes frowned. "But we won't let you do that, right Roderick?"

Roderick was looking at me with a speculative expression. Ynes smacked his arm with the back of her hand and repeated herself, "We won't let him do that, right?"

"Right, sure," Roderick said, but didn't sound like he meant it. "Besides, maybe we can convince them to just reseal his magic instead of killing him."

"Would that mean the bad luck will come back?" A shiver ran down my back at the thought.

"Bad luck?" Roderick repeated, face blank.

Sunny also looked curious, but stayed silent as she cuddled Pog.

"Are you sure it's gone for good?" Ynes asked.

I chewed my lip. "No, but I've also never gone this long without a single incident. It's been almost two days!"

"It has been very quiet," Ynes said. "The unicorns, shoe rain, and licorice grass, while weird, are pretty benign."

"Benign? You poofed the entire front of a house into feathers!" Roderick scrunched up his face and threw up his hands. "What could be worse than that?"

"Let's see," I held my fist and began ticking my fingers off as I went, "the kitchen counter cracking in half and almost smashing me under a sink, all my electronics exploding within a day or two, breaking more bones than I can count in freak accidents—" I could have gone on for a while but Ynes cut me off.

"We get the idea, Max. Trust me, Roderick, it was bad, and it seems I didn't even know the half of it." Ynes folded her arms and glared at Roderick.

"It was bad enough she thought it was a curse," I said, pointing at Ynes.

"It's true," Ynes said. She'd pulled something from her little bag of tricks and was twisting it around in her hands. "I gave him a charm to help last year. Didn't make a difference."

"Are you sure the bad luck will come back?" Roderick asked, hunching his shoulders.

"No..." I hedged. Roderick had a point.

I don't think Ynes had realized what I had known; about why Roderick was helping me. He'd tipped his hand when he'd said he'd be happy with my magic only resealed.

He felt guilty, but also selfishly didn't want me to usurp his place as heir. That was fine by me. I wanted nothing to do with my so-called father. Though I was excited at the thought of being in line to inherit as much money as it looked like the

Woolven family had, the idea of having to work with him was more than enough to overcome that excitement.

The thought of things going back to the way they had been terrified me. Even with the outbursts of magic, these last thirty hours had been amazing. Is this how things were for normal people? Buses that don't break down. No constant splinters. No sinkholes opening under my feet. Heck, I might even be able to hold down a job now, like an actual adult. No more squatting. No more relying on handouts from Brandon and others.

Still, I'd give all that up to have Brandon back unharmed. And he was right. I wasn't a hundred percent that it had been the seal breaking that fixed my bad luck.

"I guess I can risk it for Brandon," I conceded.

Roderick was looking at me now with pity, which was even worse than the dislike.

"What if..." Ynes said, sitting back up slightly. "What if that isn't necessary?"

"What do you mean?" I asked.

"You," Ynes pointed at Roderick, "are going to teach him," she pointed at me, "how to use his magic. If you can learn to use it, I have an idea."

"Ynes..." Roderick stood and paced away over to the windows. He reached for the curtains.

"Don't touch those," Sunny snapped at him and Roderick froze.

Roderick dropped his hand and turned, crossing his arms to stare down at me. "I don't think I can. I don't have the family magic. Father would be a much better teacher for him."

"Not going to happen. I want nothing to do with that loser. No offense, Rod," I said when he scowled.

"It's Roderick," he growled, clenching his fists until his knuckles went white. "And would it really be the worst thing in the world to be part of my family? Father just wanted you to come home. Yes, he went about it abominably, but still... he came to his senses. Why won't you just give him a chance?"

I stared at Roderick, totally at a loss for words. Maybe I'd misjudged that he'd wanted me gone. He must have taken my silence as encouragement, because he continued talking.

"We'll go to him, explain the misunderstanding... He's got a lot of sway. He could negotiate with the elves to get your friend back, I'm sure of it."

I couldn't stop tears from springing to my eyes. "Being part of the family wouldn't be the worst thing *if* he hadn't thrown me away like trash when I was a helpless baby!" I sprung to my feet. "And I don't trust why he suddenly wants me back." I stormed away down the hall to Sunny's bathroom to hide my tears.

I sat in the bathtub and hugged my knees to my chest, feeling very alone. I was the only one that cared about Brandon; like me, he'd grown up in the foster system and didn't have anyone. It was becoming clear to me I was going to have to rescue him on my own.

But Sunny was right about one thing: as things stood now, I would be easy pickings. I knew nothing about this new Portland that I'd discovered, let alone Faerie, which would be totally alien to me. I'd have more of a chance if I had a teacher, but I didn't want Roderick's help now.

There was a soft knock at the door. "Max, are you okay?" Ynes asked.

"I'm fine," I said, wiping tears away with the back of my hand.

"Can I come in?"

I sighed and scrubbed at my face, then climbed out of the tub to unlock the door. Ynes came in and closed it behind her. "I'm sorry about Roderick."

"It's fine." I lied. "I'm just suspicious about why my dad suddenly now wants me back after twenty years."

"I have to say I am, too." Ynes adjusted her glasses. "But don't you want to ask him yourself before rendering judgment?"

"Are you kidding me? You weren't there." I mimicked, slapping handcuffs on my wrist. "They tried to put a magic-canceling bracelet thing on me. Or I mean, they would have if they'd thought I was who they were looking for."

Ynes made a face. "It's not a bad idea, Max. You've left a trail of destruction."

"It's getting better. I felt it coming on the bus, but Rod's exercises worked."

Her eyes widened. "You didn't say anything."

"I took care of it." I crossed my arms and gave her side-eye.

She sighed. "Next time, at least let me know. I won't panic, but we need to plan just in case."

"Alright."

"That also sounds to me like Roderick's exercises worked. So why not give him another chance and come back to the living room?" Ynes left the bathroom, leaving the door open behind her.

I took a few more minutes to compose myself before rejoining the others. Sunny sat in the recliner, Pog on her lap. The wall behind the couches and chairs in the living room that I'd thought was just wood paneling had opened up to reveal a gigantic flat screen television. Some kind of realistic driving game played on the screen.

Sunny held a steering wheel shaped controller in front of Pog, helping eim drive. Apparently Pog's paws weren't dexterous enough to use it eimself.

Ynes had moved to the chair, leaving Roderick by himself on the couch.

"I'd like to apologize," Roderick said as I sat back down on the other end of the couch from him. "I didn't think through what I said. You're upset about being abandoned. It was thoughtless of me to say what I did."

He looked pretty contrite. I didn't trust myself to speak without crying again, so I nodded and rubbed my palms on my jeans.

"I can run you through more exercises," Roderick offered.

I took a few moments to breathe. My palms were getting itchy. "Ynes... my magic..." I choked out.

Sunny called without looking up from the game with Pog, "Go up to the pool if you're gonna mess around with magic. I showed you the stairs yesterday."

"This morning," I muttered as I got up. I guess she considered it yesterday since her schedule was flip-flopped, but it was still confusing.

"Pog, put down the game," I said.

"No, stay where you are," Roderick countered as he stood. "He needs to learn how to do this without your help."

Pog never even glanced up. I rolled my eyes.

Roderick and I went up to the roof and out to Sunny's pool. Clouds had moved in since we'd gotten here. The pool was a lot larger than I'd expected, almost as large as the living room below.

"Get in," Rod growled. "I don't want a repeat of this morning."

"I'm not exactly dressed for swimming," I said. I wrinkled my nose and looked down at my outfit.

"So strip." He put his hands on his hips and gave me a deadpan look.

"I'm not... can't I just sit on the deck with you?" I pleaded.

"I'm your brother. And it's not like you have anything I haven't seen before."

"My brother I only met yesterday."

"Get in or I'm going to push you in, fully clothed or not." Roderick took a menacing step towards me, eyes flashing.

"Fine, fine." I undressed, but left Ynes' charm necklace and my boxers on. After setting my clothes on a deck chair, I waded out as close to center as I could get and still keep my head above water. Then I turned to face Roderick, crossing my arms over my chest to hide my scars. My embarrassment was making my magic flare up; I could feel it pulsing inside me.

"I can still feel the magic from here," Roderick said with awe in his voice. He stood as far from the pool as he could get, standing with his back to the railing. "You're really building this much without training?"

"You can feel it even with Ynes's charm?" I asked, touching the copper amulet. That was not good news for us hiding from the elves for long.

"Yes, but I'm close. It should mask you from further away. Now, let's get started." Roderick began leading me in more of the same variations on the meditation exercises we'd done the day before.

"I don't feel like I'm going to explode, but it's not getting any better either," I said after almost an hour.

I felt wrinkly from being in the water for so long, and the temperature had dropped enough as the overhead clouds darkened that I was getting chilled.

"You won't until you release the magic you're holding," Roderick said. As we'd worked, he'd eventually tired of shouting and had moved over to sit in one of the deck chairs close to the pool.

"How do I do that?" I asked, flexing my fingers.

"Either you let it trickle back out to join the free magic around us, or you do a spell." He frowned. "I'd rather the first, if you don't mind. I don't think you're controlled enough for a spell yet."

"I've been doing spells for two days." I splashed some water in his direction. The droplets didn't even come close to hitting him, but he shot to his feet and scooted back to the fence. Guess he didn't want chlorinated water on his fancy leather shoes, since he crouched down and inspected his feet.

"No, you've been releasing uncontrolled bursts of magic for two days," Roderick corrected me after standing back up.

"What's the difference? You just said one thing I could do was release it."

"The difference is, a spell is controlled and directed. Your blasts were wild and unplanned. Ergo, not a spell." Rod smirked at me. "Releasing a big burst of magic is like..." he trailed off, his eyes going unfocused for a moment. "The difference between you drizzling water and tossing it in the air. In one of those scenarios, water goes everywhere. In the other, maybe a few drops splash up, but no one around you gets wet. Whereas a spell is like a super soaker. You direct the water to hit exactly what you're aiming at."

"You make it sound so easy." I swirled my fingers in the water and then splashed it. The analogy made sense, but I didn't have the faintest idea how to even start.

"I've been learning this since I was five. But believe it or not, it was difficult for me at first too. I almost failed my first semester because I couldn't even draw enough magic to do a single spell."

Semester? "Did you go to magic school?"

"Yeah, there are private schools for mages, and others for witches." Roderick started talking about the classes he'd taken there.

I stared down at the ripples in the water, tuning him out. I couldn't even imagine what my life would have been like if I'd grown up in that mansion. The stab of jealousy caught me off guard, and the burning in my hands suddenly increased. I hardly heard Roderick anymore; the growing pain distracted me too much to listen.

Abruptly he stopped talking, and I heard him say, "oh, shit," right before the magic tore free of me.

Water swirled up from me in a funnel until the pool was completely empty. It even pulled every drop from me, leaving me completely dry. The water swirled, forming the shape of a water gun that pointed down at Roderick. He ducked, but the water spray from the gun caught him in the chest, sending him tumbling. He landed on his stomach and the spray pinned him to the deck.

Water streamed from the deck back into the pool, but some lapped at the door that led back down to Sunny's condo, and more poured off the edges of the deck. Any pedestrians below were about to get a surprise.

By the time the water gun sprayed itself out, the pool was only half full. My clothing lay in a sodden heap on the deck and all the chairs were half-submerged where they'd been swept into the pool.

Roderick sat up, looking like he wanted to hit something. His shirt was mostly gone, blasted away by the water, and an angry red welt was already raising on his back.

I winced. "I'm sorry."

The door to the penthouse opened, and Ynes poked her head out. "Sunny wants to know why there's water trickling down the steps... oh my god. What happened?" She covered her mouth, staring around at the soaking deck with wide eyes.

"Max is what happened," Roderick snarled, stomping towards the door. His shoes squelched with each step. "God damn, you ruined my Italian leather loafers."

"You better not come in here like that. Sunny's already pissed about the water on the carpet," Ynes said, holding up a hand. "I'll go get some towels."

While we waited, I wadded around the pool and pulled out all the deck chairs. Roderick unbuttoned his ruined shirt and tossed it down on the deck. He was good looking. I tried not to stare, since he was my brother. He kicked off his shoes, then took a chair I'd tossed on the deck, righted it, and sat down.

I climbed out and then wrung out my hoodie. "I don't know what happened. Nothing. Then, boom!" I imitated an explosion with my hands.

"Powerful emotions can do that," Roderick said, running a hand through his wet hair and making it stick up all over. He sounded resigned. "I shouldn't have talked about school."

I wrung out my jeans. My shoes were another matter. I wondered if there were still any pairs left in Ladd's Addition that I could snag. The ones I'd stashed in Kay's car were gone with the carriage.

I set all the furniture back up, then took a seat near Roderick. We sat in silence until Ynes came back with towels.

"You need father's help," Roderick said as he dried himself off. "This is way beyond my abilities."

"I know you're angry at him, but I think Roderick is right." Ynes sat down next to me and put a towel in my lap.

I made a frustrated growl and threw up my hands. "Fine! I'll talk to him."

XIII

Saturn Devouring His Son

"THIS IS A BAD idea," I muttered, watching the lights of the buildings pass by out the windows.

My clothes were still a little damp from the pool incident earlier today, so I rode in the back of Sunny's hearse with Ynes and Barnabas. Roderick rode up front in the passenger seat, wearing one of Sunny's t-shirts. It was far too tight on him, accenting his chest and arms. He would have looked *less* sexy without it. I had to stop having the hots for my brother.

"You agreed to this," Ynes said, rolling on her side to face me.

"Yeah, but that doesn't mean I'm not regretting it now." It had sounded so reasonable at the time; go meet with my father and listen to what he had to say.

Roderick was sure it was nothing nefarious. I didn't have as much faith as he did, but I also needed a teacher if I was going to rescue Brandon. Roderick even thought his dad, our dad, could negotiate with the elves on my behalf.

"Roderick and I will be there with you." Ynes put her hand on my arm. "We'll leave if you feel uncomfortable. Just say the word."

Rain started falling, giving the nighttime world outside a soft, unreal feeling.

Sunny drove and Pog sat on her lap, paws on the steering wheel, pretending eiy were driving. Sunny was explaining how the controls worked.

"You push this stick up to turn on the windshield wipers once, and down to keep them on," Sunny said to Pog as the wipers started up. "Now the stick on the other side is for the turn signal. That lets other drivers know where you're going. Now, can you push that down for me? We need to turn left."

Pog reached eir paw around the wheel and hit it. "Now that light is blinking!" Pog pointed at the dash with a paw.

"Yep!" Sunny patted eir head. "That shows you what's happening on the outside."

"Why do you keep moving your feet?" Pog asked.

"To work the gas and brakes."

"Like on the controller!" The end of Pog's tail flicked happily. "Let's go really fast and jump off a ramp next."

"Sadly, you can't do that in real life." Sunny actually sounded upset about it, which concerned me. But a speed demon vampire and red panda were the least of my problems at the moment.

"Roderick, what did you tell him about me?" I asked.

"Nothing. I tried, but father didn't want to hear it. He thinks you tricked them at the house. He's still expecting to meet a girl."

Great. That was going to make this even more fun. Not.

I just nodded and turned my attention back to the road. Roderick had set up the meeting at a neutral location, the Clackamas Town Center Mall. I'd insisted on having it in the food court so that we could get dinner. Sunny hadn't expected us to come back, so she'd sent all the food home with Amelie after we'd left. Turns out vampires don't keep a lot of human food on hand when they aren't expecting guests.

"Everyone needs to shop," Sunny said when I questioned why a mall would be neutral territory. "The PCA had to break up one too many fights between supernaturals in the 80's. Hard to stay secret when shifters and vampires are brawling in the department store. So all malls are neutral, and the fighting ban is pretty strictly enforced."

"Are you sure it's a good idea to take a red panda into the mall?" Sunny asked as we all got out of the car when we arrived. I half suspected she would run off with Pog if given a chance.

"No, but I need eim with me." Pog scrambled up on my shoulder, but rather than lying around my neck, eiy sat behind my head hugging it and rested eir head on mine, with eir tail wrapped around my neck.

"Good call," Roderick said. "The familiar will help regulate your magic for you. Still, if you feel yourself losing control, run for the parking lot."

Comforting that he had so little faith in me. Worse, I agreed with him. It surprised me when Sunny joined us as we walked away from the hearse. I thought she was going to wait in the car.

"I'm coming along as a bodyguard. Can't have my favorite red panda getting hurt," she said in response to my raised eyebrow's unspoken question.

Barnabas skittered around Ynes's feet as the four of us made our way to the door, then scampered up one of the decorative trees and chittered at us from the branches.

"He's going to keep a watch out here," Pog told me.

"You can understand him?" Ynes said, surprise coloring her voice.

"Mostly. Kinda not. More like I can feel what he means?" Pog tugged on my hair and kicked eir back paws into my shoulders. "Now, yah, giddyup."

"I'm not a horse," I grumbled. Where did eiy pick these things up?

Suddenly, Sunny was no longer next to me. She was ten feet away, opening the door for us. Damn, she could move fast. I noticed she was chewing something. Gum?

"Why gum?" I asked.

"Hides the smell of blood." She popped it at me and winked as I went by.

How silly of me.

We probably looked like quite the group. Pale Sunny in her all black goth wear, Ynes in her colorful flowing fabrics, Roderick in his mismatched khaki pants and too-tight black women's babydoll t-shirt, and me in my damp art school hoodie and jeans.

Mr. Woolven and Mr. Price were already in the food court waiting for us. I'd expected Kay to be with them, but no dice. Well, if this worked out, I wouldn't need him anyway.

They'd taken one of the larger round tables in the center. In his bespoke wool suit, Mr. Woolven stuck out like a sore thumb against the backdrop of typical mall patrons. He wore a different suit than he had this morning. I snickered as I pictured him trying to pick feathers off the expensive wool. He must have given up and changed.

Mr. Price, seated next to him at the table, was dressed more casually in slacks and a polo.

Roderick and Ynes made a beeline for the table, but I wandered over towards the Popeye's with Sunny on my heels. The scent of fried chicken was irresistible. My stomach growled, and I wished I had money. Something wet dripped on my head.

"Pog, you better not be drooling on me."

"Max, I'm hungry," Pog whispered back.

"Sorry buddy, I'm broke. Maybe Mr. Moneybags over there will feed us." Maybe the food court had been a bad idea.

"Mommy, mommy, look at the red panda! Like at the zoo!" A little boy pointed up at Pog and tugged at his mother's arm. "And it talks!"

"Hehe, yeah. Technology, huh?" I petted Pog's tail and turned back to my waiting meeting.

Stomach still growling, I joined the others at the table to hear out my dad.

Ynes and Roderick had taken the seats on either side of their respective parents, and I heard the tail-end of what sounded like an epic dressing down when I wandered back.

"—you look like a homeless bum! No son of mine—" Mr. Woolven broke off as I walked up. I took a seat next to Ynes, and Sunny sat down on my other side.

I didn't agree. To me, Roderick looked more like he'd borrowed clothes from his girlfriend's closet.

"Father, I'd like you to meet Sunshine Love and Max Greenwood," Roderick said, his voice tight. "Max, this is my father, Charles Woolven, and that's Rafael Price."

Mr. Woolven wrinkled his nose as he looked Sunny over, ignoring me entirely. I wasn't sure if this was better or worse than the scorn from this morning.

Mr. Price ignored me too, but for different reasons. He was fretting over Ynes like she was a much younger child. I understood why both of them still lived at home. The apron strings in this case were more like a chain.

"Sunshine?" he finally said. "That's not the name we gave you."

Sunny responded before I could say the retort that sprang to my lips.

"Yeah, well that name was terrible," she said.

I snorted and covered my mouth. She didn't even know what it was, but she was right.

Mr. Woolven looked like he'd bitten into something sour, but he forged on. "Fine. I supposed I can overlook that, though the red hair and the attire are another matter." Mr. Woolven clasped his hands on the table. "If you're going to be part of this family again, I'll expect you to dress appropriately for your station."

Sunny arched an eyebrow and leaned back in her seat, throwing an arm around my back like we were a couple. Even through my hoodie, I could feel the coolness of her skin. She glanced up at me with an unspoken question if she should confess the mix up. We hadn't planned this, but I gave a subtle shake of my head. I wanted her to keep up the charade for a bit. However, that movement made Mr. Woolven take notice of me.

"I see. So you sent your boyfriend in with Keiichi while you stayed outside. Clever."

Sunny shrugged.

"But then, you must be brilliant indeed to trick a kitsune like that, tricksters that they are." Mr. Woolven gave a satisfied smile.

"Half-kitsune, technically," Sunny said.

"True, true." Mr. Woolven gestured to his partner. "Though still impressive."

Mr. Price pulled out a bracelet from his pocket and set it on the table. The same one they'd tried to put on me this morning.

"With all the chaos you've caused around the city, I'll need you to wear this until we can get you proper training." Mr. Woolven pushed the bracelet across the table towards Sunny with one finger, like he didn't want to touch it any more than he had to.

"What is it?" I asked.

"It will suppress her magic while she wears it, similar to the seal she was under before, but not as... restrictive," Mr. Price said to me, waving his arms in the air a lot as he spoke. It reminded me of Ynes.

"What do you think, honey?" Sunny leaned her head against my arm and reached across my chest to stroke Pog's tail.

"Dad, Max is Mr. Woolven's child, not Sunny," Ynes said.

"Ynes, dearest, Charles' oldest was a girl, not a boy." Mr. Price patted her hand.

Sunny batted her eyes at Mr. Price and blew him a kiss. He turned bright red. She was enjoying this far too much. "What do you think?" she repeated, elbowing me.

I cleared my throat. "Maybe we could get some dinner first?" I did not want to decide anything on an empty stomach.

Mr. Woolven looked horrified. "Eat here?"

"I mean, about the offer." Sunny pinched my back.

Roderick abruptly stood, sending his chair clattering backwards. "I'll get you something." He stomped off before Mr. Woolven could stop him.

"Why, after all this time? What changed?" I asked the question that had been bouncing around in my brain since yesterday. Pog's paws tightened in my hair.

"I suppose that is a fair question." Mr. Woolven sighed, looking at Sunny as he talked. "I didn't know you were alive until a few months ago. I suppose Roderick told you the story, that you'd 'died' as a young babe."

"Yeah," I said, and Mr. Woolven shot me an irritated glare.

"That's what I thought, too," he said.

Liar. I'd heard the messenger. Mr. Woolven clearly had known about the seal and that I was alive. I suspected that he just hadn't known how to find me or break the seal. Maybe both.

"But, the elf said—" I began, wanting to call him out.

Mr. Woolven slapped his hands palm down on the table. The big ring on his finger cracked loudly against the Formica, making me jump and cutting me off. Then he half stood and leaned towards me. "I'm here for her, not you. Understood?"

I widened my eyes and leaned back. He was seriously scary. Sunny's hand on my back kept me seated. "Fine, whatever." I caught Pog's long tail and crossed my arms.

"Not that I'll allow you to date my daughter after she comes home. But I admit you take after the family looks. At least she has good taste in that department." He sat back down and straightened his tie. "Now, where was I?"

"You thought the baby was dead too," Sunny prompted. Ynes tried to say something again, and again her father shushed her.

"Right. At six months, you got your magic. Total chaos. Not sure how we managed for a year, but we did. Still, I guess we weren't as discrete as we'd thought. You disappeared from the nursery. We assumed the worst."

"Still doesn't explain what changed," Sunny said, knowing exactly what I would have asked next.

"About six months ago, Kay came to me and told me he could solve my problem. You've seen Roderick's magic. I couldn't refuse. I need a competent heir." Mr. Woolven scowled. "It was expensive. Very expensive, but he had me over a barrel. I suppose I should thank you there. Only cost me the down payment after your little stunt with the feathers. Didn't have to give him the artifact."

"Thank them?" Mr. Price looked up, indignant. "There is a giant hole in the front of my house!"

"What kind of problem?" I asked, ignoring Ynes' father. Sunny kicked me under the table.

Mr. Woolven's scowl deepened, but he answered the question. "The family business... to put it frankly, it's dead soon without someone to take over."

I didn't think that was all. You didn't pay buckets of money for something like that.

"What, is Roderick a lollygagger?" Sunny laughed.

What the heck did that mean? I gave Sunny a baffled glance.

"A lolly what...?" Mr. Woolven shook his head. "No, no, he's very committed, eager to help. But he doesn't have the right magic. Totally useless."

Roderick had just returned with a tray of food and was close enough to hear. His expression twisted up. I waited for him to say something, but he stayed silent, walking around the table towards me.

I bristled. "How can you talk about your own kid like that?" I snapped at Mr. Woolven.

"It's nothing but a broad, factual statement," Mr. Woolven said, eyes boring into me.

I let it drop, though I disagreed with Mr. Woolven's assessment. Roderick's magic had proved very useful. Not flashy like mine, but it was better even, since he wasn't creating zombies and turning clouds into shoes.

By the time Roderick walked around to set the tray down in front of me, he'd smoothed his expression back out to the bland, neutral one he'd worn when we got here.

"Thanks, Rod. Roderick," I corrected, flashing him a smile. He didn't deserve the insults his father was dishing out. But by Roderick's placid non-reaction, it seemed to be commonplace.

I dug in to the fried chicken, sharing some fries with Pog.

Roderick rubbed Pog's head, then sat down next to Sunny, leaving a gap between him and his father. It said a lot to me about how much his father scared him that he'd rather sit leg-to-leg with a vampire.

"What's your power?" I asked Mr. Woolven.

Mr. Woolven was getting very irritated with me. His face turned red, and he sputtered. "I cannot believe you'd bring a mundane to this conversation. Power indeed."

I rolled my eyes and took a bite of chicken. Of course I didn't know the insider vocabulary.

"Same question, though," Sunny said. "I grew up with the mundanes, remember?" I really appreciated her doing this, though didn't know why she was helping us. Maybe she just wanted a laugh. Living for a long time had to get boring.

"The same as you." His brows knit. "Though far less powerful. Like that... thing..." he was too polite to point, but gestured at Pog on my head. "I can't create living things. And it even holds conversations. Remarkable. Though why you made it a red panda..."

"Because red pandas are the berries. I can't believe you don't like them. What are you, a wet blanket?" Sunny reached up and Pog happily climbed down into her arms.

I held back a snicker. When had Sunny become a vampire? Her slang was dated, but Mr. Woolven didn't seem to notice.

Probably he didn't know the slang of the day, and hers was old enough that he didn't know it.

Mr. Woolven attempted a smile. Badly. "I suppose they are, um, Sunshine."

"Sunny." Her tone was dead flat. I almost laughed at the juxtaposition between tone and name.

"You're supposed to be a toy, remember?" I whispered to eim.

I think eiy tried to give me the middle finger, the way eiy threw eir paw up at me, but eiy lacked fingers.

"It's a bit... conspicuous. Supernaturals try to keep a low profile," Mr. Woolven said.

"Really, Charles, she should put on the band before something else happens," Mr. Price said, pointing to the bracelet still sitting in the middle of the table.

"It's nothing to worry about. It's like that familiar you have there." Mr. Woolven used a finger to push it further across the table towards Sunny and me while leaning back away from it. He looked like he was handling a bomb. "It's just to help you contain the magic until you've learned to control it."

Sunny looked at me, her jaw working as if she wanted to ask me something. But she shook her head, picked up the bracelet, and snapped it on. Then she doubled over, gasping.

"Sunny?" I put a hand on her back and leaned over her. She'd clenched her eyes shut and her fangs had come down. I put an arm on the table, trying to block the men's view, hoping they hadn't seen. Pog wiggled out of her lap and back into mine, eir eyes wide and ears flat back.

"Max, do something," Pog whispered.

"Oh, did I forget to mention the little insurance policy we added to it?" Mr. Woolven said. "Rafa, care to explain?"

Mr. Price lifted his arm and slid back his sleeve to reveal a matching bracelet there. "This lets whoever is wearing it send you little shocks if you misbehave. Like the one you're getting right now."

"Daddy, that's forbidden magic!" Ynes went pale.

Even Roderick's demeanor cracked, his mouth dropping open.

Sunny was still face down on the table writhing, her jaw clenched like she was holding back a scream.

Fuck. They'd wanted to put that thing on me! My heart started pounding and my palms began itching.

"I suppose I should stop it now," Mr. Price said.

Sunny stopped shaking and took a few deep breaths. Her eyes, when they opened, were blood red, and her fangs were still down. After a few more measured breaths—I recognized it as a calming exercise Roderick had taught me—her eyes returned to their usual green and her fangs pulled back up. I pretended to help her sit up, and then Pog flung eimselves into her lap and hugged her chest. She clutched eim to her and looked up, her eyes flashing.

"That was a *little* shock?" she hissed through clenched teeth.

"We need to go," I said and stood, giving a wistful look at the chicken and fries that I'd only eaten a couple of bites of.

"Oh, I'm afraid not. The bracelet will also shock you if you get too far away from the holder of the control." Mr. Price smiled. "And not a little one, like that last one."

Oh, my god. Ynes' father was evil. The itching turned to burning and was shooting down my fingers as I hyperventilated.

"Ynes, Max is—" Pog flailed in Sunny's embrace.

"I know." Ynes stood. "Max, you go, now. We'll catch up."

"But Sunny..."

She'd gone stock still. Not even a flicker of life. Like a doll. It was eerie. Then she was moving again, pulling her car keys from her pocket and passing them to me in a short underhand toss. "I'll meet you at home, alright honey?" She winked at me and handed over the red panda. "And take care of Pog for me."

I nodded and ran, juggling Pog and the keys.

"No, Sunny!" Pog called, reaching back over my shoulder as I took the escalator down two steps at a time, pushing past startled shoppers.

Behind me, someone screamed, a woman, followed by a man's bellow. I kept running. I didn't even glance behind to see if Ynes and Roderick were following or if they'd stayed with their fathers.

Either they came or not. It wasn't my decision to make. If they stayed, they knew where Sunny's condo was, but I'd burn that bridge if it came to it. Hopefully, they'd both follow.

I stumbled out the doors, free of the mall. To the side, there was a little seating area with tables and chairs for the restaurants. With the rain, it was empty. Perfect. I dropped to my knees in roughly the center, put Pog down, then held the keys out to eim.

"Get these away..." gasp "so I don't accidentally change them."

Pog nodded, grabbed the keyring with eir mouth and darted off with Barnabas. I hadn't even noticed the little squirrel join us.

I hoped eiy were far enough away because I couldn't hold it in anymore. The magic tore free. Out of the corner of my eyes, I saw Roderick and Ynes flail to a stop just outside the mall doors as the magic transformed all the tables and chairs around me. The metal twisted together as the magic swept over it, leaving behind writhing chaos as the table and chair legs morphed into gray snakes of all shapes and sizes. The stone decorations crumbled and shifted into statues of demons torturing humans in various ways.

I hadn't thought to direct the magic, so the results were as much a surprise to me as to them.

"Is that... *Saturn Devouring His Son?*" I heard Ynes call as I staggered to my feet. The snakes ignored me, though they hissed and fought with each other as they moved about.

My head pounded and I could barely stand upright. I made it a few feet before I had to catch myself on one of the demon statues. It looked familiar... like a painting I'd seen once. I'd liked to go to the Portland Art Museum on their free days when I was younger, at least until I was banned—long story, not my fault—maybe I'd seen it there? Anyway, it was pretty hideous.

I waded through the snakes to where Roderick, Ynes, Pog, and Barnabas waited for me. Roderick helped me to the car, and we all piled in. I kind of liked the hearse now, because I got to ride laying down. Roderick climbed in the back with me, and Ynes got in the driver's seat.

"We need to wait for Sunny," I said, though all I wanted to do was lay down and close my eyes.

"She can take care of herself, trust me," Ynes said, cranking the key in the ignition. The hearse roared to life. "I'm more worried about my dad, but honestly, it's karma for the forbidden magic."

Roderick nodded. I reached over and squeezed his hand. Satisfied, I closed my eyes and let the roar of the road lull me to sleep.

XIV

Cue Training Montage

I BARELY REMEMBERED THE ride back or going up the elevator. I woke up briefly laying on the couch to Sunny pulling a blanket over me. Her pale skin practically glowed red and her hands were warm on my cheek.

"Is that from—"

"No, no. I just scared them into taking off the bracelet." She showed me her bare arm. "Picked up a meal on the way home."

"Thanks," I mumbled and hugged a sleeping Pog to my chest. "But I don't understand why..."

"Why I'm helping you?" Her mouth twisted up in a smirk. "Let's just say I don't like bullies. Also, the red panda definitely helps. Now go back to sleep."

I woke up to a slice of sunlight coming in through the drapes, falling across my face. I squinted at the glare and sat up. Pog was gone. No, wait, eiy sat in Sunny's gaming chair struggling with the steering wheel controller that was too large for eim. On the screen, a car silently careened back and forth before crashing into a guardrail and bursting into flames. Pog cursed quietly and restarted the level.

"Did Sunny say you could play that without her?" I said with a yawn.

"Yeah, she even made me an account, see?" It took Pog a few tries to press the button to go back to the menu. "That's me." Pog pointed a paw at the screen. The account had an icon of a red panda from Aggretsuko and was labeled 'Pog' underneath.

"Can you even read?" I asked.

"I know some letters. That spells P. O. G. Pog." Pog humphed and went back to the game. I guess it made sense that a spirit that lived with witches would pick up how to read. It just hadn't occurred to me that eiy could until now.

"Sure." I shook my head and went to the kitchen.

No sign of Ynes or Roderick. I popped open the fridge in the vague hope that food had materialized overnight. No such luck. I shut it and jumped when Sunny was suddenly there on the other side.

"I've sent for a grocery delivery," she said.

"I really appreciate everything you're doing for us."

"This has been the most fun I've had in decades." Sunny smirked. "That said, don't plan on making yourselves comfortable. I'll let you stay a few days, that's all."

I nodded. I understood.

Roderick came out of the back bedroom, yawning. "I heard voices."

"Sunny was just telling me we shouldn't make long-term plans to stay," I said.

Sunny stifled her own yawn behind one hand. "When the groceries get here, the lobby will buzz them up. Also, I've let them know you'll be staying with me for a few days, so they'll let you back in if you need to go anywhere. Now, I'm going to bed. Please try not to destroy anything while I sleep, huh?"

With that, Sunny shuffled off. The door to her bedroom shut firmly, and the lock clicked.

"Still nice of her to let us stay, even a few days," I said.

Roderick took a seat at the bar without saying anything. He had large black circles under his eyes like he hadn't slept. He was shirtless, wearing only khakis that were much worse for wear.

I rifled through the cupboards, found a bag of coffee, and prepared a pot. I might not drink the stuff, but I'd worked at a coffee shop for a few weeks before being fired, so I knew how to make it.

Once it was ready I poured a mug and placed it front of Roderick along with a few sugar packets I'd found near the ground beans. "I don't know if you like it with cream, but there isn't any."

"Black's fine," he mumbled, and pulled the mug closer.

"Are..." I licked my lips and tried to figure out what to say. "Are you alright?" I asked. If I'd felt betrayed by my father's actions, Roderick, who he'd raised, had to be feeling about a hundred times worse than me.

"No, not really." Roderick picked up the mug with both hands and sipped it. "But I'll survive. We've got a busy day."

"We do?"

"You—" Roderick poked a finger at me, "have to learn how to use your magic so we don't have another repeat of whatever the hell that was yesterday."

"And so I can rescue Brandon."

Roderick massaged the bridge of his nose. "Let's focus on not exploding first, huh?"

"That's not a bad idea," Ynes said, coming out of the hallway from the spare bedroom. "We need to come up with a plan for if—"

I glared and crossed my arms, saying, "When."

"When," Ynes amended, "the elves contact us. We need to think of a way to save both Max and Brandon. Because I'm not willing to sacrifice you, Max." Ynes embraced me, and I hugged her back.

"Thanks," I said, withdrawing after a moment. Ynes looked disappointed. "I'm not sure how we can do that, though. We don't exactly have a lot of assets." One vampire, a snarky panda, an illusion mage, a witch, and an out-of-control chaos mage versus four trained, powerful Fae?

"Well, I was thinking about how to solve that," Ynes said slowly, turning to Roderick. "We need to hit the stores and ATMs before your dad turns off your credit cards,"

"What?" Roderick said.

"Unless you have another form of income or your own accounts without your dad's name on them." She poured herself a cup of coffee and dumped in every single sugar packet I'd scrounged up, then leaned back against the counter. "You live with your dad and, you know, after yesterday... do you have any source of income independent of him?"

"Oh my god," Roderick groaned and clutched his head. "I didn't even think of that. But what about you? Aren't you in the family business, too?"

Ynes said, "I have my jewelry stand and separate bank accounts for that money. I've saved up a lot since my dad doesn't charge me rent. I'm more concerned about where we're going to live after Sunny tires of us. The jewelry stand doesn't make enough for me to afford a place in Portland, which is why I was still living at home."

"I can help you there. I've been homeless. I know all the tricks," I said and sat down next to Roderick.

"Stop saying that." Roderick put his face in his hands. "What have I done?"

"You did the right thing," Ynes said, smiling at him and giving him a speculative look that I hadn't seen her give to him before. "That's what."

The intercom buzzed. "Oh, that's probably the groceries Sunny ordered," I said and got up to pick up the delivery.

"There's stuff here for breakfast, if one of you wants to cook," I said as I put everything away. Sunny had ordered a pretty eclectic mix of food. I wondered how long it had been since she'd been human. Not that I was much better. With my former condition, cooking was about the most hazardous thing I could do. As I result I lived on sandwiches and take out.

"No, I was serious. Let's go out. We all need clothes and toiletries, at the very least. And we can plan at a cafe as well as we could here." Ynes set aside her empty coffee mug. "And I want to milk your dad for all we can before he cuts you off. Don't you?" She leaned across the counter and put her head in her hands to regard Roderick. "I'm thinking breakfast at Portland City Grill, then shopping at Macy's..."

"Does the Grill even serve breakfast?" Roderick finally looked up, his mouth quirking up on one side and eyes sparkling. "And Macy's? You aren't thinking high end enough."

"Slow down there, cowboy," Ynes said. "Let's see if your cards are even still working first."

It turned out they did. Roderick withdrew the ATM limit of cash on all of them, and then we went on a buying spree with the credit card. I was a bit worried about the elves finding us, but Ynes was sure her amulet would do its job.

We'd slept in too late for breakfast, but got lunch at an expensive little cafe with prices that made my eyes water. Ynes and Roderick didn't seem bothered, so I tried to ignore the numbers as I scanned the menu.

Between shopping, we threw around ideas on how we could work things with the elves if they ever agreed to talk to us.

I felt bad that we left Pog behind. But eiy had been happy enough to stay at the condo and play Sunny's driving game. I was worried about what would happen if I had another episode but Roderick and Ynes weren't.

"You've already caused a ton of chaos. What's one more episode?" Ynes had said and rolled her eyes.

"You'll be fine as long as you stay calm," Roderick had said with a shrug and a bland expression, as if it were that easy. Maybe it was for him.

As it was, I only had one episode during the trip. I hid out in the men's bathroom in a department store and kept the changes contained to that room. We put an out-of-order sign on the door before leaving, but the janitorial staff were going to be very confused by the fragrant clematis flowering vines now growing on every surface. I couldn't think of anything else but how bad it smelled in there, and that was what my subconscious came up with.

We only stopped when Rod's card finally got declined that evening. We dragged all our purchases back to the condo, weighed down like Santa with his giant bag of toys. Besides clothing to replace what I'd lost in the fire, I also got clothes for Brandon for when we rescued him.

Sunny was up already. She and Pog were racing each other in Mario Kart. Neither even looked up at our arrival.

"Now," Roderick said after we'd dumped the rest of the bags in the spare bedroom, "you need to train."

While we'd been gone, Sunny had set up a cot in the spare room. I think she was not-so-subtly telling us we should all sleep here from now on and not on the couch. I guess it would be annoying to have a stranger sleeping in your living room at night when you're awake.

I groaned. "Now?"

"You want to rescue your friend, right?" He scowled and crossed his arms when I nodded. "Ergo, you need to train."

"I don't even know where he is," I said when we got to the roof. Sunny had cleaned up all the furniture, but the pool was still only half full of water.

"So focus on what you can control right now." Roderick took a seat at the far end of the deck. "Learning your magic. Because if you did suddenly find out where he is?"

Or if the Fae office or the elves ever got back to us. We'd left a message asking them to call Ynes' phone, but so far silence.

"I get it." I'd been really excited for the first lesson, but so far it had been less like a cool magical school and more like a wellness retreat with breathing and meditation sessions. Still, Roderick had a point.

"No need for the pool today. You just stay over there," he said, leaning against the table.

"Okay." I settled on a deck chair away from him. "Am I finally going to learn a spell today?"

"No. I was trying to teach you exercises to keep you from gathering the magic, but that doesn't seem to be working. So instead, today we're going to work on you safely letting go of your gathered magic."

"So, a spell." I rubbed my hands together in excitement.

"No. Remember yesterday, I mentioned letting water out of your hand a drop at a time. Today we're going to work on that. Pushing it back out without fanfare."

Sounded boring to me, but I nodded.

"Now, focus on the feel of what I'm doing." Roderick held up his hands as if he were holding an invisible ball. Light flickered in the space between them for a moment. After it went out, he asked, "Did you feel what I did there?"

"No."

"You must be too far away." He rubbed his pant legs, obviously nervous. "I guess you can come sit over here for this."

I moved over next to him and he repeated the exercise. I focused, but there was only the faintest hint of a prickle on my skin.

"I maybe felt like, a flutter of something coming from your hands."

"Are you kidding me? Probably like trying to feel a drop of water when you're used to a deluge," he muttered, mostly to himself. "How about this? You try. Close your eyes, put your hands like I did, and imagine a light growing there. Then picture it dimming until it goes out."

"We have different magic, so will I even be able to do this?"

"Every mage—" Roderick cut off and shook his head. "Almost every mage," he amended, "can do little things like this. And with as much power as I've seen you channel, you should have no problem with this."

I lifted my hands, but he snapped, "No, let me go over there first."

I waited until he'd walked around the deck to where I'd been before, then tried to call light. A small star flashed to life in my hands, blinding me until I squeezed my eyes shut.

Roderick cursed, then yelled, "Now imagine it dimming! DIMMING!"

I didn't dare open my eyes. I couldn't picture what he'd said, so instead I imagined a sunset, with the sun going gradually down behind the horizon. By the time I opened my eyes the light was gone, though I was blinking artifacts from my eyes for the next few minutes.

"That was easy. What next?" I asked.

Roderick still had his hands pressed to his eyes and was cursing. "Half the city probably saw that. I told you to picture a little light, not the sun."

"Sorry." I really hadn't been picturing much of anything beyond light. I guess I should have been more specific.

"Easy," Roderick muttered, half blind and wiping tears from his eyes. "Took me nine months of practice the first time, and I can still only barely make a wisp. And Max here makes the freakin' sun on his first try."

I fidgeted with the ties of my hoodie, not sure what to say. I was pretty sure he hadn't been talking to me, anyway.

"We're done for today. Try what you did to get rid of the magic next time you feel like exploding, okay?" Roderick stood and stormed off.

I stayed up on the patio, practicing for a while before going inside. By the end, I made it half as bright, which was still blinding, though I counted that as an improvement.

What I could do to improve my relationship with Roderick, that was going to take longer. It had to be hard knowing you were always the poor second choice to a dead person, especially when that dead person showed back up.

Despite all of us sleeping in the same room, Roderick and I each did our best to pretend the other wasn't there. When I came to bed eventually, Roderick was already asleep on the cot, so I took the bed with Ynes.

The next morning, Ynes sat us all down at the bar. Sunny didn't own a kitchen table, not too surprising when I thought about it.

"Yesterday was fun and all, but we need to come up with a long-term plan, since none of us have anywhere to go home to."

"What, none of you?" We all jumped. Sunny stood at the end of the bar, leaning on it like she'd been there the whole time. She smirked. "You expect me to be asleep just because the sun's up?"

I should have expected it because she'd been up yesterday, but my mind kept thinking vampire, seeing the sunlight, and doing $1+1=2$, even though my math was wrong.

"I just graduated from high school. Father wanted me to stay at home until I could move into the dorms this fall. Guess that's not happening anymore." Roderick's shoulders slumped.

Ynes huffed. "Portland's expensive. I would have had to have roommates, and they'd have to be supernaturals because of the magic side business... and I'd need extra space for a workshop... It was just easier to stay at home."

"And you?" Sunny turned to me with raised eyebrows.

"Oh, I've been homeless for years," I said with a shrug.

Sunny, Ynes, and Roderick all stared at me.

"I thought you and your... friend, Brandon, had a house," Ynes blurted. "You said it burned down."

"We were squatting there. Ask Pog." I looked around. "Where are eiy? I got eim some presents yesterday that I didn't get a chance to give eim."

"Sleeping in my room." There was a blur and Sunny was gone. She was back a moment later with a sleepy Pog in her arms. She ruffled his head. "Pog's been telling me eiy used to be the spirit of the house you lived in, and that eiy have been feeling pretty lost without a permanent place to stay."

"Yeah, I know," I said, taking eim from Sunny's arms. "Not much I can do to help eim with that right now."

Pog threw eir paws around my neck and snuggled up to me. I carried Pog over to the couch and laid the panda down on the cushions. Eiy curled up in a ball and fell back asleep. I suspected eiy'd stayed up all night gaming with Sunny.

Sunny scowled and crossed her arms, clearly wrestling with something. "You aren't..." She stomped a foot. "Damn it. I can't let an adorable, innocent thing like Pog be homeless, and eiy's very attached to you..."

"So, I guess you and eim can stay." Sunny pointed at me.

I shook my head. "I'm not abandoning Ynes and Roderick. Thanks, but we'll figure something out." We still owed the fines to the PCA for the unicorn ride, but I was prepared to just ignore that and hope it went away. "With what Ynes, Brandon, and I have saved, I bet we'd have enough, at least for a deposit and first month's rent."

"You said you were homeless. How do you have money saved?" Roderick frowned at me.

"Money wasn't the reason Brandon and I couldn't get a place. Brandon has a good job as a welder. But, bad luck, remember?"

Roderick and Sunny looked confused, but Ynes nodded, understanding blossoming.

"Oh, yeah," Ynes said, putting a hand over mine and giving me a sympathetic smile and a squeeze. "I bet. Even if you didn't get kicked out after the curse destroyed something, no one would renew a lease with you."

Sunny's eyes darted between me and Ynes, her confused look turning thoughtful. "Max—"

I was saved from whatever she was about to say by the ringing of Ynes' phone. Ynes glanced down and her eyes widened.

"Hold that thought. It's the PCA. I need to take this." She answered, holding the phone to her ear. "Hello? Yes, this is Ynes." She glanced at me. "Yeah, he's here with me too." She frowned. "What? Wait, here, let me put it on speakerphone." Ynes set her cell on the counter. "This is Sara Williams," Ynes said. "You remember her from the PCA the other day."

Yeah, from that ticket burning a hole in my pocket. "Yes, I remember," I said instead.

Sara's voice came out through the cell's speaker. "So I've got an elf here right now. She came to collect the unicorns, but she says they're fake."

"They looked pretty real to me," I said. Just like a real-life version of the ones I'd seen in paintings and movies. White coats, cloven hooves, a white tail that ended in a puff of hair. It wasn't a horse with a horn prop.

"Not only do these look nothing like real unicorns," a musical voice snarled in the background, "they're pooping jellybeans! How is that even possible?"

I burst out laughing. Ynes, Sunny, and Roderick lifted their heads to stare at me. Sunny shook her head and wandered away.

"That doesn't make any sense!" Ynes said.

"Yes it does," I said. "Like the candy, you know? They sell it at that chichi candy shop downtown in the tourist center. It's called unicorn poop, and it comes with a dispenser shaped like a unicorn, and the candy comes out its... you know. What do they eat, anyway?" I wondered what the jelly beans tasted like too. I had to know. The licorice I'd made from the grass had been the best I'd ever tasted. I was willing to bet these jellybeans were the same.

"Unicorn... poop... candy..." the musical voice on the phone repeated in disbelief.

"You all need to get out more," I said, throwing up my hands.

"That's a toy, Max," Roderick said, looking at me with concern.

"Yeah, but those unicorns came from—" I tapped my head "—so they're not going to make sense."

"I'm sorry, I didn't catch that," Sara said over the phone. "Where did you say you got these unicorns from?"

Ynes and I exchanged a glance. "I'd... rather not say," I said. "So, what now?"

"You need to come get your... whatever these are," Sara said, her voice like ice. She was not happy with us.

Great. Where the hell were we going to put two unicorns? Sunny'd been pretty tolerant until now, but I don't think even she would let us keep two faux-unicorns here, if we could even get them in the elevator.

There was a muffled conversation coming from the phone, like Sara put her hand over the receiver, between her and the owner of that musical voice. A moment later, she came back on the line. "The elves would also like to arrange a meeting with you."

"We'll have to put a pin in that," Ynes said.

"Put a pin in which, the meeting or picking up your unicorn things?" Sara asked.

"Picking up the unicorns. We'd like to talk with the elves," Ynes said.

"Soon," I added. I hated how long Brandon had been their captive already and I couldn't stand him being there any longer.

More muffled conversation, and then Sara came back on the line. "She says the prince will call you soon to arrange a meeting. Can I give them this number?"

"Sure, yeah," Ynes said, glancing at me. I nodded.

Ynes was reaching for the phone when Sara said, "You need to come get these things today. We don't have the space to care for large animals like this. And I'm going to have to charge you—"

Ynes made a staticky noise. "I think I'm losing you," she yelled, and hung up the phone. Then she grinned up at me. "This is perfect, Max."

"We never were able to come up with a definitive plan, Ynes." I flexed my hands, hating to admit it, but, "I also don't really have control of my magic yet."

"Between the three of us—" Ynes began.

"Five!" Sunny yelled from her bedroom. "And try to keep it down would you, some of us are trying to sleep!"

"Five?" Roderick asked.

"You, me, Max, Ynes, Sunny," Pog mumbled from the couch. "Six with Barnabas."

"Six of us," Ynes amended, "I'm sure we can come up with something."

"Actually," Roderick said, toying with his coffee cup. "I might have come up with an idea. But we'll need some supplies."

XV

Even You Won't Date Me

Two years earlier

With my electronics constantly breaking, online dating had proved to be a challenge. Yet I'd eventually set up a date with a persistent woman who put up with my frequent long breaks in communication.

I arrived early to the coffee shop where we were going to meet in person for the first time. Every other date I'd gone on had ended in disaster, but this time was going to be different. I knew it.

A surge of excitement bubbled up in me as I waited in line to get a tea.

Things were not up to an auspicious start when I took a seat at one of the outdoor tables to wait for her, and the chair snapped in half, dumping me backwards onto the sidewalk. My hot tea sprayed all over my shirt, burning me, and I cracked the back of my head when I landed, making me see stars. A couple of nice people helped me to my feet.

"Should we call an ambulance?" one of them asked me as I slumped into a new chair.

"No, I'm fine," I said, taking a few napkins and holding them to the back of my head. Not only could I not afford it, if I left now I'd miss my date. I wasn't sure if she'd give me another chance.

"How many fingers am I holding up?" the man asked me. He held up his hand. My vision swum, and I squinted, trying to count.

"Um, four?" I said.

"Two," he said, lowering his hand. "You might have a concussion. If you're not going to go to the hospital, do you need help getting home?"

"It's fine, really." I waved him off with the napkins. Which were bloody, figured.

My date chose that moment to walk up. Even through the double vision, I recognized her from her picture.

"Haylay," I said, waving with my other hand, pressing the napkins back to my head again. "You look good." She did, too. She'd done up her makeup, wore a tight green dress, and she'd gathered her curly black hair up at the back of her head in an afro-type ponytail. I felt underdressed in my jeans and shirt, even if it hadn't been covered in tea.

"Geez, Max, you weren't kidding about being accident prone," she said, propping a hip on the table next to me.

"You should take her home," the guy said to Haylay.

"Him," I mumbled. Top surgery couldn't come soon enough. I'd finally gotten the paperwork done, with Brandon's help, to get Oregon Health Insurance Plan to cover it, and it was scheduled for a few months from now. Hopefully, after I might not get misgendered as much. And, much as I hated to agree with him, my head pounded and I was in no shape for a date. "And sorry to cut this so short."

"Want a ride home?" she asked.

I winced, picturing what might happen to her poor car if I took her up on it. "No, thanks. No use risking your car, too."

Her eyebrows went up at that. "If you're sure? Nothing I can do for you?"

"If you could text my roommate for me..." I said, giving her Brandon's number.

"Do I want to ask what happened to your phone?" she asked, but took out her cell and asked Brandon to come for me. Now I was extra glad I'd picked a coffee shop just a few blocks from our apartment. Next time, I should just have Brandon on standby to rescue me.

It took me a moment to focus enough to remember what had destroyed it this time. "Yesterday. Sinkhole that opened under my feet. Didn't fall in, but dropped my phone."

Everyone circled around me stared, open-mouthed.

"I'd hope you were joking," Haylay said with a shake of her head. "But..." She pushed off and turned to leave, then her phone buzzed. She stopped, glanced at it, and threw back, "Your roommate is on his way here."

I groaned and slumped back as she walked away. God, she was gorgeous, and kind, too. I wished I'd had even half a chance with her. Why couldn't things ever go right?

The Good Samaritan who'd helped me up stayed with me until Brandon sauntered up.

"I take it the date went badly. She not like your outfit?" Brandon joked as I stood.

"Psh, I wish it had lasted long enough to actually have a conversation with her." I leaned on the table and waved goodbye to the guy who'd been helping me. It would have been nice if Brandon had let me hold onto him, but as usual, he shied away from touching me.

"So what happened?" Brandon asked.

I shrugged, trying to keep how upset I was from my voice. "The usual. Happened right before she arrived. At this rate,

I'm going to be single forever!" I threw up my hand, the other still keeping the napkins pressed to my head wound.

"Too bad," Brandon said, though he sounded upbeat and not upset about that at all. I glared at him.

"You'd think being bisexual would at least double my chances," I grumbled, "but I guess double of nothing is still nothing."

Brandon merely shook his head. "Max, don't talk like that."

"You're the only person who has ever put up with my terrible luck for any significant length of time. But even you don't want to date me." I kicked a rock, missed, and stumbled, falling and catching myself on a brick wall.

"Max..." Brandon scowled. "That's not true."

"Well, after our first kiss burned down the school stadium, you hardly talked to me for a year." A few people had been hurt, and we'd only been lucky no one had been killed. I still felt guilty about it. That had been one of the worst accidents my bad luck had caused.

"I told you, that's not why..." Brandon sighed and his expression softened. "That fire wasn't your fault."

I shook my head, and we spent the rest of the walk back in awkward silence.

Roderick's plan was a good one, I had to admit. He had a tactical mind. It was better than anything else we'd come up with yesterday.

Roderick and Ynes left to go shopping. All of Ynes' potion and jewelry making supplies were back at her dad's house, and it wasn't worth the risk of going back there. Roderick's plan didn't require the assistance of Ynes' magic, but it was always worth having a fallback, just in case things went sideways.

They had left me behind, judging it safer to stay here rather than risking walking around downtown.

Ynes admitted that since the amulet I wore wasn't attuned to me, it would be possible that the elves might have been able to track me to the general area. No reason to risk them stumbling across me on accident by having me wander around the streets again.

She'd judged it safe enough yesterday, but since I'd now been in one place for over twenty-four hours, there was more of a chance that they'd have at least a general idea of where I was at.

Pog was in the living room playing Sunny's driving game, having quickly grown bored with the planning once eiy'd woken up.

"You hungry?" I asked eim.

"Max, stop distracting me!" eiy yelled back. I glanced in to see that the panda had come in last in the race. I rolled my eyes, and wandered into the kitchen.

Pog seemed to suffer no ill effects from eating human food, thankfully, since I still did not know where to get bamboo. I cut Pog's sandwich up into smaller pieces that eiy could handle, then carried the plates over to the coffee table. "Pog, take a break and come eat your dinner."

Pog climbed over and sat on the table to eat. When we were done, I went and grabbed eir present from yesterday.

"I know this isn't a house, but I hope this begins to make up for it," I said as I pulled out the game system racing bundle that my father had indirectly paid for.

"My own car game!" Pog tried to lift the box, but since it was almost as big as eim they struggled with it for a minute without success. Eir tail stuck straight up in the air, twitching happily.

Sunny spun her gaming chair around, her eyebrows raising. She wore the set of cartoon red panda pajamas I'd seen her in yesterday. I still found it odd that vampires wore pajamas.

I jumped. I thought she'd gone to bed, and she was short enough I hadn't seen her over the back of the massive swiveling gaming chair. I guess our planning session had woken her, but I was more than a little perturbed that I hadn't heard or seen her move between her bedroom and living room.

"Yeah, this way you can play after we've moved out," I said to both of them.

"What? Moved out?" Pog plopped down, eir tail drooping. "I want to stay here with Sunny."

"I know," I said, picking eim up, "but Sunny doesn't have enough room for all of us. Also, I'm sure she wants her own space back."

"That's true," Sunny agreed. "But you're welcome to visit anytime." She picked up the game system and showed it to the sniffling Pog. "Plus, now that you have this, once you have your own place, we can play together online."

"Really?" Pog perked up.

"Really." Sunny offered the red panda her hand. They did some complicated handshake thing—I wasn't even sure how Pog had done it with paws.

"Max, I need to talk to you for a second," Sunny said when they were done. Without waiting for an answer, she snagged my arm and dragged me away.

"Help!" I screamed, struggling against her grip. "I don't consent to being bitten," I hollered. Pog's face appeared over the top of the couch. Eiy waved and then eir head popped back down out of sight. Some help my familiar was.

"Settle down. I don't want to bite you. I just want to talk," Sunny said, taking me into her bedroom and shutting the door. "Okay, I lied. I want to bite you, but I won't," she said, blocking the door with her body.

Great, that didn't make me feel better. I tried to swallow down my nerves and crossed my arms to disguise my shaking hands. I did not like being locked in a room with a vampire who just admitted that she wanted to bite me.

Her bedroom looked nothing like what I'd expected, given her goth clothing aesthetic and the cozy, wood-centric decor of the rest of the condo.

No wonder Pog liked her room. The bedroom furniture matched the couch, dark-stained natural wood, but the walls were plastered with posters of cars, some so old they were yellowed with age, and every available surface was covered with painted and assembled scale model car kits. I'd bet money that a lot of them were older than me.

She saw me looking and met my gaze, challenging me to say anything about the cars.

"No one else is here. No reason for secrecy," I said instead.

Sunny raised an eyebrow. "I think you're forgetting about Pog. I like the red panda, but I doubt eiy could keep a secret to save eir life."

I gave a shaky laugh. Secrets? She wanted to tell me a secret? "True. What do you want to talk about?" I said.

"Look, I wasn't going to say anything, but your cluelessness has gone from charming to exasperating. No one likes a flat tire." She leaned towards me, getting into my personal space.

I backed up, knocking over a 50's model car that's edge stuck off the end table near the door. Sunny darted forward with lightning speed, put it back into place, and then zipped back to the door.

"Thanks, but I don't like you that way, Sunny."

"Oh, you're balled up!" She smacked her forehead. "I'm a lesbian, you ninny. Ynes! You know she carries a torch for you."

It took me a moment to parse Sunny's weird slang, and then I blinked in shock. "Wait, you're saying Ynes has a crush on me?" Now that Sunny had pointed it out, I felt like an idiot for not seeing it myself.

"Yes. Finally. I'm not saying you need to let her put you in handcuffs, but you either need to let the girl down gently or take her out on a date." Sunny opened her door and pointed. "Now out. I'm going back to bed."

Still a bit in shock from Sunny's terse truth-bomb, I stumbled back out into the kitchen and slumped onto a barstool.

Now I saw Ynes in a whole new light. The cute way her hair curled around the temple of her glasses or her face lit up when she was explaining one of her gadgets to me, or her kindness in going so far out of her way to help me over the last few days. I realized now that her crush on me had been why she'd been so willing to help me when Kay brought me by.

I did like Ynes. I'd given up the idea of dating, after every single one of my dates had ended up in disaster, beginning with my very first kiss with Brandon when my bad luck had burned down the entire high school stadium.

My lack of experience was probably why I missed the blatant signs of Ynes' attraction to me. I resolved to ask her out when she and Roderick returned.

XVI

Levitation Sounds Fun

THE ELEVATOR DINGED WITH the return of Ynes and Rod. Both of them carried large cardboard boxes.

I sprang to my feet. "Did the prince call you back yet?"

"Not yet." Ynes put the box she was carrying on the counter.

"What's taking them so long?" I grumbled, slumping down next to Pog.

"I bet they're making one last attempt to find you," Ynes said with a smirk. "But these big skyscrapers mess with magic as much as they mess with cell phone signals. I actually have a theory that cell phone technology works the same way, so they're never going to be able to pinpoint—"

"Ynes..." I gave her a significant look. "While that is super interesting, we're short on time."

"Right." She giggled and started unpacking packets of herbs and bottles of multi-colored liquids, lining them up on the counter.

"I'll write out the recipe. Roderick, you and Max will need to make as many bottles as you can," Ynes said, yanking down the notepad from the fridge and scribbling down ingredients and measurements.

"Us?" Roderick asked. "What will you be doing?"

"I'm going to be enchanting some things to help us."

"I'm impressed you remember this whole thing without your spellbook," I said, joining them at the bar as Ynes ripped off a third page and slapped it on the counter.

Ynes winked at me. "I digitized the family spellbook years ago. It's all right here." She pointed to her phone that I hadn't noticed sitting on the counter next to the pad. She finished up a fourth page and put it next to the others.

"Which recipe should we make the most of?" Roderick asked as we looked over all the pages.

"Oh, no. This is all one recipe. I just couldn't fit it on one page." She stuck the magnet pad back to the fridge and carted the second cardboard box over to the coffee table.

"This is so complicated," I said in horror. I saw why she'd had to use more than one page. Each herb had to be prepared in a certain way. Ground, chopped, crushed... And then different measurements of each.

Mage magic was much better than this fiddly mess.

"Have fun boys." Ynes waved at us, going over and dumping out her purse on the coffee table, revealing an impressive collection of random objects. Then she started taking off her bracelets and adding them to the pile.

Two hours later Roderick and I had only prepared one batch, enough to fill three of the little potion bottles, and I had a mild headache from concentrating so hard.

On top of that, I was on edge waiting for the prince to call Ynes back. At the same time, I was trying to build up my courage to talk to Ynes, ask her out.

"Ynes, we're done with one batch," I said when we filled the last bottle.

"Here, let me see," Ynes said, putting down the bracelet she was fiddling with. She popped the cork from one bottle and sniffed it. "Smells right. Good job."

"What does it do?" I asked as she packed the bottles in her bag.

"Just a safety net. For about an hour after drinking it, all your reflexes will be faster. As a bonus, it'll make you run faster too," she said. "I think Roderick's plan is good, but always good to have a quick way out."

I nodded. "Good idea."

After watching me nervously pacing the floor, while petting the fur off of Pog's sleeping back, Roderick dragged me up to the pool to "put that nervous energy to good use." Or practicing boring, repetitive exercises, as I called it.

I still hadn't gotten up my courage to ask Ynes out. Part of the reason for my nervous pacing, although Roderick didn't know that. Roderick had Ynes promise to come get me the moment the elves called her.

Roderick had me do the light exercise a few times. When I finished, he said, "I'm impressed. That was only half as blinding as last night." He didn't sound impressed, but then I knew I also hadn't improved that much.

"It's hard," I admitted. "I really have to concentrate to make it less bright."

"Nice problem to have," he said with a snort. In his new clothes, Roderick looked more like when I'd met him, put together and serious.

"I guess if you like explosions. Not so much if you just want a nightlight."

"True. When all you have is a bucket, it's hard to scoop up only a drop of water." Roderick crossed his arms, his brows contracting in thought. "I was going to have you try levitation today, but maybe you should just keep working on making the light smaller."

"No, no, levitation sounds fun. Besides, how can I mess that up?"

Roderick pursed his lips and regarded me. "Do you really want the answer to that question?"

"Yes?" I spread my hands, curious.

"Off the top of my head," he started ticking things off on his fingers as he went, "turning the object inside out instead of lifting it, throwing it sideways instead of up, smashing it down into the ground, and, based on how strong your light is, if you do actually lift it up, throwing it all the way into outer space."

"I mean, if it's just something small, what's the harm? Levitation sounds useful, and I'm going to need more than just a bright light if I'm going to help rescue Brandon."

"We'll be there too, remember." Roderick sighed. "But you have a good point. Wait here, I'll find something harmless you can practice with. Work on making a smaller light while I'm gone."

I could barely concentrate. I was so excited to try a new spell that my first light was eye-piercing, the brightest one yet. "Damn it," I swore. I'd blinded myself even with my eyes closed. By the time I'd blinked the spots from my eyes, Roderick was back holding a bag of marshmallows that Sunny had ordered because they looked like little pillows. Never let a vampire order your groceries. I think half the things she picked because she liked the packaging.

"Sugar and air. Can't get more harmless." He pulled a marshmallow out of the bag and set in on the table in front of me. "Now for this spell, picture an invisible hand moving the object for you. I'll demonstrate."

Roderick set the bag aside and then stared intently at the marshmallow. It slowly lifted off the table by about an inch. A bead of sweat rolled down the side of Roderick's face. The marshmallow floated to the left and then gently descended and settled back onto the table.

"Looks easy enough," I said.

"Let me get clear before you try, just in case." Roderick took the bag with him and retreated across the deck until he stood as far from me as he could get. "Ok, now!" he yelled.

Invisible hand. I stared intently at the marshmallow, unconsciously imitating Roderick's expression. Hand, meet marshmallow. A ghostly hand appeared in the air in front of me, power sparking off of it.

"Wait—" Roderick yelled.

I pictured the fingers reaching down and grasping the little cube. As the fingers contracted on it, the marshmallow exploded, sending little chunks of molten sugar splattering all over my face and my brand-new clothes.

In the background, Roderick laughed uproariously.

"What the fuck." I wiped sticky marshmallow ooze from my face. Or tried to. It stuck to my hands and eyes, so I mostly ended up smearing it around. "You didn't mention that the object might explode."

"I've never seen that happen," Roderick said around his laugh. I heard his steps coming across the deck then he pressed a towel into my hands.

"But how...?" I asked as I scrubbed at my face. I didn't even bother trying to scrub off the shirt. It would need a couple of runs through the washing machine at the very least.

"You used far too much power. When your hand touched the marshmallow, the extra magic transferred." Roderick laughed again and set another marshmallow on the table. "Just like the light exercise, you need a lighter touch. I tried to warn you."

"How did you know?"

"Your 'invisible' hand had so much power behind it, it wasn't actually invisible." Roderick tapped the table and retreated again.

"I thought it was just my imagination." I sat back and shook out my hands. "Alright, round two."

Two hours later, marshmallow goo covered me from head to toe, and the bag was empty. I didn't even want to see what I looked like.

"It's them, it's them!" Ynes yelled as she burst out the door. She stopped dead, her eyes wide and phone held high. "What the heck happened up here?" She shook her head. "You know what? It doesn't matter. I've got them on hold, but I don't know how long they'll wait." She set her phone down on one of the deck chairs, since I'd covered the table in marshmallow goo, and dropped to her knees next to it, gesturing us over and taking the phone off hold.

"Hi, I'm back. I've got the mage you're looking for here with me."

"Finally." The musical voice was a different one than we'd spoken to this morning. "This is Prince Wynne. You've given us quite the little chase, young mage."

I glanced at Ynes and Roderick, who both looked back at me expectantly. I guess it was up to me to talk to him.

"Why are you even after me?" I asked.

There was a pause on the other end. Probably the sound of my voice was not what they'd expected. "Isn't it obvious?"

"... no?" I said after a moment.

"Your magic is far too powerful. There was a reason we sealed it away."

"Ah, that."

"Yes."

I took a breath, not sure how to bring up Brandon. Might as well just get right to the point. "My friend, Brandon, the one who broke the seal. I want him back."

"That is not an option."

"What if I make a trade? Me, for him."

Another pause. In the background, I could hear a conversation happen in a language I didn't know, full of musical trills and clicks. The same as what I'd heard at my house.

After a bit, the prince came back on the line. "We gain nothing from this. We'll find you soon enough on our own." Despite his confident words, his tone didn't match, his words growly and frustrated.

Ynes covered her mouth to smoother a laugh. She must have been right about them not being able to track me here. I pictured the elves running all over downtown, following magical tracking that was bouncing off skyscrapers and sending them to the wrong place.

"I'll come with you quietly—no more chasing me around the city, no more chaos—and let you seal my magic again, as long as you let Brandon go unharmed." My hands shook, but I think I kept my voice steady. We had a plan to stop that from happening. Hopefully.

Someone said something in the background in that same musical language. Prince Wynne said, "No fighting? No tricks?"

"Yes. No fighting."

"This is acceptable," the prince said. "Where are you? We'll come get you right now. I will release Brandon once we return with you to Faerie."

"No, this will be a trade," I emphasized the word. "You bring him to us. My friends will be there to make sure he gets home safely."

"He is in Faerie. It will take us time to retrieve him."

"That's fine. We can meet at midnight, if that's enough time." I said. That was roughly five hours from now.

The prince hummed, and someone said something in the background. "Yes, that will work."

"Then let's meet at midnight in Pier Park, by the moss-covered house."

We'd chosen Pier Park after a lot of discussion. Forest Park was larger, and less accessible to the public, but Ynes said that since the PCA headquarters was there, it was often filled with shifters and vampires at night.

Pier Park was full of large old-growth trees that would conceal our activities from non-magical folk.

"Acceptable. We'll be waiting," the prince said.

The line went dead.

"It's done," I said, rubbing marshmallow goo from my face.

"I hope this works," Roderick said, his voice trembling.

"Me too..."

XVII

Unicorn Poop

"Good, enough time for you to shower," Ynes said, looking me over. "What the heck happened to you anyway?"

"I was trying to levitate marshmallows," I said to Ynes as she trailed me downstairs.

She wiped a finger along my cheek, taking a blob of marshmallow fluff, and then licking it off her finger while giving me a sultry look. Geez, I was oblivious. How did I miss that she liked me?

Covered in goop wasn't exactly the best look for me. I knew I should wait, but I needed to do this now before I lost my nerve. If things went wrong tonight, this might be my last chance.

"So, uh, Ynes, I..." I stammered, not sure what to say still. "You and me, is, I mean, how long..."

"Your red face is cute," she giggled. "Or what I can see of it. But you mean liking you? Ages. But you weren't part of the supernatural community. I mean, it's not forbidden, but..." she shrugged. "I don't know. It's so hard to date someone who doesn't know about half your life. Easier to just date other witches."

"Yeah..." That seemed like it would be a recipe for disaster. "But don't witches and mages not get along?"

"Eh," she see-sawed her hand. "Mostly traditionalists like our dads. And even they can put things aside when needed, as you saw."

"Would you like to go on a date when this is all over? Assuming—"

"Don't say it! It's bad luck," Ynes said. "And yes, though I was starting to wonder if you were gay. I saw the looks you were giving Kay."

"I'm bisexual. He's cute and a flirt. I'm not made of stone." I squirmed. "Me being trans doesn't bother you?" I asked. It felt almost too good to be true. In less than a week, the bad luck that had plagued my whole life was gone. I'd found my birth family and arranged a date. The only things marring my high were Brandon being a captive of the elves. That and I guess them trying to kill me.

She bit her lip and blushed, shaking her head. "I've never dated a trans guy before, but, no, it doesn't bother me."

I leaned towards her.

She pecked me on the lips and then stepped back. "Let's save more for after your shower."

I couldn't stop humming to myself in the shower. When I came out in fresh clothes, I found everyone, including Sunny, gathered in the living room.

"We just finished catching her up on the plan," Ynes said as I plopped down on the couch between her and Roderick. Barnabas sat on the arm of the couch, and Sunny was in her gamer chair with Pog in her lap. Ynes gave me a half smile and took my hand.

"I have to admit, it's not a bad plan. I'm sure we could come up with something better, given time, but given the time limit..." She flashed her fangs and I jumped. "But I'm still unclear on why we're bothering to retrieve the unicorns on the way."

"An extra bit of insurance," Roderick said. "A getaway vehicle. Those things are *fast*. No offence, Sunny, but Ynes couldn't get your hearse to go over fifty when we drove it home."

"I don't drive it for speed. It's an aesthetic." Sunny scowled. "And I don't know why you all assume I don't have another car."

"Do you?" I asked. Everyone's eyes turned to me. "Have another car, I mean."

"Of course I do," Sunny snapped. "We can take that if the hearse doesn't meet your needs."

"No, the hearse is fine," Ynes said. "But I want to get them sooner rather than later. I'm afraid if I leave them there any longer Ms. Williams will blow a gasket."

"What the heck are we going to do with them after?" Roderick asked.

"I wonder what unicorn blood tastes like?" Sunny mused.

"I suppose that's one solution," Ynes said, bumping my shoulder with hers.

I didn't like the idea of Sunny killing my unicorns, but I didn't have a better solution.

We still had some time before we had to leave, so Sunny and Pog went back to gaming. Roderick turned to ask something, saw our clasped hands, and grinned.

"Finally. I was beginning to think Ynes was going to have to tackle you to get through to you."

"Look, with my bad luck, I didn't exactly have an impressive track record with matters of the heart." I flushed red.

"I think it's adorable." Ynes hugged my arm, then reached around, grabbed the front of my shirt, and pulled me around to kiss me. I tensed at first from the shock, but then relaxed into her.

I felt the cushions shift as Roderick got up.

Her tongue probed my lips, and I opened and let her in. I shifted around to straddle her lap, sliding an arm around her back, and cupping the back of her head with the other. Her chest was soft against mine, warm and inviting. I could have kissed her for hours.

Too soon, Sunny was poking my shoulder, telling us it was time to go. By now we were vertical on the couch, Ynes on top, my legs tangled in her skirt. Ynes ran to change to a more appropriate outfit, and I tried to calm my pounding libido. Hopefully there'd be more time for that later.

Once we'd gathered up all our supplies, we all piled into Sunny's hearse.

Sunny dropped the three of us off at the PCA's front gates before roaring off with Pog and Barnabas. They were going to meet us at the park... I hoped. I didn't think she'd really take off with eim, but I still had a twinge of worry as I watched them drive away.

The gates were shut. I went up and rattled them. Locked. A massive wolf trotted up to the other side, staring out at us with amber eyes. I staggered back with a cry of surprise. Ynes' hand on my back stopped me.

"Evening," Ynes said. "We're here to pick up the unicorns."

The wolf opened its mouth in what looked like a laugh, tongue lolling out. "Those are yours? I'll be sad to see them go; they're hilarious."

The voice sounded growly, but still human. I stared open-mouthed at the talking wolf.

"Yeah, yeah. Can you let us in, please?" Ynes put a hand on her hip.

"Is that someone's familiar?" I whispered to Ynes.

She elbowed me. "Be nice. She's a werewolf."

"Hold on. I don't exactly have hands like this," the wolf said. "Hope you don't mind a bit of nudity." The wolf's fur pulled back in and its limbs stretched out. A moment later, a naked woman, hair the same color as the wolf's fur, stood where the wolf had been. She stood up, shook out her fingers, and then walked over to the side of the gate, out of sight. A moment later, it rattled open.

Ynes pushed me along and Roderick trailed behind us. After we entered, the gate reversed, shutting again with a clang.

"Hey, handsome," the woman sauntered over to us and took Roderick's arm. She was still naked. "My name is Zoe."

Ynes pointed to us all in turn. "Zoe, nice to meet you. I'm Ynes, this is Max, and his brother Roderick whose arm you have."

"Roderick. So distinguished. Let me walk you over there," Zoe said, winking at Roderick.

Roderick's face turned bright red. "We know the way up to the office," Roderick said stiffly. "No need to escort us."

Zoe sighed and let go with a scowl. "Another gay one, huh? You know, my partner's gay and single."

"Not gay..." Roderick's blush deepened and he kept his eyes fixed to the side. "Just... maybe you can change back into a wolf?"

"Ohhh... Just a prude? You know nudity is nothing to be ashamed of." Her gaze traveled down Roderick, then she shook her head, giggled and stepped back. Fur sprouted as she fell over onto all fours. By the time she landed, she was a wolf again.

"The unicorns aren't up at the office. They're in the shed down here," Zoe said. "Follow me."

She trotted off, tail wagging, through the lines of cars. There was a little shed at the end of the yard, and she stopped next to it. "You'll have to open the door yourself, you know, with the paws and all." Zoe lifted one front leg and shook it.

Ynes and I each grabbed a door and rolled them open. The two unicorns were inside munching on a pile of hay. A massive pile of jellybeans sat in the corner next to a shovel.

As we watched, one unicorn raised its tail. Jellybeans came tumbling out the back end.

"I really want to know how you did this," Zoe said, padding over and nosing the jellybeans. The unicorns didn't seem bothered by the giant wolf moving around their legs. "I haven't been brave enough to try them, but they smell just like jellybeans. And wolf noses don't lie."

"Is that right?" I asked, walking over to stand next to her. I crouched down and picked up a pink and white jellybean from the fresh pile. "Still warm. Smells good too," I said, sniffing it.

Curiosity seized me.

"Max, no!" Ynes howled as I put the jellybean into my mouth.

"Oh, my, god," Roderick said, retching.

"Strawberry cheesecake," I said as I chewed. "It's good." Like the licorice had been, it was probably the best candy I'd ever had.

I grabbed handful after handful, stuffing them in my pockets until they were overflowing. Everyone was staring at me as I stood up, even the wolf. "What?"

"Just for the record, Max, that's disgusting," Ynes said, taking the bridles from a hook on the wall. "You saw where those things came from."

"Whatever." I popped another one in my mouth. If we were going to be keeping the unicorns, I'd have as much of this as I wanted. More than I wanted, if the piles already in the shed were anything to go by.

God, I could make a fortune with this. Unicorn Poop Candy Store. Had a nice ring to it. No way was I going to let Sunny eat them.

"Gross," Ynes said.

That name might need some workshopping.

Ynes pressed the bridles into Roderick's hands. "You two put these on the unicorns. Zoe, can you show me where the carriage is?"

"Carriage?" the wolf's ears pricked forward.

"You know, red, silver trim, round, pulled by horses, or unicorns in this case..." Ynes said, gesturing her hands in a circle.

"I don't know anything about a carriage," the wolf said, one ear flicking back. "Haven't seen one."

"It's gotta be around here somewhere. I'll go look," Ynes said, and went outside.

"I can assure you it's not. Nothing but cars on the lot," Zoe said, following her. "I think I would have noticed something like that."

Roderick tossed me a bridle and got to work, putting it on his unicorn. I turned mine this way and that, unable to even figure out where to start with it. Roderick finished with his and came over and took the bridle from me with a shake of his head.

"I'll just get the... middle things that hold the unicorn to the carriage," I said, as he untangled the mess I'd made of the leather straps.

"They're called a harness," Roderick said. "Haven't you ever worked with horses before?"

"No." I decided Roderick would be better suited to put the harnesses on. I crossed my arms and watched him work instead. "None of the families I fostered with had pet horses."

"That's too bad."

I couldn't tell if he was serious or joking. I had meant mine as a joke. But Roderick had taken me seriously, I decided after watching him work for a moment. He looked like a pro as he carefully fitted the bridle over the unicorn's head. To me, it had just looked like a random collection of leather straps, but in his hands it looked easy.

"It's gone!" Ynes yelled, storming back into the barn.

"I told you," Zoe said, trotting at her heels. "While you searched, I went up to the office and looked at the logs. A Keiichi Miura picked it up. He had a title that matched the VIN. Though why a carriage had a VIN... It was even an Audi brand. I thought they just made cars." One of the wolf's ears cocked back, and she tilted her head.

"I'm gonna strangle that fox," Ynes growled.

"How'd he even get it out of here? Who pulled it?" I mused.

Zoe shrugged furry shoulders. "I don't know. Wasn't here for that."

"I'm going to call Sunny to come back and pick us up," Ynes said.

"Why?" Roderick said, patting the neck of the unicorn he'd just bridled. "We can ride the unicorns over there. Two of us will just have to double up."

"No, no." I waved my arms and backed up. "I don't know how to ride a horse."

"All you'll have to do is hang on," Roderick said, as if it were that easy. "You know how to ride a horse, right?" he asked Ynes.

"I took riding lessons at the clubhouse." Ynes took the reins of the other unicorn. She fiddled with one of her rings, then jumped smoothly up four feet onto its back. Good thing she'd changed into pants, I don't know how she would have ridden it in a skirt.

"Damn, that's some vertical leap. You should play basketball," Zoe woofed.

"Magic ring." Ynes showed the back of her hand so Zoe could see her ring. "I sell them at the Saturday Market, if you want one."

Roderick led his unicorn over to a stool and used it to climb on. "You want to ride with me or her?" he asked once he sat on its back.

"Walking's an option, right?" I asked, staring up at the massive beasts.

Ynes checked her watch. "Not if you want to be on time. It's already past eleven."

Fifty minutes to midnight. I knew from experience that it would take me longer than that to walk all the way to the park from here.

"Fine, Ynes, I'll ride with you."

Roderick shrugged. I picked up the stool and carried it over to Ynes. Even once I was on it, I looked up, and up, and up at the unicorn's back. It seemed a lot higher now that I was contemplating riding it.

"Hurry up, Max," Ynes said. The unicorn shifted, sensing her impatience.

I gave a couple of attempts to climb up, but even with the stool and Ynes' assistance, I couldn't get on.

"Guess you're riding with me," Roderick said, prancing his unicorn over to the stool, then he thrust a hand down to me. "Here, I'll help. Just lift your leg really high and fling it up and over while I pull."

The muscles on Roderick's arm bulged as he practically hauled me one-handed up onto the unicorn's back. Once I was on, my legs felt like they were being forced into splits by the unicorn's broad back. My groin already ached, and I'd only been on this thing for a few seconds.

"Put your arms around me, Max."

I gingerly put my hands on his hips.

"No, around me. I don't want you falling off when we move."

I put my arms all the way around his middle. This meant I had to press my chest against his back. Goddamn it. I would have loved to sit with Ynes like this. Why were horses so damn tall?

"Good. Now hold on," Roderick said.

I'd thought my groin hurt before. As the unicorn moved, its spine jammed into my crotch with each step. I hugged Roderick tight and prayed this didn't last long.

"Wait," I said, remembering why we'd brought Roderick along. He was going to do an illusion to hide the carriage on the way over to the park, but he needed to concentrate to do his spell. "If you're driving, who's going to do the illusion spell to hide the unicorns?"

"You ride a horse, not drive them," Roderick said. I couldn't see his face, but I could practically hear the roll of his eyes.

"I don't have anything with me to make an illusion," Ynes said. "We'll just have to risk it. It's late. Hopefully, not too many people will see us," Ynes said, her unicorn prancing under her.

"I'll just pretend I didn't hear that." Zoe woofed as she trotted beside us back to the gate to let us out. I shrugged. What was one more ticket?

XVIII

The Exchange

By the time we arrived at the park, my guts felt like they'd been through a blender and the insides of my thighs pulsed with pain.

"You can let go now," Roderick said with a laugh. "We're here." I tried, but my hands refused to unclench from each other.

"And ten minutes early, too!" Ynes said, hopping off with a bounce in her step. She looked far too cheerful.

Roderick pried my hands apart. "Ynes, come help Cityboy here get down so I can get off."

"Just lift your leg over and slide off. I'll catch you," Sunny said, suddenly standing next to the unicorn. Where had she come from? I started.

The unicorn snorted and pawed at the ground at her appearance, but Roderick put a hand on its neck and stroked it, calming it down. I wondered why the wolf hadn't bothered them, but the vampire had. Maybe because Zoe hadn't scared me, but Sunny did.

I did as she instructed, practically falling backwards off as my legs refused to work. Sunny's slim, but surprisingly strong arms caught me from behind and lowered me to the ground.

"I may never walk again," I groaned as she helped me stand.

Roderick slid down a little less gracefully than Ynes had, landing with a thump and almost falling, but he grabbed the unicorn's mane and managed to stay upright.

"You'll be fine once you walk around a bit," Roderick said, patting his unicorn's neck.

"Where's Pog and Barnabas?" I asked, bending over to rest my hands on my knees.

"I left them keeping watch," Sunny said, taking off into the park.

Roderick summoned a little wisp of light that hovered over my head. I shot him a dirty look. "I thought I was going to make the light."

"It's pitch black out here," Roderick said, pointing at me. "And if I let you summon one, we'd all be blind."

"But why put it over my head?" I grumbled.

"Because you're the bait, remember," Roderick said.

It would have been cooler floating in my outstretched palm rather than above my head, but I let it drop.

"Wait, everyone drink these." Ynes passed us each one of the potions Roderick and I had made earlier. The one that would make us move and react faster.

I made a face as I drank it; it tasted like vinegar and grass.

I had to lean on Sunny, hobbling with pain shooting up my groin with each step. Ynes and Roderick each led one of the unicorns. No reason to leave them on the street and risk someone stumbling across them. Sadly without the carriage they wouldn't make a good escape plan, too hard to get on.

When we arrived, Barnabas chittered at us from the roof of the moss house. A few bits of moss dislodged as Pog's head poked over the edge next to him.

"Pog, how'd you get up there?" I hissed. "Get down here before you fall and break something."

"I put eim up there," Sunny said.

"I'm a lookout!" Pog announced proudly. "I haven't seen anything yet, and Barnabas hasn't either."

"Great, keep up the good work," Sunny said.

Pog's head disappeared back over the roof.

"I'll be watching from the trees over there," Sunny said. She pulled the hood of her black hoodie up and then covered her lower face with a black mask. In the dark, she was practically invisible. Then she vanished. In the distance, I saw movement scurrying up a tree, fast as a squirrel. Vampires were terrifying. I was glad Sunny was on our side.

I took up position with Ynes, waiting for the elves to arrive. Roderick held the unicorns around the side of the house, out of sight. His part in this plan required him to concentrate, and we didn't want him interrupted. The plan was simple, which I hoped meant nothing would go wrong. Knowing my luck, that was just wistful thinking, but still.

The elves arrived about five minutes later, right on time. By then I was shivering in my thin hoodie. I'd been warm on the ride over, between Roderick and the unicorn's body heat.

The prince led the procession. Behind him, the massive troll carried a large birdcage with a cloth cover over it. The other two elves brought up the rear.

"Where's Brandon?" I yelled. "That was the deal!"

The troll lifted the birdcage by the ring at the top with one hand, sending it rocking. The bird inside screeched.

"Your friend is right here." The prince pushed the cage, making the bird scream again.

I exchanged a baffled glance with Ynes. "You turned him into a bird?" I asked.

"What?" The prince sneered. He was so pretty, that even that expression was beautiful.

"I told you, Brandon's a bird." Pog's head popped over the edge of the roof over my head.

"If you say so." This week had been weird, might as well roll with the best friend I've ever had turning out to be a bird.

"Let's make the exchange." The prince flourished his sword. "Unless you've changed your mind."

I hoped all these preparations would be enough. Too late to worry about it now. "Let me see him first," I yelled.

Prince Wynne must have been expecting that because he stepped back and used his sword to cut the cloth cover off of the cage. It fluttered to the ground, revealing a red feathered vulture with a long plumed tail more like a peacock. With the cover gone, the tail fell out between the bars, draping all the way to the ground.

When it saw me, the bird let out a trilling cry and fluffed its wings. I could have sworn the cry sounded like the bird had said, "Max." Fire sprang up along the bird's feathers, bursting into an inferno that completely engulfed the cage.

"That bird is on fire," I said in disbelief, stating the obvious.

"Phoenix," Ynes corrected me. "It's a phoenix."

"How is that not burning the troll's hand?" I asked no one in particular.

"Magical cage," Ynes said. "Obviously."

Obvious maybe to people who grew up in the magical world.

"That's Brandon," Pog called down.

"Thanks, Pog," I shot back without taking my eyes off the elves.

"I assume you are satisfied?" the prince called across the open space between us.

"Yes. Let's make the exchange," I said. I still couldn't believe Brandon had really been a bird all this time, but I trusted Pog. "I'll come to you, at the same time, you bring Brandon over to Ynes."

The troll walked forward a step. Ynes pushed at my back and whispered, "Go. You know the plan."

I nodded and started walking. The troll matched me. I monitored the light over my head, taking slow, measured steps. When it bobbed forward before I moved, I froze, holding as still as possible. The troll passed by the light, moving in time with the illusion of me that Roderick was creating underneath. I held my breath as she went by me, and not just because of the smell. Roderick had warned me he could only make visual illusions. If I made a sound, the troll might notice me under Roderick's illusion of invisibility.

The illusion of me was almost to the elves, which meant that the troll was almost to Ynes with Brandon. Maybe we were going to pull this off after all. With slow steps, I began backing up.

In the distance, wood cracked. A blue glimmer shone through the trees. Everyone whipped their heads around to stare in that direction. A red carriage came crashing through the trees, pulled by a horse-sized, two-tailed golden fox. Kay! He had absolutely terrible timing.

Five blue balls of flame swirled around his head and the carriage careened along behind him, bouncing off rocks and scraping the trees.

Mr. Woolven sat in the driver's seat. "There he is!" he yelled, pointing at the illusion of me under Roderick's light. The charging fox had been headed right for me, the real me, standing in the center of the two groups, but changed direction to head towards my illusion.

"Are you fucking kidding me?" I muttered, turned, and sprinted back towards Ynes and the moss house. Even with having to dodge through the trees, the carriage would be on us in a moment, and the jig would be up. So forget the plan, the plan was bust.

The troll set the cage down and turned to watch the carriage. Her eyes widened as I sprinted past her. I think Roderick's illusion had broken.

When the troll took a step after me, Ynes darted forward, grabbed the cage and tried to drag it away, but it was as tall as her. The phoenix—I still couldn't wrap my head around it being Brandon—screamed at her.

"He's saying to open the door and let him out, Dummy!" Pog yelled from the roof.

The troll roared and turned, diving for the cage.

"Oh, right!" Ynes unlocked the door.

Before she could get it open, the troll grabbed the ring at the top of the cage and jerked it out of her reach. But that had been enough. The movement flung the cage door open. The bird burst free with a shriek. Fire trailed from its feathers as it flew up and away.

I sprinted for the side of the moss house where Roderick and the unicorns hid. Ynes scrambled to her feet and ran after me.

The elves started screaming. I risked a glance behind to see the carriage skidding on two wheels, barely missing the elves as Kay made a hard turn towards me. The illusion of me vanished into smoke as Kay ran it over.

The ground shook under our feet as the troll stomped after us. We weren't going to make it; even with Ynes' speed potion, the troll was faster, taking one step for every five of mine or Ynes'. My legs still ached from the unicorn ride over too which wasn't helping me to run any faster, although the terror helped.

A unicorn charged from behind the moss house, Roderick whooping on its back. The unicorn lowered its head as it galloped past us. The spiral horn glinted blue from the light of Kay's magical fire.

The horn slammed into the troll's chest. The troll let out a bellow so loud that it knocked me off my feet. Green blood spurted out around the impaled horn, staining the unicorn's glowing white coat. Roderick jumped free and rolled to his feet on the other side of the troll.

Kay and the carriage were almost to us.

"Run," Roderick yelled, and then turned, chanting a spell and throwing out his hands. A shimmering yellow wall went up in front of Kay. Fox Kay hit it nose first and bounced off it with a yelp of pain. In the carriage, Mr. Woolven and Mr. Price were thrown forward.

The second unicorn was still hidden behind the moss house, and I briefly considered running for it, but I honestly didn't think I could get on it without Roderick's help or Ynes' jump ring. I should have asked to borrow it. Hindsight. Instead, I scrambled to my feet and ran towards the entrance of the park, Ynes on my heels.

The unicorn that had hit the troll let out a scream and then there was a massive crack, loud enough that I stopped and looked back. The troll grabbed the unicorn's head and twisted, snapping its neck before it tore the horn free of its chest with another spurt of green blood.

Poor thing. I hadn't even named it yet.

She tossed the unicorn's lifeless body aside and started after me with a roar, drawing her axe from her back as she charged. Frost curled out along the dirt behind her.

Shit. I turned and ran. It was so dark I could barely see, and I kept tripping on roots and rocks, slowing me down. I didn't dare make light, I'd probably blind myself, like Roderick had pointed out.

The second unicorn charged past me with Pog and Barnabas on its back. Pog had the unicorn's mane twisted in eir paws, steering it. Barnabas waved at me as they rode past.

"Wait... for... me..." I gasped as they disappeared into the darkness ahead. "What the hell, Pog!" I yelled after them.

The roaring troll was getting closer, but then it fell, screaming, with a black form on its back. Sunny's red hair was bright against the black of her outfit as her hood fell back. The troll shook itself like a dog, tossing Sunny away off into the darkness. But her attack had at least bought us a few more seconds.

I paused to throw some jellybeans at the troll, attempting to levitate them as they hit. Sadly, unlike the marshmallows that had burst into flaming molten chunks, the jellybeans just popped. Very anti-climactic.

Ynes and I were almost at the entrance to the park when the oncoming headlights of a car blinded me. I shrieked and jumped off the path to one side, Ynes to the other, just before Sunny's hearse barreled past.

"Push the gas down farther, Barnabas," Pog yelled from the driver's seat, steering the car with eir paws. "We need to go faster!"

How had Pog turned the car on? Where had they gotten the keys? Maybe Sunny had left them in the ignition? One hoped. Otherwise, it meant my familiar knew how to hot-wire a car.

The hearse smashed into the troll's legs. It was like hitting a brick wall. The front of the car crumpled in, and the back bounced into the air. The air bags went off with a bang, and smoke poured out from under the hood.

Great, now I owed three people cars. But I really didn't care about that right now.

"Pog!" I ran back towards the crashed car. The airbags had gone off; I hoped it had been enough to save them.

Before I could take more than three steps, the troll screamed and smashed her giant axe down into the roof, cutting the car almost in half.

"Pog, no!" I screamed, skidding to a stop on the dirt path and putting my hands over my mouth in horror.

"My car!" Sunny screamed, stumbling out of the woods, holding Pog and Barnabas. Green liquid stained her mouth.

"Pog, you're okay!" I grabbed the red panda out of her arms. Barnabas jumped down, chittering, and scampered across the path to Ynes, who scooped him up.

"I'm not dumb, Max. We jumped out before it hit." Pog hugged me back.

"You should run," Sunny said, grabbing my arm and forcefully dragging me down the path.

"I'll try to slow them down, Max!" Ynes yelled. She flicked out her switch-blade wand, chanted, and pointed it at the troll. Fire swirled from the end. It crashed into the troll, leaving a burned streak, but the troll didn't even react, focused on pulling her stuck axe from the engine block.

"I'm not going to make it! We need to stop and fight," I said, slowing.

"Max, you're no match for them. You need to run." Sunny dragged me away. I fought, but her grip was like iron. "The rest of us will be fine.

"But what about Ynes? And Roderick?" I yelled.

"They'll be fine. Their dads won't let them get hurt." Sunny kept going, towing me along.

Kay and the carriage came charging down the path behind the troll. A blue wisp of fire zoomed from his head and smashed into the troll's back. She bellowed in pain, but kept tugging.

Behind the carriage, the three elves were running hell bent, waving their swords. There was no sign of Roderick. I hoped he was okay. Of course, he could use illusion to make himself invisible. I hoped that was what he'd done.

The troll put her foot down on the car and heaved, ripping her axe free with a tearing of metal, taking out pieces of the car along with it. She used the flat side of the axe to flip the car off the path, then hefted her axe high again and charged.

The giant fox ran past the troll and then swerved to the side, ramming her in the side with the red carriage. She tripped and her axe came smashing down on the tresses that connected Kay to the carriage. With a roar, she backhanded the side of the carriage, sending it tumbling over on its side and crashing into the trees. I hoped Mr. Price and Mr. Woolven were okay. I didn't like them, but I didn't want them dead, either.

Pog had eir paws wrapped around my neck, clinging to me for dear life as I stumbled after Sunny.

The giant fox sped up, snarling. His eyes burned blue as he barreled down on us. The troll with her axe was only a few steps behind him. Ynes' continued lobs of fire weren't having any effect.

"You owe me," Kay growled, baring his teeth. "I'm going to turn you over to your father and collect the rest of my fee."

Kay and the troll were almost on us. I had to do something.

"Sunny, Pog, cover your eyes," I hissed. It was hard to concentrate with all the noise and while trying to keep my feet under me, but I'd been practicing.

Light bloomed in my hands. Bright as the sun, searing even with my eyes closed. Sunny screamed and let go of my arm, staggering away, her skin sizzling.

Kay howled, an animal sound, and the troll bellowed. I hugged Pog to my chest, blinking the spots from my eyes.

That had been my brightest one yet, maybe because my emotions were so high right now.

Blinding them would slow them down, but not for long. There was no way I could outrun any of them, especially with the car now totaled. I could always escape on the other unicorn, but I wouldn't leave my friends behind.

XIX

The Fight

YNES SCREAMED FROM THE darkness. A fox snarled and the troll bellowed, along with sounds of a scuffle. The ground shook. I blinked, squinting, and made out white fur and blue skin rolling around on the dirt, lit by occasional flashes of blue and red fire. The giant fox wresting with the troll.

Ynes, backlit by the carriage headlights, circled the fighting fox and troll, headed for something behind them.

There was a clash of steel on steel and a man yelled something that I couldn't make out over the din. In the distance, I saw two suited forms standing by the overturned carriage, flinging magic at the three elves.

One suited figure held up what looked like a stick of wood. It shimmered, turning into something that glittered in the light.

He flung the brand new dagger at the prince, who barely deflected it with his sword. That must be my father.

Mr. Price, the other suited form, spun a chain over his head. Bolts of lightning crackled from it. The other two elves dodged and rolled, barely avoiding being hit as they flung magic back at the men. But Mr. Price's spinning chain lightning zapped away each bolt before they could hit. The fight seemed to be at a stalemate, but it probably wouldn't take much for either to get the upper hand.

"I need to turn myself in. Stop the fighting," I yelled. I didn't want anyone to get killed, neither my friends, their fathers, or even the elves.

"Turn yourself over to who, your father or the elves?" Sunny yelled back, climbing to her feet. Black burns covered her face and hands.

"Honestly, at this point I don't care. I just don't want anyone to get hurt."

"Too late for that!" Sunny snarled, pointing at her face.

I winced. "It'll heal, right?" I guess my sunlight had been a little too real.

She gave me a dirty look and bared her fangs at me, eyes glowing red. "When I feed, yeah. Still hurts though. You're lucky Pog likes you, and that there are better meals around." With that, she blurred off towards the fighting. A moment later, a dark shadow grabbed an elf and dragged it off into the woods.

Sunny had a point though. Two parties, and neither was likely to let me go with the other without a fight. But I had to do something.

I crouched and pried Pog from around my neck. "You stay here. Stay safe. I have to go save my friends." I stood and ran back toward the fighting, drawing magic into me.

"No, Max, no!" Pog chased after me, but eir little legs were too short and eiy couldn't keep up, especially with the potion speeding me up.

This was the first time I'd tried to do this on purpose. The magic built quickly. I imagined the light switch was off, and let the tingle build in my palms.

A bird screeched down from the sky, trailing fire. It landed between me and the fighters, then spread its wings out. Little licks of flame danced along its feathers.

I stumbled to a stop in front of it, the heat from the fire singed me. "Out of the way, bird," I yelled.

The bird's feathers pulled in as the bird's form stretched out. Its beak flattened into a human face, the feathers of its head turning into long red hair. Then Brandon was there, standing in front of me, the last bits of flame dancing on his tanned skin for a moment before dying.

"Brandon?" I said, blushing and very glad the light was behind him, leaving most of his front in shadow, because he wasn't wearing any clothes.

"I'm sorry I never told you," he said, taking a step towards me. I backed up a step. Hurt flashed in his eyes.

"How long have you known I was a mage?" I whispered, barely able to talk past the lump in my throat. I loved Brandon so much. He was like family to me. The only constant in my life growing up. Seeing him transform like that, knowing he'd kept something so big about himself from me, twisted a knife in my gut. The fighting happening behind him faded to a dull roar. All I could see was Brandon.

"Since the day I met you." He sighed and his shoulders slumped. He looked to the side, not meeting my eyes. "I could feel the magic gathering around you. But some force kept it from you, an invisible barrier between you and your heritage. That magic denied had to go somewhere, so it manifested around you in the bad luck you suffered your entire life."

I felt faint and slumped to my knees so I didn't fall. "Why didn't you tell me?"

He knelt in front of me and took my hand. I didn't stop him. Magic burned in my palms, almost as hot as his skin. "Would you have believed me?"

"Probably not." I gave him a crooked smile. I still barely believed what had happened this week, and I'd lived it.

"I broke the seal so we could be together." Brandon leaned in for a kiss, but I put a hand to his chest.

"We could have been together before," I reminded him. "Remember high school?"

He shook his head sadly, a lock of red hair falling across his face. "No, we couldn't. Every time we touched, the seal zapped me. It couldn't distinguish between my magic and yours." He gave a deep sigh. "And high school, that fire was me. That was the day I manifested my phoenix for the first time."

"You should have told me." I balled my fists. "I'm hurt you lied to me." But now his insistence that I shouldn't feel guilty about the fire made more sense.

"I'm sorry. You're right." He looked away, eyes guilty. He swallowed and glanced back, expression flashing back to hopeful. "I did this for you, Max. Can't you give me another chance?" He leaned towards me again, and this time I let it happen.

We kissed, long and deep. A little thrill went through me and I leaned into him. Followed by a stab of guilt. Ynes.

We broke apart. I could still taste Brandon on my lips.

"Brandon, I can't. I have a girlfriend." Well, we hadn't had that conversation yet. "A girl I like," I amended.

His eyes widened. "What? You didn't tell me..."

"Like you didn't tell me about Kay?" I lifted an eyebrow and he at least had the grace to look chagrined.

"I didn't mean to keep seeing him secret from you."

A warm furry form collided with my back, and then Pog was clutching my leg. "See? Bird. I told you," eiy said.

"What the heck?" Brandon rocked back, eyes wide as he stared down at the red panda.

"Oh, yeah. Pog, meet Brandon, my roommate. Brandon, this is Pog, our house ghost." I paused. "Former house ghost, you know, now that they burned our house down and Pog is a red panda."

Brandon's eyes widened. "The house is what—"

I pushed Pog into Brandon's arms. "Take care of eim for a minute, please. I need to stop this fighting."

"No, you need to run!" Brandon dumped Pog into the dirt and scrambled up after me.

"If I do that, my friends are going to get hurt!" I pushed past him, drawing more magic into me until it felt like my arms were on fire. I'd need to do something with it soon.

Kay's giant fox form had the troll on her back, his teeth around her throat. Meanwhile, the prince had Roderick on his knees in front of him, holding a knife to his throat, while Mr. Woolven had the female elf hostage, protected by Mr. Price and his lightning chain. Sunny had an arm around the third elf's throat, her bloody teeth bared. Ynes stood next to her. All parties watched each other warily.

A standoff.

"Let my son go," Mr. Woolven yelled to the prince.

"Not until you call off your dog!" Prince Wynne's musical voice somehow still sounded furious.

Kay's ears went back and his tails flicked up and down. He growled, but could not say anything with his teeth around the troll's throat.

"And your vampire!" he continued.

"The vampire is not mine. She's working with my idiot daughter... son... that we're both trying to catch," Mr. Woolven snapped.

"I want Roderick back," Ynes yelled from next to Sunny.

"Everybody, calm down!" I raised my fists and imagined a firefly buzzing around each palm. Bright light flashed and pulsed on each fist for a moment, far brighter than I intended. All eyes turned in my direction.

Brandon ran up behind me, but when the light flashed, his eyes widened, and he stopped. Pog ran past him and hugged my leg, drawing out some of the magic and giving me a bit more time. I gave him a quick smile.

Now that everyone was looking at me, I didn't know what to say. I swallowed, nervous, and my magic blazed, almost escaping. Only the practice of the last two days kept me under control.

"Now we are going to solve this *without*," I emphasized the word, "any more bloodshed. What will that take?"

"It will take you returning to Faerie with us, like you promised," the prince yelled, tightening his fist in Roderick's short hair. Roderick whimpered.

"Do not hurt my brother," I warned him, lighting my fists up again.

"No, what it will take is you putting the bracelet on and coming with me," Mr. Woolven said. He shook the shoulders of the elf he had hostage. Mr. Price lowered his spinning chain and pulled out the bracelet that he'd put on Sunny the other night. He tossed it into the dirt a few feet from me.

"I can't do both of those things," I said. "And honestly, I don't want to do either of them."

Kay growled low in his throat.

"Okay, to start with Kay, why don't you let her go, and Sunny will let her elf go?" I glanced at the fox. His ears flattened to his head. "Your boss still has a hostage. And this way you can talk."

Sunny shoved her elf away. "Whatever. Turns out elf blood tastes like shit."

The elf fell to his knees and crawled towards the prince.

"Kay, your turn," I said.

Kay snarled, but opened his jaws and backed off the troll. As he did, his form shrunk down, fur pulling in, until he was human again, blond hair almost glowing in the ambient light of the carriage headlights. He stomped over to the mage and wizard, flicking his long blond hair over his shoulder and sticking his nose in the air. What a drama queen.

That left two: Prince Wynne holding Roderick and Mr. Woolven holding the last elf.

"Let's get one thing straight." I kicked dirt on the bracelet. "I'm never putting this on and two," I looked at the prince, "I'm not letting you seal my magic again."

"Who said anything about sealing it?" The prince sneered. I widened my eyes.

"Then what..." I trailed off, remembering what Roderick had said about them killing me as an option.

"Your magic is an abomination. We only resorted to sealing before because you were just a babe and because of your father's request, but now there is no reason to hold back. Once we get back to Faerie, we will try you for your magical crimes, and probably execute you."

God, not them too. First the PCA and now the Fae. My magic was my magic. It wasn't my fault what my powers were.

"I will never let that happen." Brandon growled, stepping forward to stand shoulder to shoulder with me.

The prince tightened his hand on the sword. A line of blood trickled down Roderick's throat and a tear trickled down his cheek. Shit. Mr. Woolven did the same to his elf. This was escalating fast. I had to do something now, but my mind was blank. All I could think of was light and marshmallow levitation; the two spells I'd been practicing. My magic tore free.

Marshmallows rained from the sky. The prince and Mr. Woolven's swords tumbled apart in their hands as they turned into marshmallows. The lights from the carriage winked out as it burst into millions of fluffy red marshmallows.

Luckily, everyone was still dressed, except Brandon, and he'd been naked before I started. Though I'd turned everything else within ten yards of me into soft white cubes. All the weapons. The carriage. The trees. A tidal wave of marshmallows engulfed everyone as the branches-turned-marshmallows dropped from the trees.

Brandon extended his arms, and fire blazed from him, forming into the shape of a bird. It was hot enough that it burned the surrounding marshmallows to ashes, but I was far away enough that it merely melted the marshmallows around my feet, covering my lower legs in goo.

"My fur!" Pog wailed, standing on hind legs.

"What the fuck, Max!" The yell came from Roderick as he emerged from a mound of marshmallows. He waded through them in my direction. Then he let out a cry and disappeared back under, his legs pulled out from under him. The marshmallows rolled as he fought with someone under the piles.

"I'm coming, Rod!" I lunged in his direction, tossing marshmallows away by the armful. Many of them stuck to the melted remains covering me and slowing me down.

The troll burst from a pile behind me, roaring and scattering marshmallows everywhere. She reached for her axe, but it was gone, turned into silver and blue marshmallows. Brandon turned to face her, making his fire bird blaze higher and brighter. She flinched back from the flames, holding her hand in front of her face.

The heat began melting more marshmallows, covering those of us closest to him in melted goo.

Kay and an elf appeared above the marshmallows, briefly wrestling with each other before disappearing back under the mess.

"Everyone, stop fighting!" I yelled, barely able to move.

"He said to stop!" Brandon yelled. A fire bird flew up from him, screeching loudly. The heat singed my eyebrows and melted more of the marshmallows, revealing everyone and covering them all with sticky goo. One by one, each of them got to their feet. One elf made a halfhearted lunge for either Mr. Price or Mr. Woolven—I couldn't tell who was who under the white marshmallow fluff, but Brandon let out another screech and they rocked back on their heels.

The prince stood up in disgust, trying to comb the mess from his hair with his hands. "What is this?" he said, horror dripping from his words.

"My suit is *ruined*." That was Mr. Woolven as he scraped at the goo on his leg, but only smeared it around.

"These are marshmallows," I said in answer to the prince, rubbing goop from my eyes. "I'm sorry. I panicked and couldn't think of anything else." I shrugged sheepishly. "At least you all stopped fighting."

The prince gave up on his hair and put his hands on his hips to glare at me. He looked like an anime character with his white-streaked brown hair sticking out in every direction.

"Here's what's going to happen." I glared right back at him. "You are going to go back to Faerie without me."

"Why would I do that?" the prince said. "You need to stand trial."

"For what!" I threw up my hands. "I haven't done anything."

"Those unicorn abominations, for one." The prince said.

"That was an accident," I said. "But I don't think it's anything I need to stand trial for. I've already got way more control, thanks to Roderick's lessons. And you can't fault me just for being born with magic."

"You call this control," Mr. Woolven yelled, throwing a marshmallow at me.

"Compared to what it had been? Yes," Roderick said. He waded through the marshmallows towards me, as did Ynes and Sunny.

I felt better with them all—and Brandon—at my side.

"We can't just let you go," the prince said. "We need reparations." He pointed at Brandon, "for the damages caused by that one in Faerie and by your misuse of magic." I still wanted to argue with that last one, but I let it be for now.

"Reparations? Like money?" I asked with a frown. Brandon gave a little shake of his head.

The prince laughed. "Money? What would we need with human currency? No, reparations. Something to make up for everything."

"You'll have to forgive me. I don't know what that means." I turned to look at the others with a question.

The prince rubbed his hand through his hair and tossed a handful of melted marshmallow on the ground with a sneer, where it landed with a plop. "Considering the circumstances, I can consider payment as a favor to be paid at a later time."

Ynes's eyes got wide, and she shook her head. Brandon and Roderick both looked alarmed, but I didn't see that I had any other choice.

"Agreed," I said before any of them could stop me.

"No, Max!" Brandon shouted. But it was too late.

"The bargain is struck." The prince nodded and gestured to the troll and the rest. "You'll be hearing from me later." The elves and the troll stalked off into the darkness, trailing marshmallow goo.

"Max, you don't make deals with Faeries!" Ynes hissed. "Especially elves."

"We didn't exactly have a choice," I said back, turning to Kay, Mr. Price, and my father.

Kay looked at me with interest while the other two scowled at me.

"And you, Mr. Woolven—" I started.

"That's Father to you!"

"Not going to happen." I set my jaw. I didn't really want to do this either, but I could tell that working with Roderick was only going to get me so far. But there was something I had to know first.

"Before I tell you the deal, I want to know the truth about what happened with my magic." I squeezed my fists, trying to steady myself. "And how I got into foster care."

Mr. Woolven scowled, clearly not wanting to tell me the story, but wanting to hear my demands. "I made a deal with the elves for them to seal your magic. We were overwhelmed. We could have other children. Try again." He shrugged and spread his hands. "We thought that this would be the best way."

"Why not do something temporary?" I asked, thinking of Ynes' suggestion.

"We tried. You kept breaking even the strongest artifacts I could make," Mr. Price said.

Huh. What made them think this time would be any different?

He must have seen my skepticism, because he scowled. "I've had a lot of time to perfect my artifacts since then."

Mr. Woolven didn't look so sure, but it was hard to tell under all the marshmallow fluff. "Well, be as it was, we weren't going to last until you were old enough for control." He shook his head. "It was an act of desperation."

"Which part, sealing my magic or giving me up?" I asked, barely keeping my voice even. I could feel the tingle of magic building at my rising emotions, but I was still too fatigued from the last one and it slipped away.

"Both. I hadn't known about the side-effect of the seal. Caring for you was impossible, if even more difficult than before," Mr. Woolven said.

I could imagine. "Even so, tossing me away like that? And not even keeping track of me?"

"I had to. Otherwise, your mother would have come looking for you. So I told her you'd died in one of your accidents and dropped you off at a hospital with a fake name."

So he had lied about that. The worst part was that he didn't sound regretful in the least. I hated the way he treated Roderick, and I had a feeling it would have been even worse for me being assigned female at birth. Guys like him tended to be misogynists. I *really* didn't want to do this.

I took a deep breath, hoping I wasn't making a mistake. "Fine, here's the deal. I won't call you father, or wear the bracelet, but I will come work for you in exchange for a salary and magic lessons."

Mr. Woolven didn't look happy, but that was the most I was willing to give him. He looked around himself with a shake of his head. "Appalling," he muttered, kicking at the marshmallows. "But fine, agreed."

I clapped my hands together, though with the marshmallow goo it just made a squishing sound. "That's that then? Can we all go home and get some sleep now?"

"So that means I get my fee?" Kay perked up, looking pleased.

Mr. Woolven snarled. "Yes, yes. Call my secretary in the morning so we can arrange for transfer."

"Wonderful." Kay then turned to me and made a finger gun. "You still owe me a car, but I'll collect on that later." Kay swirled into fox form and bounced away into the trees.

"Roderick, come with me. We'll get a cab home," Mr. Woolven said, snapping his fingers at Roderick like he was a dog.

"No." Roderick put a hand on my shoulder. His voice was firm, but I could feel him trembling.

"What did you say?" Mr. Woolven said in disbelief.

"I said no, Father." He gripped me like I was all that was keeping him upright. "I'm moving out."

I grinned over my shoulder at him and put my hand over his. I was proud of him. It obviously took him a lot of courage to stand up to his father.

"Not you too, Ynes?" Mr. Price asked, his eyes pleading.

"Me, too." Ynes stood up straight and crossed her arms. "I can't believe you would be party to this. I'll come get my things later this week."

"Let's go, Rafa," Mr. Woolven said, stomping away. Mr. Price followed him, though he kept shooting glances over his shoulder at us, or more likely at Ynes.

I didn't relax until they were out of sight, then I turned to my assembled friends.

Brandon opened his arms, but Ynes hugged me and pressed her lips to mine for a brief moment. Brandon's eyes narrowed as Ynes put her arm around my back and hugged my arm. Ynes glanced between us, curious.

"I thought you said you weren't dating?" she asked, tightening her hand on my hip.

I gave Brandon a hard look. "We weren't. Although if someone had confessed his feelings, we would have been. You have no call to be jealous."

"I couldn't touch you while the seal was active," Brandon growled, but then his shoulders slumped and he let out a deep sigh. "But where are my manners? Thank you all for helping Max. Ynes, I recognize from the Saturday market, but I don't know the rest of you."

"Oh, I should introduce you. Everyone, this is Brandon." I waved at him, and then went around and made introductions.

"Max, I don't want to get between you. I know how much you love him." Ynes tried to step away, but I put an arm around her shoulder and kept her there.

"You won't," Brandon said. He came over and put his arms around both of us, hugging us tight. "Though I can't promise not to be jealous."

His hand got stuck in the marshmallow goo covering my back. He stepped back, wrinkling his nose as he looked down at the goo now covering his hands. Fire whooshed over him briefly and then he shook off the ash. I kind of wished I could do that. Then again, it would probably ash my clothes too.

"You know, Max and I, it's not exclusive. We aren't even officially dating yet," Ynes said, glancing at me. "I don't mind sharing, if that's what Max wants?"

What did I want? I was so tired I could barely think right now.

"It's been a hard night," Sunny said. I gave her a grateful smile. "Maybe we should get home. Let him sleep on it."

"Where is home, anyway?" Roderick muttered, clearly having second thoughts.

I laughed, Brandon hugged me from behind. Ynes squeezed my waist, a second warmth on my side.

A white-furred and very miserable sticky red panda sat at my feet and pouted.

"Not my place, at least not until we've all had a shower," Sunny said, looking us over. "We look like we lost a fight at an orgy. Is there a hotel around here?"

That was certainly a vivid description. I suddenly remembered my other problem. "Pog, where did you and Barnabas leave the other unicorn?"

Sunny perked up and licked her lips. "Leave that to me."

"No!" I glared at her. "Don't you dare. I'll figure out something."

Epilogue

WE ALL HUNCHED AROUND a laptop sitting on Sunny's coffee table. The couch was a tight fit with all four of us—Brandon, me, Ynes, and Roderick—but we managed, partially, by me sitting across Ynes and Brandon's laps.

Ynes scrolled through the houses for rent, our discussion of pros and cons of various listings punctuated by occasional shouts from Sunny or Pog as they trash talked each other over their racing game.

It had only been two days since the showdown in the park, but I could tell we were wearing our welcome out with Sunny, especially since we'd added one more to the already over-full spare bedroom.

Roderick took the cot, while Ynes, Brandon, and me shared the bed. I'd declined to decide on dating, telling Brandon that since he'd declined to share his feelings with me earlier, he'd have to deal with Ynes and me dating at the same time I was dating him. Maybe I'd have to go exclusive with one of them eventually but, so far, I'd only caught a few jealous glances from Brandon when he saw me with Ynes. Ynes didn't seem bothered.

For now, we'd taken the unicorn back to the PCA. Ms. Williams was letting us keep it in the shack until we could find a house.

With my upcoming job with Mr. Woolven, plus Brandon and Ynes' income, we had enough to rent a place together.

The requirement of a yard with a tall fence was slowing down our search, but the other option, of having it killed, did not appeal to me. Besides, it made the best jelly beans I'd ever tasted. I'd make a fortune if I could figure out how to sell them.

Since Roderick had worked for his father, he was now unemployed. I'd told him I could talk to Mr. Woolven about coming back, but he'd soundly rejected that notion.

And Roderick, we were going to let him stay with us until he figured out what he wanted to do with his life. Father had planned out his college major and classes, but all of us encouraged him to think about if that was really what he wanted.

I was happy for Roderick. He looked much more content and at-ease than he did when I'd first met him. Going out on his own was probably just what he'd needed.

I still wasn't sure I hadn't made a deal with the devil when I'd agreed to work for Mr. Woolven. We'd see. I was going to start lessons in a few days once we'd gotten housing sorted. For now, I was keeping the attacks at bay with the light spell. Anytime I needed to release magic, I went up to the roof and made the biggest light I could. Management of the condo building had gotten some complaints, but so far they hadn't figured out where the flashing lights were coming from.

As for the prince, he hadn't asked for my contact information, but Brandon assured me he'd find me when it was time to collect on my debt. He was worried the prince might use the favor to kill me, but that was something for future-me to worry about. I don't know if we would have been able to prevail without one of us getting hurt if I hadn't made the deal.

ALSO BY ROAN ROSSER

The Changing Bodies Series

- Book 1 – Ritual of the Ancients
- Book 2 – Bloodline of the Ancients
- Book 3 – Goddess of the Ancients
- Prequel – Jackal of Hearts

The Chaos Menagerie Series

- Book 1 – Red Pandamonium
- Book 1.5 – Diamond in the Rat
- Book 2 – Pandora's Fox – Coming Soon

ABOUT THE AUTHOR

ROAN ROSSER

My urban fantasy novels mainly feature the trans and queer protagonists grappling with things like identity and found families that I wished I could have read about growing up.

I escaped from the bowels of Utah (namely Provo) and now live in the sunny Pacific Northwest of the United States.

When not writing, you can probably find me beating up pixel baddies or in front of one of my sewing machines adding to my overstuffed closet or my army of homemade plush dolls.

If you find yourself blinded by the vivid colors and loud patterns of my homemade shirts, know that I'm only trying to warn you that I may be poisonous. Or venomous? Or both? Probably both.

Learn more at RoanRosser.com

www.ingramcontent.com/pod-product-compliance
Lightning Source LLC
Chambersburg PA
CBHW030136180626
46812CB00002B/710